Look for all these TOR books by André Norton

THE CRYSTAL GRYPHON
FORERUNNER
FORERUNNER: THE SECOND VENTURE
GRYPHON'S EYRIE (with A.C. Crispin)
HOUSE OF SHADOWS (with Phyllis Miller)
MAGIC IN ITHKAR (edited by André Norton and
    Robert Adams)
MAGIC IN ITHKAR 2 (edited by André Norton and
    Robert Adams)
MOON CALLED
THE PRINCE COMMANDS
WHEEL OF STARS

ANDRÉ NORTON

FLIGHT IN YIKTOR

TOR

A TOM DOHERTY ASSOCIATES BOOK

FLIGHT IN YIKTOR

Copyright © 1986 by André Norton

First printing: May 1986

A TOR Book

Published by Tom Doherty Associates
49 West 24 Street
New York, N.Y. 10010

Cover art by Victoria Poyser
Cover design by Carol Russo

ISBN: 0-312-93245-6

Library of Congress Catalog Card Number: 85-52253

Printed in the United States

0   9   8   7   6   5   4   3   2   1

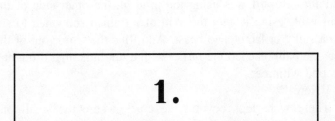

1.

Cold, cold. Fold in the legs—do not move.

Cold—pain—the big one was using the prod again—pain. Stand—jump—but it is cold—so——cold.

The small body edged between the two large woven baskets uttered a mewing cry. Then one claw hand flew to provide a gag against any more sound. But shivers continued to shake the too thin body.

Cold—where is cold—where is pain?

The curled body jerked as if a tormenting lash had been applied to the wrinkled greenish skin only too visible through the tatters which were not true clothing. No one had shouted those words. Yet they had come as clear and loud as if Russtif his ugly self were standing over the hider. In the head—not in the ear. Talking in the head!

The small one tried to wedge even more out of sight, and now the shudders of fear were worse.

Where is cold? Where is pain?

The demand came again, imperative—to be obeyed. Wrinkled hands covered ears, but that did not keep the questions from opening like dry and curled leaves under the touch of water—an opening in the head. Once more the body jerked—

Pain—Russtif was using the prod on the other side of the tent wall, using it with the skill of a trained showman to stir up a sulky or frightened beast. And, like the words out of the air, the pain reached the lurker with a hot burst that brought a second whimper.

"Here!"

There were legs beyond the crack where the small one crouched—two pairs of them in space boots.

"No harm—there is nothing to fear."

A pallid tongue licked cracked lips. But there was something that made the fear less, lulled it a little. Beyond the wall Russtif growled and spat threats. His anger and love of tormenting that which could not fight back was like a spurt of fire.

"Nothing to fear." Again the words spun into a mind that had to listen even if the ears were stoppered against sound. Nor did either pair of boots move toward or away from the lurker. Crouch, wait for a hand to reach down and jerk out the small body, perhaps cuff hard for being there—for existing at all.

But this was not Russtif and the boots did not move. Slowly the head, covered with dry tangles of thick hair, came up, drawn against all will by the new note—the very strange note—in that mind voice. Large eyes looked up and out.

Very far from Russtif these two. There were always strangers about, some of them as odd in their way as Russtif's imprisoned performers. So it was not their difference, rather the way they stood shoulder to shoulder looking down. Not with disgust nor cruel curiosity but in another way the lurker could not understand.

"Do not be afraid." It was the male who spoke now, uttering words in the trade lingo that was common speech all through this quarter which catered to the entertainment of ship people.

He was very fair of skin and his hair was white—though he was not an old man. Those eyebrows so pale even against his skin ran up at the temples to join the hairline, and his eyes were green, luminous as if there were tiny fires behind each.

"There is nothing to fear." That was the other one, the female, who spoke now. Beside the fairness of her companion she was a fire glowing—hair as red as one of Russtif's oil lamps was braided and looped about her head to look like a heavy crown. She was—

The small body uncoiled. Claw hands went out to the big basket and drew the hunched body up as far as nature would let it. For it was a very crooked body, hunched forward by a misshapen burden at shoulder level, so that the head had to be raised to an uncomfortable angle to see the other two at all.

Arms and legs were thin, their greenish skin encrusted with dirt. The mass of uncombed hair was black, gray with dust at places, but black underneath.

"A child." It was the spaceman who said that aloud. "What—"

The woman made a gesture with one hand. There was a listening look about her. Could she hear Toggor, too?

"This one, yes," she said. "But also another. Is that not so, little one?"

The answer was pulled out by the intent gaze of her eyes—coming before thought muffled it with caution.

"He—Russtif—he would make Toggor play. It is cold— too cold. Toggor hurts from the cold—from the pain whip." "So?"

She stooped to set a hand beneath the chin of the small, bent and maimed figure. From her touch, from the tips of her fingers, something warm and good flooded right into the shaking body.

"Toggor is what?"

"My—my friend." That was not quite the way of it either, but they were the closest words could be found.

There was a hiss of breath from the man; the woman's lips fitted tightly together. She was angry—not like Russtif, all noise and quick to aim a blow—but neither was her anger turned toward the one before her.

"We may have found what we seek." She spoke above the bowed head to her companion. "And who are you?" Again warmth flowed from her.

"The Dung one." Long ago had that name of the lowest been accepted. There was no other. "I run errands. I do what I can." A pride which was seldom felt made shoulders hunch a little higher.

"For Russtif?" The man indicated the tent behind.

Dung shook his head. "Russtif has Jusas and Sem."

"Yet you are here."

"It is Toggor. I—I bring him—" The claw hand fumbled in the front of the single ragged garment. Once more truth was pulled forth by that warmth of the other. "I bring this." He held an unwholesome-looking lump of stuff. "Russtif does not feed Toggor enough. He wants him to fight for food. Toggor will die"—the sharply pointed chin quivered —"there!"

They could all hear the crackle of the prod and a rising mutter of obscenities from beyond the tent wall.

"Toggor fights and they bet on him. Russtif never had so good a clawed one before."

"So," the man said, "let us see this fighter, Maelen. Also Russtif. He interests me."

The woman nodded. She dropped her hand from beneath the pointed chin to lace a hold in the tatters which crossed the bowed shoulder hump.

What did she want with Dung?

"Come." Her hold unchanging, she urged him forward just behind the man who walked with the swing of one who has spent most of his years in space, and who was now heading toward the entrance to Russtif's domain at the other end of the tent. Whether or not the lurker wished to accompany them was not asked. There was no breaking that hold which was drawing Dung along. Somehow the thought of fighting for freedom had vanished.

There was the thick and nasty smell which was Russtif's— one of uncleaned cages with weak and sickening captives—to fill the nose as soon as they had pushed past the open flap. Things rustled and squeaked until Russtif roared and the silence of fear snapped down.

He was a big man who had once been proud of his strength but now was entombed in rolls of greasy fat. His bare skull shone with oil in the light of the lantern he had set on the table where there was also a cage—Toggor's place of prison. Now he looked up with a sullen scowl. Then that changed, by a visible effort, into a showman's ingratiating grin.

"Gentle Fem, Gentle Homo, how can I serve you?" His back was to the table now, and he had dropped the prod on it. It was then he caught sight of Dung.

"Has the trash made some trouble?" He took a ponderous step forward, his hand lifted as if to aim a blow at the hunchback.

"What trouble is this one noted for making?" asked the woman.

"A thief, a piece of walking dung, a monster like that? Why, whatever comes to hand to upset honest people—"

"Such as Beastmerchant Russtif perhaps?" asked the man.

Russtif's smile slipped and slid but still he caught it. "Such as me and everyone else. I caught this sewer scum tampering with a cage just two eves ago. Luck was with him then, or else he would have smarted for a good lessoning. Trash should be thrown away and not come to annoy others.''

"Opening a cage? Is perhaps the cage that one?" The man pointed to the one on the table.

Russtif's smile did vanish then. With the hand in sight he made a fist which might have fallen like a hammer blow on the hunchback.

"Why do you wonder that, Gentle Homo? Has the trash been spewing out some vomit that you would believe?"

"You have a fighting smux is what I believe," the woman cut in, and Russtif hastened to draw on his showman's smirk again.

"The best, Gentle Fem, the best! There have been stellars wagered on this one—not just market coppers—and stellars won!" He moved along the edge of the table now so they could better view his possession.

The woman stooped a little so she could see most of what looked like a ball of hairy rags squatting in the center of the cage. Under her hold Dung gave a quick start and then stood very still. She was mind speaking to Toggor. The smux did not answer. It was as if he did not or would not listen.

"These be—good." Unknowingly at first, Dung's mind reached out to become a part of that other steady stream of reassurance.

Toggor's answer never came in words such as those that had struck Dung. Rather it was feeling: pain, fear, and sometimes but very seldom, a rough kind of contentment. Thus Dung thought "good," even "help," which Toggor somehow seized upon avidly, as if Dung had indeed flung open his place of hopeless captivity.

The handful of legs folded tightly to the haired body was visible. Those vicious-looking claws at the end of the first four were clamped together as the creature answered Dung's reassurance rather than the more concise broadcast of the woman.

The smux was no thing of beauty. Had he grown larger he

might have been such a monster as to set human kind to flight. His body, covered with spiky hairs thick enough to look like quills, was a grayish red like a fire coal smoldering in ashes. Each quill was tipped also with a darker red as if blood-dipped. There were eight of the long hairy legs, the fore pairs equipped with claws which were sawtoothed on the inner sides.

His body was two ovals attached, the smaller fore one to larger hind one with a waist no thicker than two of his legs held side by side. His eyes—all six of them—were now retracted into his ball of head, concealing the stalks on which they were mounted. All in all he was ugly, and, with that ugliness, he gave off the promise of quick and vicious attack.

Now his abdomen dragged on the floor of the cage, and Dung knew Toggor was both filthy and hungry. To be dropped into a rounded half sphere with another of his kind and a piece of raw meat flung in for a victory prize should arouse every fighting instinct of the smux. At Dung's thrust of thought he raised one foreleg and clicked the claw there in entreaty—a friend had food.

Russtif kept his hand well away from the prod. Would he dare to move when these two strangers were here? Dung did not know, but breaking the long-held rule of his own survival, he wadded together the bit of offal he had sneaked from behind the butcher's and, measuring the distance carefully, while Russtif was watching the woman, his small eyes leering, Dung threw the bit of food into the cage. Toggor was on it in an instant, grasping the unwholesome-looking piece and bringing it to his mandibles.

Russtif roared and swung one of those hammer fists at Dung, but it did not crash against the side of the hunchback's head as he expected. It was the woman who swung her lightly held captive out of the way, and it was the man whose hand came down in a sharp chop across the beast seller's wrist, bringing an angry cry out of him.

"What you do?" Russtif seemed to swell as if his bulk had suddenly increased.

"Nothing."

"Nothing? You let this trash throw poison to my smux and it is nothing? Ho, let the wardens decide whether this is nothing."

That Dung had not expected. That Russtif would allow the law such interference was unheard of. Yet the beastmerchant was slipping farther along the edge of the table, his eyes turning from the spaceman standing at quiet ease, to Toggor, to the woman, almost as if he expected they were about to unite against him. Dung made a second attempt to wring free of the grasp which had brought his misshapen body into the tent, fruitlessly. Though that hand twisted in the rags across the hump did not tighten, yet moving away was impossible.

"The smux—quote a price on it." That was not the man but the woman who said that quietly. Russtif grinned a little, showing broken, black, rotted teeth.

"There is no price for good fortune, Gentle Fem." He had stopped his crabwise retreat from the two, standing now at the end of the table with Toggor's cage between them. The smux had finished the bit of near-carrion Dung had scraped out of a discarded *E* tube and had closed himself once more into ball form which was his only protection, since Russtif had soaked the poison from his claws only an hour ago.

"There is always an end to good fortune," said the woman, standing tall so that only the tips of her fingers touched Dung, yet light as that touch was now, captivity remained. "Also for everything there is a price. You have fought that smux ten—double ten—triple ten times, starving it between so that it will come to battle as you wish. There is a flicking of life force in it now. Would you kill it rather than profit?"

Dung's dark tongue swept across pale lips. "Toggor." He was not aware that he had spoken aloud until he heard his own word.

The spaceman moved his wrist out into the open, closer to the lantern. That light showed a cal dial, its light steady. As Russtif saw that, his small eyes held a new glitter. Everything this off-worlder said was true. The smux was—or had been—a strong contender, the best he had ever been able to find. He had marked the day he had had it out of the hands of the drunken crewman who had wanted to raise a stellar to see him back to his ship, as a fortunate one for him. But who knew how long the thing would continue to live? Russtif was greedy, but there was an undercurrent of sly profit sense in him, too.

"Off-worlders cannot run gaming," he pointed out. He was absentmindedly rubbing the wrist the spacer had struck with the fingers of his other hand.

"We have a license to buy," the woman cut in. "We do not choose fighters as such, but only strange beings or creatures."

Now Russtif made a wide gesture that took in the other cages and prisoners. "Take then your choice, Gentle Fem; we have such in abundance here. There is a hopper from Grogon, a dry tongue sucker from Basil, a—"

"Smux from—from where, Beastmerchant? From which world comes your lucky fighter?"

Russtif's thick shoulders arose in a shrug. "Who knows? By the time such come—and they come seldom—they have been traded perhaps a dozen times. And surely the thing itself is not prepared to snicker out its home world. It fights— fights to eat. It sleeps. It lives after a fashion, but no one can bring charges that Russtif deals in a thinking species. These are all below the official recording, and the records will tell you so."

Dung could have protested. Alone among Russtif's captives had the hunchback made contact with Toggor. The creature's mind pattern was different, very hard to follow. It wove in and out when he tried to communicate more than the most primitive messages or emotions. Yet he was sure that smux had more powers of thought than Russtif believed.

The spaceman tapped the edge of his cal dial with a forefinger, the small click-click underlining the restlessness of the caged creatures about. Russtif's own cal dial showed.

"The thing brings in a stellar—"

Now the woman laughed, and there was a note of scorn in that sound. "A stellar a battle? And for how much longer? It is weakening, is it not? At the last fight did it not nearly lose a claw?"

Russtif's eyes narrowed. He stared at her insolently, though he was careful to keep his voice at a respectful pitch as he answered.

"I did not see you there among the wagerers, Gentle Fem."

"Nor would you," she replied. "But I speak the truth."

Again Russtif shrugged. "A stellar this bit of ugliness did win. And he will win again."

"Two stellars." That was from the spaceman and it came crisply.

Dung gasped and then raised his stick-thin fingers to cover his betraying mouth. Two stellars—it was a fortune beyond imagining in the haunts of the outcasts where the hunchback sheltered.

"Two stellars, um?" Russtif rolled the words around in his mouth as if he could taste the sweetness of such an offer. "Three." A brainsick fool who would make such an offer could perhaps be edged upward yet again.

"Do not bargain." The woman's voice was not raised. It was neither harsh nor threatening. Yet Dung shivered and sunk his head lower, not wishing to see her face. Though the hunchback had scurried away from threats all the years of harsh memory he had never heard such a tone before. What was this woman? Certainly some great lady, such as one would never think might venture into such a hole. She should

come carried on the shoulders of stout chair veeks with
outrunners and speakers-for-the-great in attendance. Who or
what was she?

The effect her order had on Russtif was made plain in the
way his fists fell upon the table and his eyes took on a
reddish glare. Dung expected to hear foul words ordering
these two out of the trader's sight. Yet no words came.
Instead, a purplish flush covered the beastmerchant's oily
jowls and he looked as one who might be choking on his own
spittle.

"Two stellars," the man said again, and his speech was as
quiet as the woman's, although with none of that compulsion
in it. Yet it was also not to be denied.

Russtif made a noise like the honk of an enraged grop, the
purpling color still in his cheeks waxing deeper. He gave a
sharp shove to the smux's cage, sending it skidding along the
greasy tabletop.

"Two stellars." He choked out the words with the same
enthusiasm he might have given had the offer been only
copper.

The man began tapping out on his cal the transfer from his
own holdings to Russtif's.

The skidding cage was about to dive over the edge of the
table. Dung's skeleton hand caught it, and for the first time
the hunchback dared to try to reach Toggor again.

"These are good." Anyone would be better than Russtif,
to be sure, but there was the additional promise in the mind
touch of the woman. One could not lie with thoughts as one
could with words.

The woman did not try to take the cage, but neither did she
loosen her hold on Dung's rags. Instead, she gave a slight
pull which brought him around and started him for the open
tent flap. Then they were out in the twilight where other
tents' smoky torches and impulse lamps gave a measure of
sight.

A moment later the man joined them.

"Trouble?" The woman did not use speech, but had mind touch that Dung found easy to catch.

The man could not laugh in that mind-to-mind communication, but there was something in his answer which was light as laughter.

"Trouble? No, he will be slightly puzzled perhaps for a space, and then congratulate himself on a bargain that *he* made. I wish we could clear out that whole den of his."

"Think freedom?"

Dung caught not only words but a picture—a picture that showed paws, and insectile legs, and tentacles looping through wire, mastering the catches on the cages in the tent behind. "Bend so—push. Go, little ones, go!"

Dung felt a touch on his own grime-blackened hand. The smux had thrust a foreleg through the wire netting, was grasping with a claw the catch of the cage. Like those in the tent, Toggor had caught that message and was following the promise that was like an order.

Gasping, Dung held the cage against his body. But that gesture came too late. Toggor had already freed himself and caught with all four claws at the rags across the pinched chest of the hunchback. Dung dropped the cage, then nearly stumbled over it, except a strong hand caught at his bony shoulder, pulling the small figure back on balance.

Dung cupped both hands about Toggor, having no fear of any cutting slash from those claws, for the smux fitted itself into the hollows of his palms as if those were a safe home nest. Now those hands swung out to the man who stood so straight and tall that Dung had to stretch his neck painfully to see his face, offering Toggor to him who had paid that unbelievable sum to free the smux.

"Hold him well, little one. Bring him that we may tend him—he still hungers and thirsts. And"—the mind speech was softer than any Dung had ever heard in a short hard life—"so do you."

Thus one who had always slunk through shadows now walked as straight as an ungainly and broken body would allow, a friend sheltered in hand and a stranger on either side acting as if one was as tall and well formed as themselves. It was beyond belief yet it was the truth!

2.

Twice when they passed some patrolling guard, sent to keep the peace among the dealers in the strange and rare who gathered like an untidy fringe about any space port, Dung hung back, and would even have dived for the shadows, but for that grip on the rags across his hump, steering him straight ahead until they passed the invisible boundary which kept those in the Limits from the respectable portions of town.

The lingering twilight was enough for Dung to see the stares which greeted their party. Passersby, used to strange sights issuing from the Limits, seemed to judge their small group even stranger. Yet neither of the spacers appeared aware of the comment they caused, and Dung was brought along as one who had every right to walk there.

They came to one of the large shelters for travelers, light beaming richly from its wide doorway, house guards on duty. Dung, straining his neck upward, ready to twist away from a blow or kick, saw that the guard on the right did move forward a step as if to question their passage, but retreated again when the spacers paid him no attention.

Together the three crossed the wide lobby with its ring of luxury shops, its throngs of people, making for one of the transport plates Dung had heard of but had never seen. They had it to themselves, other people drawing back as they approached. Their carrier whirled upward and then sped into one of the open hallways three stories above the lobby. It was stomach-turning for Dung, who gulped and gulped again. The invisible plastaglass sides did not give any suggestion of protection.

Dung swallowed hard for the third time as they stopped before a door and the spaceman put out a hand to press against the lockplate, letting the door withdraw into the wall to give them entrance. Toggor stirred and pushed against the sudden involuntary tightening of Dung's hold. This was such luxury as trash from the Limits had never seen. His misshapen feet sunk into a thick carpet that was a lush green and gave forth a tangy, spicy smell.

There was no smoking torch or lantern here. The walls themselves glowed, and that glow grew more brilliant as the door rolled shut behind them. A wide couch heaped with cushions ran along the left-hand wall, and other cushions were piled one upon the other at various points here and there— each flanked by a low table or double sets of shelves on which were a number of things Dung did not have time to study, for that grasp on his rags drew him to one table which the spaceman swept free of tapes and a queerly shaped bowl.

"Put the smux here." The woman did not use the mind touch but the trade tongue, and loosed Dung to gesture to the now clear surface. "Or will it run?"

Dung licked lips dry with that never-ending fear. They had bought the smux. Perhaps Dung had only been necessary in its transportation here. Now there might be no longer any need for this one misshapen and twisted body.

Obediently his thin fingers uncupped and set the spike-covered body in the place the woman had indicated.

"Stay," Dung thought. "These are good." Though how he could be sure of that!

Toggor crouched, drawn into a ball with legs hugging his pulpy body. The eyestalks on his bristly head extended a fraction with all the eyes facing outward and around, ready for attack from any direction.

The man went to the wall and tapped on a row of buttons there. There moved out a section on which sat a tray with a number of small covered boxes and dishes. He brought the tray to the table on which Toggor crouched.

"What does it eat?" Trade speech again.

Dung's own mouth watered and his belly pinched with longing as the spaceman snapped off the lids of the dishes and showed a variety of food.

"Meat," Dung said and stood, hands behind his own body lest they move of themselves and snatch some of that bounty.

"Well enough." The spaceman moved two of the dishes a fraction closer to the smux, but Toggor made no attempt to try their contents. That in-and-out pattern which could reach Dung spelled out the smux's wariness.

"Toggor wishes to know where he must fight," Dung interpreted.

"There is no fighting, only eating. Tell him so!" The woman no longer had any hold on Dung, but her hand moved to the upbent head, touched lightly between and above the reddened eyes.

"No fight—eat." Dung strove to fit his thoughts to the pattern Toggor could catch.

For a long moment it seemed the smux did not understand, or, understanding, did not believe. Then a claw flew, with a speed which made it hardly visible, to the nearest dish to seize upon a cube within and transfer it to clashing mandibles.

When the smux had fed a second time and was now using both foreclaws to empty the dish, the woman spoke again, this time no trade talk but words that were clear in Dung's head.

"Eat you also. If there is other which you want, just say it so."

Dung felt as Toggor must have moments earlier: that there might be a threat to come. Why had he been brought here and offered— But also, as it had with Toggor, hunger got the better of wariness and he grabbed for a flat round of bread-cake already spread with lumpy gor-berry jell. It was crammed swiftly into mouth. His eyes were not on stalks, able to watch all sides of the room, but Dung used them as best he could while he ate, ate so fast that the taste of the food was lost in the swift chewing and swallowing.

There seemed to be no trick. He ate more slowly when no hand came forth to snatch away food, no foot raised to boot his bag-of-bones body. In all the seasons Dung could remember never had he been offered freely such a wealth of food.

None but well-cleaned dishes were on that tray when smux and Dung were done. The smux balled up, his legs wrapped about his body. He might doze now for several hours. Dung eyed the piles of cushions and wished he could do likewise. But those who had brought him here were not yet through.

This time the spaceman caught Dung's shoulder and drew his captive to a wall, over which he passed his hand. A second door opened. There was a tight little room therein—no cushions, nothing but bare walls and floor.

Ah, rightly had Dung feared them. He was to be shut up in there. Twisting his body did no good; there was too strong a hold on him. His rags tore as the spaceman stripped the rotten cloth away from the hump, away from Dung's body. Bare so that all the bruises mottling the greenish flesh could be seen, the hunchback was placed well inside, and the door closed before he could throw himself at it in one last despairing attempt to escape imprisonment.

Out of the wall shot streams of water, warm against the

skin. Two metal arms unfolded from the shining surface of
the cell and caught him. To hold him under that flood to
drown? No, they were brushing down the small body, rubbing to dislodge the grime which had always been a part of
Dung. No more struggle. Standing still, a faint pleasure grew
within him—clean as never any such as Dung could be. Even
the wild matted hair was washed and combed back, its wet
and curling ends brushing the hump.

The skin of the hump was different from the rest of the
grimed hide which covered his body. He had never seen
himself in any mirror, but his fingers had long ago told him it
was thick and hard, almost like the covering on his nails,
with a ridge down the middle of the back which only by
painful contortion Dung could touch. Through it he had little
or no feeling.

The water shower died away, and the door which had
sealed came open again. But the spaceman did not drag Dung
forth. Rather, he stretched an arm above Dung's head and
pushed a thumb tight to the wall.

Water had come before, now it was wind, warm and
drying. Dung swung slowly around as he realized its purpose. Even the hair which had lain so lankly back arose and
answered, to fly up and out.

Then the wind was cut off, and when Dung looked up in
disappointment the hand of the spaceman reached inside the
place of water and air, holding toward him a folded piece of
cloth. Dung took it and shook out a small robe, clean and
white and of a soft wooly texture unknown to any beggar in
the outer Limits.

To be fed, and clean, and wearing a whole garment—
Dung's wildest dreams had never taken him so far before.
Regretfully the claw fingers caressed the soft folds about the
top-heavy body. One walk into the night known to Dung, and
that covering would be snatched by the more powerful.

He came out of the washing place blinking. It had been a

long time since tears had come to Dung. There was a far memory of a time when sobs had choked his throat and shook his body, when there had been pain and more pain. Then there came the day when there was a door left unguarded because Dung was a useless unknown thing, unneeded. Strength had come, enough to creep away and begin life in the shadows. But there had been a time before—so far away and dim now. Being clean and clad again triggered that memory. However, fast on it followed fear so deep that Dung dropped to the floor, folding in upon himself, waiting again for what had ended that other good time, blows and hurting in the head with the threatening thoughts . . .

"Why do you so fear, little one?"

Dung would not look up. The words in his mind did not hurt, but who cared what became of Limits trash or would want to know the past of such a one?

"*We* wish to know, little one. And there is no need to fear."

Dung struggled to raise his head the higher slantwise.

"I am Dung." He said it and thought it—thought the vileness which had given him his name.

"Never so. You are what you believe, little one. Do *you* call yourself by that name for filth?"

She was too clever, she guessed, she knew.

Now he allowed his hands to cover his face. His face, yes, but who could hide thoughts? And both of these could pick his thoughts out as Toggor picked scraps of meat from within an orker shell.

"Farree?" She spoke that name aloud. Now they would laugh and push him out the sooner into the coming night, the outer Limits which would be the worse because he had left for a space.

"Dung!" He corrected aloud, his voice rising squeakingly high. "Dung!" If he did not claim that other name, perhaps he would be allowed to escape all but the jeers.

The woman dropped to her knees, bringing them near face-to-face so he need not hold his head at such an angle to view her. Her hands reached to gently touch the grotesque shoulders.

"Farree. Hold by what birth gave you, little one. Do not accept what unseeing ones force upon you."

Dung's head shook uncomfortably from side to side. What did this one who lived in luxury know of what one faced in the Limits?

"You are not of Grant's World?" It was the man who spoke.

Dung shivered. In truth he did not know from where he had come; the early days were so overlaid now by the terrors and torments that had followed.

"I am Dung." He must hold to that, to do otherwise was to stand bare of body and defenseless in a ring of Limits bullies. He had seen the weak kicked and pummeled to death for daring to show any spirit.

There was a pulling at the clean robe about him, and he looked down to see Toggor catching hold with his foreclaws, drawing himself up the cloth. Dung had never handled the smux before this twilight, but there was nothing to frighten or disgust him.

"Good." Not a word, a feeling projected by the smux and filling him with warmth—it was like a burst of shouting. The smux might be living for the moment, but he was triumphant in the joys of that moment. Dung wished that he could share the creature's relief and joy.

"You can, if you wish."

Dung stared at the woman fronting him still at his own level.

"If with this stranger-brother you can communicate, then—" She looked around and up at the man and straight-away he opened another inner door of the room.

What came dancing into their presence then was a creature

the like of which Dung had never seen, although those who dealt with strange life forms had given him his only shelter. Among the bizarre his own affliction had seemed less conspicuous.

"Yazz. I am Yazz." The words seeped into his mind as the newcomer pranced around him, uttering sharp mouth sounds into the bargain.

Its body was as tall as Dung, its head topping him. Four slender, golden brown legs supported smoothly rounded flanks and a sleek-haired barrel. The head was triangular. A mane with a froth of frizzly hair near-covered its large eyes and then rose to curve down its long, slender neck and shoulders.

Those eyes peering carefully at him were a bright red like the gems a Lord-One might wear, and its muzzle was open far enough to disclose gleamingly clean teeth of a golden yellow several shades lighter than its coat.

It had a wisp of tail, which fluttered from side to side as it stood, still now, viewing Dung. "What are you, brother one?" Its head tilted a little to one side as it surveyed him. "No, there are two of you." It had apparently sighted Toggor. "Large, small. Different. What?"

The words came into Dung's mind smoothly but less forcibly than those of the man and the woman.

"I am . . ." Dung began to reply and then suddenly hesitated. Never before had he had to explain what he was: a wretched mistake in a world which named him trash. "I am—me," he answered dully. "This"—he had taken the smux into his two hands again—"is Toggor. He is a smux."

That he was answering the questions of what was manifestly an animal seemed now no stranger than anything else which had happened since the two off-worlders had found him.

"What do you do?" Yazz returned. The creature was bubbling with what Dung realized very dimly was content—happiness—though to define happiness was beyond him.

What did he do? Fight to live and yet every day come closer to the knowledge that for him there was little reason to go on struggling at all. "I—live." He said that aloud, not in thought.

"You live." It was not as if the woman was agreeing with him, rather that she was confirming some necessary belief. "Now comes a time when you may do more. Since you can talk with the Little Ones—there is a place for you, Farree—"

"I am Dung," he corrected her again, but inside him there was a small spark of wonder aflame. Did these two—could they— He did not even want to think of the brightness which might just be true.

But it would seem that this wonder of wonders might be after all, for the man said then: "You have no kin, you are apprenticed nowhere?"

Dung laughed, a broken cackle which had seldom left his lips. "Who wants Dung? I am of the trash of the Limits."

The woman's hand suddenly laid fingers across his lips. He could smell more strongly the spicy scent which seemed as much a part of her as her skin or the glory of her hair.

"You are Farree. Say not that other name. And now you are apprenticed if you wish. We welcome one who can talk with our small ones."

So it was that Dung became Farree, though to him it remained like a dream from which he might awaken into the despair of the real day. He ate voraciously what they provided, never knowing when they might tire of their careless generosity. He learned to keep his body clean and to answer to that other name, but he shrank from going out, from leaving this refuge from all he had ever known.

Though these rooms in the towering rest place for travelers were not the home of the two he had learned to call Lady Maelen and Lord-One Krip (even though they objected to his names of state), to him they were greater palaces than any of the nobles' of Grant's World, whom he had only seen at a distance. No, this was only a temporary resting place; these two were truly out of space. They had a ship of their own finned down in the repair field where various changes on it were being made. Strangest of all was the fact that these changes were being made to accommodate bodies which were not human nor even of human shape. They were to hold in comfort animals!

Once or twice he wondered if they looked upon him also as an animal, one with superior talents for communication. But better to be an animal, with such a life as they were giving him, than Dung. Always they talked to him as if he were straight and tall and of as fair a body as they. At length (though he never asked any questions, lest by doing so he would offend) he learned that it was in their minds to gather together animals, even such as Toggor, and to transport them from world to world showing that indeed all life was kin and that creatures were to be welcomed as brothers and sisters rather than be kept in such slavery as Russtif had held the smux.

So far they only had three such—for the venture depended, Farree came swiftly to understand, on the ability to communicate by the mind touch. There was Yazz, who also had been bought from a showman and remembered a past in the high mountain country before she was entrapped by hunters; there was the smux; and, kept in a hut near the ship, there was a bartle the spacers named Bojor.

Had Farree not seen the bartle loosed from a chain and coming to pay homage to Maelen by licking her feet, he would have raced from the hut as fast as his bent legs would carry him. For a bartle was one of the menaces in stories of the early days on Grant's World. He had seen bartle claws strung on ident disc chains and worn with pride by any fortunate to have them.

When the bartle arose on his hind paws, he topped Lord-One Krip. His body was massive enough to make three of the

man's. This being the shedding season, great patches of
coarse hair lay on the floor of the hut, and the sleek underhide
shone through in green-gray spots.

The off-worlders visited the bartle for many hours each
day, the man grooming out the dead fur, both of them
communicating with the beast. Farree, who knew that only
one of those huge paws needed to descend on him to leave a
smear of broken bones and blood, kept his distance at first.
But, caught up in the mind exchange that held the other, he
began to think of the shaggy beast as another person—odd
and queer to be sure, but no different in that respect from
many of the aliens which he had viewed from hiding around
the port.

The alterations in the ship were slow, and soon Lord-One
Krip spent more time there, urging on the fitters, for it would
seem that for some reason he and the Lady Maelen wished to
be in space as soon as possible.

In space! Farree's thought shied away from that, and he
refused to think again into the future. Then he would be back
in the Limits again. This time—this time when there was no
more—

Sitting in the doorway of the bartle's place he had begun
that train of thought that he could no longer shove away.
They would go with the bartle, Toggor, and Yazz, and
he—he would—

"Come with us!"

Farree gave a start. His hands clenched and his head
swung at a painful angle so he could see the Lady Maelen's
face. He had thought her busy with clipping the bartle's
claws. The big beast had been biting at them, being no longer
able to wear them out upon the stones of the distant canyons.
No, she was not looking to Farree but he was sure that he had
caught that thought.

"You did. You come with us."

"Off-world?" He swallowed, and it hurt as if his inner throat was raw.

"If you wish it, it is so." She did not look at him even now, but there was such certainty in her thought that he had to accept that she meant it.

"If I *wish*—" He could not quite believe. This was more of the dream from which he hoped there would be no more waking. "If I wish—Lady—" His hands twisted the robe across his misshapen breast. "There is no other wish in me—"

"Then it is so." Now she did look at him, and she smiled. He felt as if he were Yazz, and wished to creep close and nuzzle at her hands and signal with a tail he did not have. The dream was continuing!

"There is trouble again with Kem-fu." Lord-One Krip had come up without Farree noting. "The fittings must be re-laid." The man was frowning and tapping his fingertips on his cal as he did, Farree knew, whenever he was disturbed.

"Yet he set those himself." Lady Maelen got to her feet. "Why now this difficulty?"

"Ask me not. It was almost as if—" Farree saw the frown on the man's face deepen. "As if," he continued after a moment, "he was deliberately delaying us. And the moon—"

"Why would he deliberately delay us? There would be no reason for it."

"No reason except Sehkmet and what was wrought there. That was a raider snatch first, and, when we spoiled that game and uncovered the great treasure, the Guild did not take it kindly. It depends upon how far the true story has been spread. And who was really behind that operation to loot the tombs of the sleepers."

"But what would they get from us? Our share of the finding fee is safe now, and they would have no chance at it. What we do here has nothing to do with any Guild or raider plotting. That is finished, and on Yiktor there is nothing which would draw them. They seek large returns, not the looting of a small planet where lordling has fought lordling until nothing flourishes to tempt even a Free Trader.''

"Revenge, perhaps, or for us to furnish a lesson. I will have the inspectors out before we up ship, and that is the truth if I ever spoke it!''

The Lady Maelen smiled. "It is probably just that this contractor deals with such a ship as he has never seen before. Thus he goes slow and makes mistakes.''

"The moon," returned Lord-One Krip shortly.

Now it was Lady Maelen's turn to frown. "We have allowed time; surely we have allowed enough time.''

"True enough, but time runs fast. We must lift ship in the next seven days if we are to make it.''

"Kem-fu—'' Farree did not understand all this about moons and treasure, but he did know much of what went on in the Limits. "He loses much at the tables in the Go-far. It is known that he is in debt to Gerog L'Kumb.''

Lord-One Krip looked down, startled. "What else do you know, Farree? This is of importance. Great importance.''

3.

Though Farree had half, or maybe more, of the lore of the Limits collected mindwise, he had to do some sorting before he answered.

"It is said . . ." He stopped. He wanted to be very careful to separate rumor and what he knew from observation and actual overhearing of news. Such a one as he was so much a part of the general trash of the Limits that few watched their tongues when he crouched or shuffled nearby.

"It is said," he began slowly once again, "that Gerog L'Kumb has as much power in the Limits as the Lawspeakers of the Great City. Yet he is seldom seen or heard to use it. For one to speak his name is enough to make a desire an act. He has his own eyes and ears everywhere. And, Lord-One—"

"Krip," the other corrected him mechanically.

"K-Krip." Farree stumbled over the saying of that name without any honorifics. "If it be his wish to delay the work upon your ship, then it will be delayed. It is said that oftentimes he does such until he is paid more, and then out of the ground come the needed men and straightaway all is done as was first ordered."

"Extortion." The Lord-One's mouth became a thin line.

The Lady Maelen nodded. "And we are fit victims for such a game. Perhaps that he also knows."

Farree drew as deep a breath as his constricted lungs would allow. "Let this one," he said then, "put on rags and go back to the Limits. To no one he matters, and that he has been gone for days—that would not have been noted. While he was sheltered by you, few here knew it, either. Is that not so?"

"And if it has been noted and reported to the Lord of the Limits, and you appeared again, what excuse—"

Farree lifted his head as far as he could. "There are Lords in the upper town who keep twisted ones such as I for as long as we afford them a certain amusement. When we are no longer of interest we return to the Limits—if we are lucky."

"And if you are not lucky?" asked Lady Maelen.

Farree shivered and doubled his fists. "There are other ways of amusement, Lady. To them such mistakes of birth are to be used and discarded at will."

"I do not think that I like the customs here," she declared. "So, little one, you could return to the Limits as one who has served your purpose with us?"

"As long as I stay well away from Russtif, yes, that I could do. And men talk before beasts—though you have shown me that perhaps the beasts might also undo plans if they met such great ones as you thereafter. In the Limits I am such a one as is not worth as much as Toggor would win in a battle match."

"I do not like it," she returned promptly. "To put you into such danger as that—"

"Lady, I have had ten seasons in the Limits and still I live." Farree held himself as erect as possible. "I am not lacking in a game of peering and prying. If time is what you fear, then it is best for you to use any tool to hand—such as

Dung.'' For the first time in days he used his old name, the one he had hoped to forget.

Lord-One Krip looked to the woman over Farree's upward-straining head. ''If this is meant to hold us planet down as he thinks, the Guild may be behind it. They would not have taken kindly to our interference with their looting on Sehkmet. And if we are bucking the Guild—the sooner we know it the better. What do you know of the Thieves Guild, Farree? And are you still as willing to venture in, if it is a matter of theirs this L'Kumb busies himself with now?''

The Thieves Guild! Farree's pointed tongue caressed his lower lip. To go up against the all-powerful Guild—yes, that was a different matter. Yet he believed that he could sink once more into the Limits and pass from sight of anyone save perhaps some grotesque scavenger such as he had been.

''You will take me, Lord-One, to the gate. Perhaps you should drive me forth with kicks and curses, having discovered that I stole from you. That would be as they expect.'' He put a hand out to the door of the bartle's hut. ''It is moon dark for three nights, and the shadows are my old home. I can listen very well.''

A small body thudded against his own, and, as limited as that force was, he near lost his balance. Toggor had crawled out of Lady Maelen's belt pouch to spring at Farree. He scuttled up to that unsightly hump and squatted in the narrow hollow between head and shoulder. When the Lady reached for him, he hissed sharply, warning her off.

Farree strove also to dislodge the smux, but the mental contact came sharper and clearer than he had ever received it before, as if the days spent with the off-worlders had honed a weapon to an edge fit to shave a hair.

''Go with. Hide, but go with!''

The Lady drew back and nodded as if the smux was suddenly one of her own kind with whom she was in full communication. Perhaps contact with the creature for some days had given her that power. But Farree was afraid.

"Russtif—" He made a mental picture of the beast seller.

"No see—hide." With that the smux burrowed under the edge of Farree's robe, his claw tips tickling as he made his way from hump to breast and there settled himself, the stiff bristles of his hair rasping Farree's skin as he clung to the inside of the garment.

"So be it," the Lord-One said. "Two days we shall wait, while I also shall try to discover why our work goes so slowly. Then you will return, whether you have learned anything or not." He slipped one of his long-fingered hands under Farree's pointed chin and stared down into the hunchback's wide eyes with such command that Farree was forced to agree, knowing well that he could not deny that order. These two were not like any others he had known, and he could not guess what form their control might take—even an unrecognized molding of his own mind to obey.

He stood as soon as the Lord-One released him and scooped up some of the dust and straw by the door, smearing it with a careful hand down the fore of his robe.

"You shall shout evil after me, kick me forth—" he told the Lord-One. "Do this with no lightness. Any who watch—as you may be watched—must be deceived."

"Well enough!" The Lord-One reached down to grab his knotted shoulder and hurled him out of the hut. As Farree sprawled forward on the ground, one hand curved over the hidden smux to protect it from harm, he felt the pain of a well-placed kick. Loud in his ears were curses noted in the trade lingo and others which must be in the Lord-One's own tongue.

A booted toe scraped along the side of his tousled head, and he uttered a cry of fear as he scuttled, first on hands and knees, and then on his feet, away from the hut across the field toward the gate. Behind him came the Lord-One, yelling curses and accusations that this was a thief no honest man would want around, and when Farree slowed by the gate the boot caught him again, this time in his side and with enough force to leave a bruised hurt. The two guards on duty only laughed, and one of them swung the stock of his gas rod, thudding it home with such vigor above the hump that Farree nearly lost his balance again.

He ran as he had run many times in the past, heading for the nearest straggle of buildings marking the Limits. Out of somewhere a clod of hard earth struck his ear and brought another cry out of him.

He scuttled between buildings, twice slipping in the noisome scum that marked all but the main ways of the Limits, and kept on running until a sharp pain under his ribs brought him up to hold a tent rope, gasping.

Though his robe was not tattered, it was bespattered with dirt and foulness, and he believed that his appearance was little better than when the lordly ones had led him forth from this place of ever-abiding terror and despair.

However, his wits had not been dimmed along with the cleanliness of his robe. Now, even as he breathed in gasps, he looked about him, trying to fathom where to lurk to learn what he had come to pick up. To keep well away from Russtif's section of the Limits was also necessary.

This was a section of drinking booths ready to catch the lower ranks from any ship which finned down on the landing field. Though it was not alive with custom as it would be later on, there were enough men in the shacks to make a din that Farree found loud after his days in the upper town. He dodged a staggering, singing couple who wavered out of the nearest den and slunk along behind the crude buildings.

Toggor was riding right under his chin now, eyestalks were extending over the collar of the robe. The smux seemed to be watching their surroundings with a purpose, Farree thought, equal to his own.

He approached L'Kumb's gambling establishment and squatted down near its door. There was an old superstition which he loathed—that to rub the hump of such as he would increase a man's luck. He had never willingly allowed it before, but now he had a purpose in which he could accept debasement. Thus, he squatted with his thin knees poked up, both hands resting in the dust of the ground, his head turned up as far as he could. His back was to the wall of the shack. He tried to tune in the voices inside, but he found them too muffled to follow—save for the cries brought about by success or failure.

A man wearing the worn leather of a space officer—lighter spots on the breast from which insignia had been ripped away—trod purposefully forward. Farree recognized the type: a planeted junior officer who had been fired from or missed his ship and was on the downward road into the floating trash of the Limits. He was darkly browned as became an off-worlder—even his scalp, for it had either been shaved or he was naturally hairless.

In spite of the evidence of his worn clothing, he did not look like one of the lost. There were no dribbles of Graz from the corners of his wide mouth and he walked with the alert stride of one who had purpose in life. As he came, Farree saw that he shot sharp glances about him, even over his shoulders, as if he thought he might be under surveillance. From one of the Limits guards who wanted a larger bribe than could be gotten out of that shabby belt pouch? The pouch was not flat, Farree saw, and he noted that the spacer's hand was never far from it. Therefore he must be in funds—and so would be welcome in L'Kumb's establishment.

Then those keen eyes, which seemed to belie the role the other was playing, caught and held on Farree, and the spacer swung a little out of his way, his hand dropping to thump the hunchback sharply between his bowed shoulders.

"Wish me luck, Dung." He fumbled inside the vest he

wore and from an inner pocket produced a bit, a section split
from a well-worn stellar, snapping it to the ground before
Farree's bare toes.

"Luck." Farree mouthed the word obediently but absently
for he was surprised. To his memory this off-worlder was a
stranger. How could he use the noisome name known to the
Limits? How many strangers might then have heard of Dung
and would mark his coming and going?

The man had already turned away and was passing through
the doorless entrance of the shack. Farree's hand closed over
the fragment of metal he had been thrown. Though he wanted
to hurl it from him, that gesture would be foolish. He needed
to eat if he stayed for any time in the Limits, and this would
provide him with a bowl of stew at Hangstna's tent, as long
as he was content to enter the kitchen half and bestow it on
Mug the waiter-bartender.

Toggor moved and wriggled out of the neck of Farree's
tunic, swinging down onto the hunchback's knee where he
squatted, retracting three of his eyestalks and whirling the
others about in a way which could make a viewer a little
dizzy to watch.

"What? What see?"

Perhaps his association with the two spacers and their
communication from mind to mind had strengthened Farree's
own powers. The swing of touch in and out that had always
been a part of his contact with Toggor was less, and he had
caught what was surely a question much more easily than he
ever had before. A thought of his own struck Farree, and he
touched the smux on his bristled back just below the head.
Could he use the small creature to go where he could not
venture without risking an end to his mission?

"Toggor see?" He shaped the message so that it was a
question, and promptly enough came the answer.

"Toggor see—what?"

"In." Farree jerked a claw thumb at the shed. "Hide—see?"

But it was not going to be easy. The smux drew together into a ball as always when threatened by something greater than himself. The sense of refusal struck without words to center it.

It had been only a passing thought. Farree resigned himself regretfully. All kinds of parasites and vermin roamed the Limits—some of them deadly. He had fought twice for his own life against the slashing-toothed vir that hunted in packs and, when forced by hunger, were known to have set upon sleeping drunks and left nothing but well-stripped bones behind.

For the first time Farree was startled himself. The smux apparently had followed his chain of thought, though it had not been deliberately aimed at him. For Toggor curled up three eyestalks, turning one lidless appendage to watch the door of the shack and the other two on Farree. The message followed the direction of the pair of eyes.

"See—in—what?"

Yes, what? He was sure that he could not implant in the smux's very alien mind the purpose of spying. But he could try something as a test—a watch on the spacer who had just entered, perhaps.

"See—him." He pictured as best he could the man who had just thumped him for luck. "What he—do."

"Toggor be caught."

"Toggor small. Hide, watch." Farree scooped up a handful of the evil-smelling dust of this path between shacks and poured it on the lifted edge of his already much befouled robe, mounding it there with busy fingers. "Toggor covered with this." All of the eyestalks had arisen again, and more than half of them watched that dust sifting through the hunchback's fingers.

Farree did not add anything more. He was no Russtif to command obedience from the smux. He had asked; now it was up to Toggor whether the other would agree or not.

The smux reached out a foreclaw and dabbled it in the dust

that Farree had mounded on the edge of his robe. The claw scooped up a fraction and let it slide again through its hold. Then brought up a second lot to toss it over the bristles on the back.

Farree needed no other reply. Delicately, so as not to drop any motes to irritate the outstanding eyes, he took up pinches and spread them on the smux. The creature hopped from his knee hold, landing out in the dust, and proceeded to draw in his eyes and then roll across the ground. Moments later the smux looked like a clod of earth.

Farree picked up the small creature carefully and set him by the open doorway. Putting out foreclaws, Toggor pulled himself in and out of sight.

Farree was suddenly rocked back by a wave of mixed fear and rage. He would not have believed that so small a creature could have projected that to him. There was a frazzled mind picture a part of it, something dark and ugly and—

There was only one thing, he believed, that could have brought that response out of the smux: Russtif!

Instant agreement sped thought-swift. The beast seller was there—with a wavery figure that Farree thought might have been the man he saw enter moments before. There was a third bulk, but Farree could pick up no more than the fact someone else was present.

Farree drew himself tight against the rotting timbers of the shaky wall. When he put out a hand and scraped his nails along it splinters loosened. If he could just—

"Near you?" he asked Toggor. He was sure that the smux had not gone far into the room inside. And if those three were in good sight then they must be not too far from the partition against which he now huddled.

"Here," Toggor beamed in reply—though where "here" could be Farree could not be sure.

He put an ear to the boards where he had scratched. But he must also keep an eye for any passing by who might sight

him. There were voices right enough and words—but not the
words of gamblers. He treasured what he might catch.

"—no pilot."

"See that remains so."

"Stellars, stellars like bits." That was Russtif; Farree
could never forget that growl.

"Tell—"

"Why share?" Russtif again.

"L'Kumb knows. Never get away with—"

"His plan—why always his?" That voice was raised a
little. There followed a thought which broke through Farree's
concentration.

"This one comes. Trouble moves—"

And come the smux did, slipping through the hole in the
board and leaping for the folds of Farree's robe. Then he
scrambled within at the neck.

"Bad one. Look. See."

Fear froze Farree in turn. He jerked back from the wall and
scrambled on hands and knees around to the back of the
shack. There he forced himself to halt and watch around the
corner he had put between himself and the alley. If the beast
seller had indeed sighted the smux, he might be issuing forth
to get him.

Russtif did come out, but he did not glance down the alley.
Tramping heavily across its mouth, he was gone. Farree's
heart ceased its leaping beat and settled down to steady
rhythm again. The animal dealer was followed by another
man—not the spacer Farree had wished luck but a tall fellow
wearing the uniform of a guard, one who stood for a heart-
stopping moment at the mouth of the alley. But he, too,
failed to glance down it. Rather, he looked after Russtif and
then shrugged at some thought and turned in the opposite
direction.

Farree settled down to wait for the spaceman. Somehow he
believed that this off-worlder had importance to his own

mission. He had to wait for quite a while—perhaps the man was trying his luck after all.

When he came out he strode across the alley mouth in two steps, but Farree had already planned ahead how he could follow. There was a back way he had spied out and, though his pace was not a run, he had learned to be fast in his own way. Stones and blows had taught him much about the need for speed.

He was always the length of a tent or a shack behind the spacer, keeping to the shadow which had risen fast as the sun had gone down. There was more activity on the "street," and that would grow with the night. As long as it was not more than now, Farree could follow.

The man turned, heading along one of the crooked ways that led through the Limits to, at length, give upon the respectable streets of the upper town. If he crossed into that Farree dared not follow. There he would be as visible to the first passerby as a scarlet lurpa among dudan lilies. He was growing breathless and tired also, for he was not used to long stretches at his highest speed. And he had to pick always a shadowed way which often led him off the right path.

To his relief the spacer did not cross over into the upper town, rather turned in at the door of one of the more respectable buildings of the Limits—one which offered lodging to such travelers as could still pay half a stellar each morn. Rubbing his ribs where a sharp pain bit at him, Farree hunched down in the nearest pool of shadow, unsure of his next move. Why he had chosen to follow this stranger he was still unsure, but the man was an off-worlder, a spacer plainly down on his luck, for no spacer would stay planetside for long if he could help it. Farree had heard the Lord-One Krip say that their own ship needed a minimum of crew or it could not raise. He had hired one crewman, a spacer who had been planeted when the captain of a prospecting ship could not afford a needed rebuild. The crewman had been willing to sign on for his own need to get to a more traffic-filled field on another and richer world. Was this man Farree had followed such a one?

4.

Could he play the role of a beggar at the back of the rest place? It was well known that the trash did this from time to time. However, should the spacer sight him, the man might think it was too much of a coincidence that he had seen Farree by the gambling tent and saw him also here, more than halfway across the Limits. What had he learned? Little enough—that there was a reason why someone would have difficulty in finding an off-world crew. There was only one trying to hire such now—the Lord-One Krip.

Farree hesitated, trying to plan his next foray for knowledge when he saw another come down the street, walking boldly and swinging a silencing club. The guards had tanglers and stunners, but most of them relied on their clubs to keep order, preferring to leave a half-dead, beaten victim in the street rather than take the time and trouble to bind and deliver a prisoner to their general headquarters.

Farree squeezed backwards as far as he could go, careful not to catch the eye of one trained to sight just such a disturber of the uncertain peace as the hunchback was deemed to be. He breathed slowly and shallowly, with as long a pause between each breath as he could manage. There was the wreckage of a crate of more than usual substance pulled into this space between two structures, and Farree made the best use of that that he could.

The guard did not hesitate, turning directly into the rest house as the spacer had earlier. Farree tried to think clearly. Perhaps this one carried some message—one that would mean much if he could report it to those who waited for him near the port. But how might he worm his way into the building, see those he must spy upon? Though it was now heavy twilight and only the few and far between street lanterns gave any glow, he knew better than to try and win past that doorway yonder.

Bristles scraped against his chest. The smux—could Toggor give him partial sight, a fraction of hearing, as he had at the drinking hole? Farree put his hand gently into the front of his befouled robe and felt the claws grip so that he could draw the smux out.

Farree's night sight had been trained to the peak of what his species could achieve during the years in the Limits. There was coming and going in the crooked street now. And at least four of the passersby turned into the rest house. He watched for his chance and crossed to shelter once more against a slimed wall, bringing out Toggor as soon as he settled himself in the best shadow concealment he could find. The smux's eyes were all up and out, fanning about his head at their farthest extent.

"What—do?"

Toggor seemed free of any fear. Farree studied the wall against which he crouched. The lowest story of the building was stone, very old and fitted block upon block with crumbling mortar in between. It might once have been an important building like those of the upper town. The second story was squared timbers, also rough. Farree thought that his own thin fingers could find openings there to draw himself up.

But the weight on his back was not meant for a climber, and would hinder any such attempt.

Instead, the hunchback held the smux closer to his own head as if the proximity would better broadcast the thought he labored to send.

"Man." Laboriously he pictured as best he could the spacer, not sure that the alien mind of the small creature could pick up the identification. "Find in—" He patted the stone of the wall with his other hand.

A little to his surprise the smux seemed almost eager to go, climbing over his fingers to latch foreclaws into one of the mortarless divisions between the blocks. Farree leaned as far as he could backward to watch the creature climb easily aloft. He reached the narrow sill of one of the slitlike windows. But apparently there was no entrance there for him. Instead he scrambled around to the wood and pulled up claw over claw. Then he was gone!

Farree looked around wildly. Had Toggor lost grip and fallen? No—there was a beam, not of thought, but emotion. Hunger, hunt—the smux had come into the runway of a vynate. Farree felt the bitterness of defeat. Once on the trail of one of those pests he could not hope to turn Toggor aside.

But neither would he loose the thin thread of mind touch that tied them together. The smux's hunger became strong enough to make Farree's own belly rumble, and he thought of a meat cake, rich, dripping with gravy, such as he had eaten only that morning. Hunger—then the attack—

He shivered, still making himself share the frenzy of Toggor as the smux tore into flesh, was spattered by blood, and then feasted to the full. Never before had Farree shared minds with a hunter, and he found his body trembling, his own hands clawing out as if he were faced with good food. Now the smux was satisfied. He must either summon it back somehow or—

Would Toggor now wish to sleep after his kill? If so, how could Farree retain any control over him?

He clasped and unclasped his fingers, drew a deep breath, and probed.

Perhaps his very uneasiness added strength to that call, for he reached the twittering mind of the small creature on the first try.

"Eat. Good. Eat!"

Farree began to despair of getting below that satisfaction of the successful hunt. He held on and kept trying though he felt that the smux was finding him an irritation but apparently not one Toggor could throw off. Deliberately Farree made his demand.

"Find. Find the man." Into that order he tried to pour the full extent of his mind hold.

"Eat!" The ecstasy of the hunt still held, and Farree could have beaten the wall beside him in his frustration.

"Find!" There were beads of sweat on his narrow forehead, matting the heavy thatch of his hair. "Find."

His mind touch wavered in and out more and more. The smux was caught up in his own world, triumphant, free to be himself perhaps for the first time since he was captured. What power could Farree raise which would bring Toggor again under his control, light as that control was?

"Find!" Though he realized that it was dangerous, Farree loosed his awareness of the world about him, built up the picture of the spacer, and beamed it savagely to the creature in the walls above. "Find!"

There were only the thinnest of threads uniting them now—and those Farree could not be sure of. The smux might continue where he was in the wall runways of the vermin, hunting and slaying to eat. Why should Toggor answer or want to come out again?

"Find!" Farree's full attention was on building that thread, on attempting to rouse the smux out of his lethargy. Then, suddenly, the thread was broken. There was only emptiness. Farree's head touched the wall up which Toggor had gone, failure making him weak. The smux had chosen his own way. He was gone!

Somehow Farree got to his feet. That the loss of the creature was his fault he understood only too well. He had been so intent on gaining his own ends that he had forgotten he was dealing with an assistant who had really no common interest with him. The smux could live for days, he was sure, scouting the runways, a killer such as no vyn could escape.

"Find!" He sent a last desperate and despairing silent cry into the nothingness where Toggor had been. Dared he wait and hope? He could not make up his mind. The spacer and the guard—there was manifestly a tie between them, one into which Russtif was also drawn. Then, out of the nothingness, there came a weak signal.

"Man!" That fuzzy picture was so bad it could have been either the spacer or the guard. But Toggor had been set to locate the spacer, so—

Wild with relief, Farree had to keep a tight grip on himself to allow his thoughts to simmer down to calmness, then to sharpen into the meet prod.

"What do—?" That he had been wrong about Toggor made him feel a little dizzy.

"Man. Man."

Twice? Maybe that signified another meeting—the guard and the spacer. If he only had a hearing hole such as he had found back at the shack. A few words might make all the difference!

Two fuzzy shapes were beamed to him now. They were close together, facing one another. Then they grew sharper as if the smux were making a supreme effort.

Anger. Anger and threat. The smux could not report words, but the emotions he picked up were warning enough. Whatever those two planned meant trouble. Trouble for the off-worlders? Farree could not be sure, but he believed that it pointed to such.

There was an alteration in the scene the smux projected. One of the fuzzy figures stood up, disappeared out of range. The other remained where he was—that was the spacer, Farree was sure, since it was he Toggor had been sent to track.

"Come." There was nothing further to be learned, Farree was sure, as long as the smux could not provide him with ears.

"Another comes," the creature on spy aloft returned.

"Show me. Show me this other as well as you can!" Would that plea bring him anything? Toggor's sight was not his, and what was clear to the smux was badly blurred for him. Yet another figure did join the spacer now. To Farree's joy there was a distinguishing mark to this one. He wore the uniform of a spaceman, yes, but across the breast was a splash of vivid color. Smux's sense of color was also not human. He registered in shades of red and yellow seemingly, having no other shade or hue to project. This splash was yellow.

"Come!" He wanted to get Toggor away from the tempting runways hidden in the inn's walls. Now he wondered if he *could* draw the smux away from so rich a hunting ground.

There was someone coming out of the front door of the inn, humming as if he were free of a burden. Farree cowered as the guide went by. It was sheer luck that the man turned north instead of south, heading toward the narrow way where the Limits touched the upper town.

Toggor had broken off touch again. Farree could only hope that that meant the smux was returning to him, not starting another hunt. Twice more he beamed, "Come," without any answer. It was dark enough now so that the wall above him was shadowed. Those lanterns which lit the street did not send any beam this far back. And there was a hum of noise carrying up from the other side where lay the bulk of the Limits—that district was coming into its nightly life.

Then Farree saw movement within the shadow which lapped against the wall. Before he had more time than to draw three breaths the smux leaped from the sill of the narrow window above to land on his hunched back, running lightly around to burrow again into the neck opening of his robe.

Farree raised both hands and clasped them gently around Toggor, so relieved that the smux had returned to him that he could have gone forth humming as had the guard. Into his mind shot an impression of two wavering figures moving out from a room above. He crouched low in the dusk, his eyes upon the doorway of the inn. Then they came: the spaceman he had followed here, together with the other who wore the badge, which was not as brilliant as Toggor had pictured it for him but certainly was vivid.

Anyone in the Limits knew the meaning of that. Unlike the one who accompanied him, this second off-worlder still belonged to some ship's company. Yet Farree was not knowledgeable enough to know which.

Unlike the guard, the two headed downslope toward the distant landing field, and Farree again slipped through the pools of dusk between the lanterns, tracking them. He caught words now and then, but they were not in trader lingo, and he did not understand. Save that the spacers were talking earnestly as they went.

They did not pause at the gaming places nor the drinking dens but threaded a way straight for the port where the brilliant lights about the ships provided a beacon against the murky ways of the surrounding territory.

There were three ships on the landing apron, spaced well apart. That which belonged to the off-worlders, Farree knew, was the closest to the gates, and there was scaffolding about its outer skin though no workmen were visible at this hour. Beyond was a small Patrol skimmer, a messenger vessel which had landed only two days earlier with information for the local League council. Beyond that stood a merchant-class vessel, larger than that which the off-worlders had claimed, with a battered, space-scoured insignia on one fin.

The two he followed passed the gate, and the guard there asked no questions as they went on toward the ship under reconstruction. Farree must follow them. But to get past the light, which was full at the gates, and the guard there—could he?

Hunkering down in a noisome pocket between two of the nearer Limits tents, Farree bent his head forward until his forehead rested on his crossed arms. He strove with frantic need for an answer.

It was as if he whirled out into a space that was filled with almost invisible ribbons floating and spinning, seeking the right one to guide him to his needed goal. There were flashes of thought, which he tried earnestly to shut out that he might seek single-mindedly. Then—

"Little brother!" Not the muddled response he got from Toggor, but as clear as if the words had been spoken in one of his prick-pointed ears.

"In." Certainly he had little to report—only the two meetings. Yet he also had a strong feeling that the news he carried was needed, and there was little time. "Bring me in."

For a heart-shaking moment he thought that he had lost contact—that it was as it was between him and Toggor—his talent was too limited, too diffuse to hold. Then there came strong and steady the answer: "Be ready—near the gate."

He went forward on all fours, feeling the prick of Toggor's claws and bristle hair as the smux rode in the fore of his robe. So he reached the edge of the shadows—beyond which lay only the merciless light of the gate.

There was someone approaching from the opposite side, and he saw the hood of a cloak slip back from the head of that brilliant hair as deep as any Milisand ruby in shade. The Lady was coming for him herself.

She halted before the guard and spoke, the murmur of her voice carrying but not her words. Her right hand was up, and she twirled something between her fingers with a rhythmic movement.

"Now!"

Farree had to trust. He ran forward on his spindly legs, both hands pressed over the smux lest he lose Toggor. When he stumbled over a stone and it moved with a click, the guard did not look around. Then Farree dared the gate itself, putting all his strength into a dash which carried him by the Lady Maelen and the guard with a speed that near sent him sprawling forward. But he kept to his feet and hurried toward the hut where the bartle was housed.

Outside of that was the Lord-One Krip, and with him the two men Farree had followed from the Limits. The hunchback pushed himself behind the hut, hoping that he had not been sighted. Why the guard had not seen him when he was in plain sight at the gate he could not guess.

He lay nearly flat now as Toggor climbed up and back to squat upon his hump. The Lady was still at the gate, with the guard listening to her as if his position depended upon her words. But she had dropped her hand and the shining thing had disappeared. Finally the man saluted and she turned away, coming back toward the hut.

Farree drew a deep breath and huddled where he was. He heard a little chirping call. The smux scrambled down and scuttled to the fore of the hut, leaving Farree for a moment or two a little angry that the creature would so readily obey that summons from another.

"Well enough. If you bring a quittance from your captain then we shall deal." That was the Lord-One Krip talking. "We sign only until first planetfall, you understand."

"That is to my advantage also, Captain." It was a new

voice—that of the spaceman who wore the insignia? "Also the *Dragon* already carries a senior astrogator. When do you lift?"

"Soon enough. See me tomorrow with your papers. And yours, Quanhi—have you full clearance for hire?"

"I will bring a statement from the councilor. I am fit again and want nothing more than to be free of Grant's World. Few enough ships touch here to give me much chance."

"We will consider."

"Right enough!" Together, the two Farree had followed turned and went back toward the field gate.

Farree crept around the side of the hut, putting it between him and the gate. He made a last dash and took himself inside before Lord-One and the Lady Maelen entered. The bartle moved uneasily, and Farree heard a low growl out of the dark. But another shape stood over him, licking at his face—Yazz giving her usual exuberant welcome.

"What have you learned?" The Lady Maelen came first, and at a twist of her fingers there was a dim light in the hut.

What had he learned? Bits and pieces. Perhaps none really were of importance. Yet Russtif had a place and a part, and the dealer in beasts was for Farree the symbol of evil, an evil that could reach out and touch these two. He could not have found words to explain what the Lady and the Lord-One meant to him, he could only offer all he could summon to their service.

"Those who were there," he began in haste so his words were almost a gabble. Then he caught hold of himself. "One, he who wears no badge, met with Russtif and a guard. They said—" He summoned the few words he had caught: "No pilot—stay that way—stellars like bits—and L'Kumb—he plans something. The badgeless one meets with a guard again and then with he who wears a badge."

"Stellars like bits—" Lord-One Krip repeated. "Where would such a speech *be* the truth?"

"On Sehkmet," the Lady Maelen returned promptly. "That tale is one of the legends of the star lanes now."

"But that world is fully guarded. No raider, or even a Guild-owned vessel, could set down anywhere there."

"Yet those who found it first could carry away information of perhaps other finds—a danger we considered from the first. And the clutching fingers of this Guild extend far. Perhaps they think to plant one—two of their own among us."

"We would read them."

"Would we?" the Lady Maelen asked then. "It is well known that the Guild has access to many discoveries that even the Patrol does not know. Remember, on Sehkmet there were mind shields which we could not break."

"But those were—"

"Of the dead old ones, you would say? We cannot be sure they do not otherwise exist. What mankind has once discovered can be found again." She turned to Farree.

"You heard no more?"

He shook his head. "It is said that Russtif would link with L'Kumb if he could. It was in a gambling hut that he met with the badgeless one—"

"Pitor Dune of Chamblee, suffering with spotted fever, was left here when his ship lifted four months ago. And this other, Quanhi, who wishes a full berth for himself as astrogator," the Lord-One Krip said slowly. "We have a half crew at least. And now the rigger has his men on the jump to get finished, saying frankly he must have the money."

"It links," the Lady Maelen said slowly. "We have had trouble in finding men. Yiktor is no major base, even now when the League plays more a role in her current history."

Lord-One Krip laughed. "Ah, but they do not know what powers the Thassa have—the Thassa and She Who Slept."

The Lady shook her head almost violently. "Not so, Krip. Nothing did I learn from her. She was—the real part of her—long dead or gone elsewhere. I but banished the will which kept her waiting. But we bewilder you, small one."

She smiled down at Farree. "Know that we are Thassa, a people so old we have forgotten our beginnings. It was given to us to find a mighty treasure of the Forerunners on the planet Sehkmet and there was trouble there, for the Guild would also plunder it. The Guild lost and the winning was ours. We seek a ship of our own and so here we found the *Far Seeker* for sale, one which will serve us well. But the time is short. The three rings will shine on Yiktor our home world, and to that world we must go. It is a tangled tale in our past—you will have the hearing of it some time."

"I?" Farree strove to lift his head higher. As if she knew what frustration moved him, the Lady knelt and laid her hands one on each shoulder.

"If you wish to come, little one, then it shall be so," she repeated the earlier promise.

Farree drew a deep breath. To stride the stars as if he were straight and strong and stood as tall as the Lord-One himself—that was something he had not dared trust.

"Yes—oh, yes!" His own hands flew to his shoulders to cover hers where they rested warm and welcoming. "Oh—yes!" He could have shouted that aloud.

"So be it." She nodded. "Now let us think concerning this man Quanhi who seems so willing to come—"

"He thinks we lift for Greater Marth," said Lord-One Krip.

"Let him continue to think so. The voyage tape I hold myself," she answered. "And we need no astrogator in truth once the tape is locked in—only the port authorities require we have one aboard. As for those trying some tricks with us—'' Now it was her turn to laugh, raising her hand to gesture to the rest of them, Farree, Yazz, and Bojor the bartle as well as the smux clinging now to her own shoulder. ''I think we may have some surprises for them.''

5.

He whom Farree had spied upon came again to the bartle's hut. The hunchback shrank to the rear of the hut, trusting the big animal. Toggor sat on his shoulder, eyestalks aloft, and beamed what Farree already guessed—that this was the one he had watched.

The man was young, though it was always difficult to tell the true age of any spacer since ship time and planet time were different and those who spent most of their days within the hulls of the sky ships did not age so swiftly. His badgeless uniform was shabby, but he seemed clear-eyed and quick to answer, not as if he were someone rightfully grounded.

"For the voyage only, Dune," Lord-One Krip repeated. "And are there any more willing to take service?"

"I can get you twenty," returned Pitor Dune. "That you would want them is another question. They may have been grounded for more than illness or ill luck. Quanhi is, however, a good man."

"I have said we would take him, as you heard, but to change ships in mid voyage—" Lord-One Krip began.

"May be the sign of an unsteady crewman, yes. What

55

excuse does he offer to *you*?'' Lady Maelen asked of Dune. She might be checking stories.

"None, except he can expect no further promotion within the *Dragon*, and that is an outland trader which does not set down on many worlds with larger ports and more traffic."

"We shall take him when he brings quittance," Lord-One Krip returned. "In the meantime, you also bring your papers as you promised."

The crewman started out across the field. On Farree's shoulder the smux moved, and the hunchback caught a fraction of emotion once more—uncertainty, shadowed by fear. Behind him Bojor gave a deep grunt. Instantly Lady Maelen turned her head to observe the tall beast. Farree caught her questioning concern.

It came as with the smux—no words, only the feeling of wrongness, of the need for being aware.

"We are warned," the Lady commented. "It seems that there is something about our new shipmate which the small ones do not like." She was beaming soothingly, promising that there would be no trouble with the strangers.

Once more Lord-One Krip questioned Farree.

"Russtif, yes. His interest I can understand. He was over-paid for one of his slave things," the Lady mused. "Yet had we bargained, that would have given him time to wonder, to think . . ."

For the first time Farree dared question the off-worlder.

"Lady, he will think, does think. From him perhaps others have learned."

She made a face and shrugged her shoulders. "I lose my caution when I answer a help cry. Perhaps we were wrong. But the man was ugly enough to have killed this little one." She held out her hand, and the smux extended a long curl of tongue to touch the tip of her finger.

"You have fitted the tape?" Lord-One Krip changed the subject.

"Last night when the workmen left," she answered. "I have learned much, and perhaps even this new body of mine retained some level of knowledge. When we lift we do so for Yiktor."

New body? wondered Farree. What story lay behind that? But he dared not question now.

"There has certainly been a change in the fitters," her companion returned. "They have kept on the job steadily this afternoon. Tomorrow we can move Bojor aboard. By the next sunrise we shall lift ship."

"Providing we get this astrogator Quanhi. But, Krip, of this I am sure, we shall get him, and for no reason which means us well. Our only protection is our sealed tape that cannot be withdrawn by any except my own hand."

"And that tape was bought on Ballard. The *Dragon* last raised from that world," the other answered her. "That is an open port—"

She nodded. "If we go threatened from the left, we can only hope for aid from the right. On no other world are such tapes for sale, and we had to deal with those outside the law of the League in order to get it. News travels near as fast as thought. Ah, here comes our new shipmate and with him Quanhi—you are sure that this is the one who met him in the Limits, small one?"

The Lady moved aside a fraction from the doorway and Farree could see out into the lighted field. He would be certain of that emblazoned badge anywhere, but as for the man—he could not be sure. So he reported.

"Quanhi," Lady Maelen repeated the name. "And of no world—perhaps a Free Trader then."

"Not so," Lord-One Krip snapped. He was frowning now, his attention all for the man coming toward them. "We shall see how much this one desires to become one of the crew," Lord-One Krip observed. "Stay in the shadows," he spoke now to the hunchback. "It is better that they do not see you and perhaps speak of you."

Farree speedily hunkered back, Toggor riding on his shoulder. Bojor moved aside as if ordered, giving only a snuffing sniff in the hunchback's direction. Yazz was lying full length, lost in the shadows at the back of the hut.

The man from the other ship looked even younger in this stronger light than the other—with an open expression which Farree found hard to think of as belonging to a plotter. He answered Lord-One Krip's questions freely and openly but—

In spite of the order given Farree and his own uneasiness, he sent a single tendril, thread fine, toward the other's mind. And he met—

Nothingness!

Not a barrier, not the swirl of alienness which marked the smux, the bartle, and Yazz. Simply an emptiness, as if no one stood there at all. That was so frightening that, for a full moment, he shivered and strove to the edge even farther away. Yet when he opened the eyes he had squinted shut, there was a man like any other walking the Limits or the upper town.

He had heard tales—always told with gusto but never believed—of how, on some distant world, there were beings with the look of men but who were in truth machines. Those would even think when properly supplied with the right tapes, just as a ship could be guided, once in space, to a chosen world. Was he now fronting one of those fearsome things neither living nor dead?

Like their bargain with Dune, this other one was quickly struck, but, as the astrogator left, Maelen spoke softly, using a language Farree did not know. He heard harshness in the Lord-One Krip's quick answer.

The Lady looked over her shoulder to where Farree crouched. "Mind touch?"

He knew what she meant and first shook his head and then, fearing she could not see, answered in words.

"There was nothing. Nothing at all!"

"A shield," Lord-One Krip said then, "and that is surely Guild. But if they knew us they also know that we would detect such at once and be warned off."

"A machine one?" Farree ventured.

"What do you know of such?" Lady Maelen asked.

"Only stories," he answered. "No one believes them true."

"Yet once such things were," she answered slowly. "Once the Thassas knew such. But also I do not understand why they would send us a well-shielded one."

"They may think that it is only with each other and with the animal ones we can communicate," Lord-One Krip said slowly. "Yet the Guild have the reputation of taking nothing and no one on trust. There are many races and species in space. The Zacanthans in their rolls of history have only a partial listing of such and their attributes both physical and mental. They did not even know of the Thassa until we met on Yiktor. There may be many others—even a race born with a natural mind shield. Still, it argues planning on their part. This is a warning, for it goes with all we know of the Guild."

The Thieves Guild had spread and entwined world after world—where star rovers went, sooner or later the Guild followed. They were reputed to be masters of strange knowledge and devices which they stole or bought before the Patrol realized that such existed.

Farree ran his tongue across his lips and then asked in a small voice: "Could it be known that time is of importance to your plans, Lord-One, and that you would chance taking whoever offered because of that?"

"Yes," Lord-One Krip replied, "that makes sense. However, these two may have defenses or weapons of which we know nothing. And to blast off with such aboard—''

Toggor moved. His eyestalks were all extended to the farthest limit and swung so that they pointed after the man who had just left.

A fuzzy picture in Farree's mind. One which the Lady Maelen must have picked up as quickly as the hunchback.

"He is not a machine—that one," she said. "The smux finds true life there and danger."

"Yazz, Bojor." The Lord-One looked to the two other animals.

"Live. Like Yazz. Live," answered that one at once. The bartle growled, sitting up on his broad and weighty haunches, making gestures of holding something in his front paws.

"I think," Lady Maelen said slowly, "that we may have our own warning alerts from directions which our new ship-mates will not guess. They can accept animals performing because of threats or promises, but not little ones who share with us that true life of all that is equal in Molester's scales of being. We shall mount our safeguards. You have made your own lock installments on the cages?'' She turned to Lord-One Krip.

"Yes; we shall test them this night. It will serve that our little ones are firmly housed and yet''—he smiled a little grimly—"that will be only a cover.''

Farree had been in the ship before, but that had been a hurried visit and only to that section meant to house those the Lady Maelen called her "little ones.'' Though she used the same term for Farree himself, there was a difference which was subtle but which he had caught. He was perhaps as ignorant of worlds beyond this planet as the animals, or even more so, for those had roved the wilds far beyond the Limits. Yet to these two off-worlders he was common kin.

Now he lay in the bunk which had been assigned to him. For the off-worlders and their live companions had chosen to

go within the ship though it was still fin down. However,
what he was thinking had nothing to do with the events of the
past two days. Rather he was caught up in what he had never
experienced before: a waking dream of wonder. That was
centered upon something he had seen in the Lady Maelen's
quarters.

A cube which seemed transparent and clear of any content—
one which was only slightly larger than what he could hold
comfortably in his two hands. When the Lady touched it,
there had come a swirl of color within as he watched in
astonishment. He might have been poised in the air above
another land—one so far different from the Limits that dream
was all he could find to call it.

There were wide plains—small within the limits of the
cube's space, yet the longer one looked at the scene the wider
those spread, as if one became smaller than a sand jumper
and had been pulled into the picture. There was green—great
stretches of green growing things, starred here and there with
brilliant splashes of color, some widely separated, some massed
together. Growing things also, but the like of which Farree
had never seen before.

Far down in his cramped memory something stirred even
as it had when they had asked his true name. Color, growing
things— There were none such in the Limits, yet he recognized them for what they were instantly: a mantling of rich,
tall-growing grass and—flowers. Faltering memory produced
a name for him.

His nostrils expanded. Yet there was nothing save the air
of the ship to fill them. He had expected something else:
clean, strong, unlike the sour stench of the Limits. Why did
he think of that?

"Yiktor." The Lady Maelen's word had cut through his
searching of memory. "The Thassa wander wide over these
plains, though their own private place is near desert." She
was, he saw by an upward glance, concentrating on the cube

with an intent stare. "We shall be in Yiktor! In the circling
of the rings."

The scene within the cube swirled again from clarity into a
fog of mingled color. Farree gave a small exclamation of
protest. But the cube did not clear entirely. Now there hung a
ball of light within it, and around that three distinct rings of
radiance grew and held.

He felt a greater wonder than even the flower-studded land
had given him. This was a thing out of the sky—a miracle of
light unlike any he could have imagined. The sight brought no
faint recognition with it; it was totally alien to anything he
even had heard described.

The Lady reached out long fingers and caressed the cube
as she had done at times the bartle and Yazz, as if she needed
the reassurance that they did exist. Farree felt a strong wave
which was both of sadness and of joy—though, before this
moment, he could not have believed two such diverse emotions could be interwoven.

Then she lifted the cube and instantly the picture was
gone. She took a soft piece of spider silk and wrapped what
was now only a clear and colorless artifact, then placed it in
one of the wall compartments.

Farree longed to see again that flowery land, to feel that he
had been drawn into the dream and become a part of the
whole, accepted and at—at home—

"You saw," the Lady spoke slowly as she turned from the
compartment she had locked with her thumb seal. "Yiktor,
which I . . ." Now her voice failed for an instant before she
added, "which I long for and to which we go."

She clasped her hands together, rubbing one over the other
as if some substance had escaped the cube to moisten her
fingers. "Yiktor," she breathed for the third time. Then her
glance wavered from the compartment door, and she looked
directly at Farree.

"You saw. But there was something else—you remembered."

Oddly enough he felt suddenly threatened by her words. It was as if her probe could pierce easily into an inner part of him—a far inner part which cowered away from light and knowledge. There was a growing pain within him, which he found hard to handle.

"I did not remember," he countered quickly. "There was always the Limits—just the Limits."

"Your kin—your father—your mother?" She was not going to let him escape. But she need only keep mind touch with him to know the answer to that. The Limits, always the Limits—but then the man—

For the first time in years Farree was remembering the man. He was only a shape, faceless, to be feared, yet all-powerful. He had died drunken and Farree had fled. He himself had been even smaller then, a misshapen lump of flesh which no one could look upon except with distaste or fear. Like Toggor, he had been alone. His kin? Who would claim kin with such as he? He had never seen his like even among the beggars, some self-mutilated to arouse pity. From them he had kept apart, moved by the queer feeling that were he to seek a place in their stinking, shambling guild he would be, in a strange way, lost.

He was stronger than he looked, and there was a core of determination within him to keep him going on his own. How long had it been? The refuse of the Limits did not reckon years, only seasons—hot and cold. And he did not add those up.

Before he realized what she was about to do, Farree felt the Lady's hands at the neck fastening of his robe. She pulled at the cloth, bringing it down to bare his hump.

He flared with a thrust of sick anger. Then her mind speech touched him quickly. At least she had not put hand to that monstrous roll of flesh which he bore always with him.

"This is no hurt, yet it looks as if it were old scarring."
She shook her head. "A healer I once was—a Moon Singer
who could bring good out of ill. And much have I seen of
bad wounds and injuries. The Thassa have their own dangers,
which do not equal those of other species. This looks more
like a shell—"

Farree jerked the cloth of his robe, fastened it tightly once
again. "No Singer can make me straight," he answered
sullenly.

But she did not let him go. Though she did not touch him
again, yet he realized that he must answer her. For the first
time he resented with more and more bitterness this mind tie
between them. What had once seemed to him to be an
opening gate to understanding now took on the bars of a
cage.

"No, I think not. But for everything there is a reason. Do
you suffer pain?"

He had to answer with the truth. "No—except the pain of
its weight. It grows heavier with the passing of time."
Against his will truth came out of his mind. He had suffered
the pain of kicks and cuffs aplenty, but the weight on his
shoulders which curved him forward had never hurt. There
was an itching which came at times, more often recently. He
had been driven once or twice by the force of that to rub his
back against the stone walls of the inn within the Limits.

"If you suffer pain, Farree," she addressed him now as
she might the Lord-One Krip, "come to me. Though I am an
exile from the Thassa, yet I still hold some power in these."
She held up her hands and flexed her fingers.

Now, as Farree lay circled on his side in his own place (for
he had been given a small cabin of his own, to his unvoiced
wonder), every bit of that came back to him. She had meant
it, and he knew also that it was an offer he could not take. Or
at least he thought at this moment that he could not. The

burden was his own, and none but death might lift it from him.

Yet he kept remembering the pictures in the cube and his inner excitement grew. It was necessary for these two he held in unbreakable awe and reverence to go to that world of flowered plains and three-ringed moon, and they were taking him with them.

That they took off a day later with two on board who must be watched did not alarm Farree. He knew too well how to keep wary eyes and those thoughts which tied the rest of that company into a force none without mind touch might even deduce existed.

He who had the mind shield could be seen, and the other, though they were careful not to probe below his surface thoughts, could well be open to search if it became necessary. There had been a flare of protests from the astrogator when he discovered that they were traveling by a sealed tape. But on a privately owned ship that was not too uncommon, and his arguments had been few enough.

It was Toggor who provided their first sentry. Though they were in free-fall for a goodly space of time and Farree was miserably sick and fought to conceal that fact, the smux loosed its legs and swam in the air, catching at fittings for anchorage from time to time.

The Lady Maelen stayed with Bojor, who suffered the most for lack of proper weight and had to be constantly reassured that this was not something that would last forever.

Once in hyperspace the weak gravity of the ship gave them at least a chance for footing. Farree, out of some inner uneasiness, made it a point to learn how to get about without help—wishing that he had the smux's confidence.

There was no time except that rigidly marked by the ship's instruments. They kept to a series of watches wherein either Lord-One Krip or the Lady Maelen was on duty with one of their hastily assembled crew. For Farree there were no stated duties, but he would lie on his bunk for unknown periods of time, linked with Toggor, learning more and more how to channel the smux's foggy sight so that he so went exploring through the ship by that remote means.

Separated by division into watches which the off-worlders had devised, there seemed to be no reason for the two crewmen to get together. Nor did they.

It was during the tenth sleeping time that Farree awoke out of a troubled doze. He did not know what had haunted him so that he had not rested as deeply as he usually did. Then he looked out into the middle of the small cabin and saw, scuttling across the floor, Toggor, who had just pulled himself through the crack of the door. The smux's claws reached up and Farree put his hand down for the creature to climb.

Just as Toggor had once registered pain and cold, so now he registered again fear. Whipping up the hunchback's body, he sought a hiding place at the neck of his robe.

Farree sat up and dangled his thin, stunted legs over the side of the bunk, both hands over the smux's lump on his breast.

"What—?" He began and then realized again that the direct mind touch was not clear. Instead then he strove to disentangle emotions. He got what startled him first and then led to a flare of anger.

Toggor's picture was very fuzzy and it had been at floor level. There was something which was clearly part of a pilot's seat and then—then a boot, metal plated as were all in space, swung out and over the questing eyestalks, aimed to crush the smux. There was a quick flurry of movement, which Farree could not untangle, but it was plain that one of the crew had attempted, or had chanced, to nearly crush the smux, who had fled in a burst of fear.

Which of the crewmen—and why?

Patiently Farree struggled to subdue that fear, to get through the icy curtain of it for an answer.

Crewman—he could get no clearer answer than that. To Toggor perhaps both men looked alike. The fuzzy figure bent over, trying to claw at the wall of the command cabin. At least Toggor saw it so.

Farree had no idea of the duties aboard ship. The man might have been busied at some regulation task. But he was shaken enough by Toggor's report to try to raise Lord-One Krip whose watch should be ending about now.

What he found with the mind touch—nothing!

That nothingness was as strong as it had been for Quanhi. It was as if the off-worlder had ceased to exist.

The answer brought a fear as deep as Toggor's had been. Farree swung off the bunk, reached in to one of the compartments below. He brought out something which he had discovered in his earlier exploration of the ship: a stunner. The weapon was not made for hands as small and weak as his. But he could carry it. Though his inability to take hold with both hands would slow him on his travel through the weak gravity, weapon held butt to his chest near the lump that was Toggor, he left the cabin. Mentally he sought Bojor and Yazz as he went. Both of them reported no trouble.

Lady Maelen—dare he try to reach her or would that betray him in turn to the one with the mind lock?

6.

Farree scented it first in the central core, which held the ladder rising from one level of the ship to the next. It came as only a trace of a cloying sweetish odor which reminded him instantly of the noisome stews of the Limits and had no place in the sterile air of a space vessel. It wafted through the air from ducts on the next level, and Farree felt dizzy as if he floated out in some vast space with no ship to enclose or support him.

The Lady Maelen! Her cabin was here. He reached the door port and was stopped short. Across the surface, wedged well into the frame, was a bar making a prison for one inside. He put down the stunner. Then he swung his full weight on that bar. It was immobile as if it had been welded into place.

Panting, he huddled there, daring to use mind touch. Though he was sure that she whom he sought was inside, he touched—nothing! Just as the same answer came to his search for Lord-One Krip. Yet he could not believe that either of the off-worlders was dead.

Not up to the pilot's central cabin—not yet. Taking up the stunner, he pulled his distorted body down instead, seeking

69

the special quarters which had been installed for Bojor and Yazz on the lower level. His eyes smarted and he felt a burdening need for rest that he was sure was a part of the drugged vapor which had been fed through the air duct. However, as he went lower, trying to breathe as shallowly as possible, the traces of that sickly sweetness vanished. By the time he had reached the lower level all he could smell was the odor of the bartle, the acrid scent of its shaggy fur.

"What happens?" Yazz's quick demand caught Farree as he swung from the final hold on the ladder and approached the cage of the larger animal. Pressed tightly to the wall between them was Yazz, bright eyes ashine in the gloom of this level, lips drawn back to show fangs near as formidable as those of Bojor.

Farree came quickly forward.

"Trouble." He could only advance his own fears but that was enough to alert both animals instantly.

There came a single yap of reply from Yazz, a deep-chested growl from Bojor. Both of them now planted themselves, ready to issue forth were their doors opened. Outside the ship, planetside, both would have been formidable opponents. Within the confines here, it was another matter. Farree crouched down before the two animals and mind cast as well as he could what he had discovered, intensifying his fear of the pollutant in the air supply. Both of these were quicker to touch than the smux, and the channel between them and the hunchback was clearer.

"No food," came from Bojor. "Since last sleep no food."

Farree could guess the reason for that. To the crewmen there would be no reason to feed either the bartle or Yazz, the two animals having no value. The hunchback dragged himself across to the far wall. There were the levers he had seen tested and retested by the Lord-One Krip before they had lifted from Grant's World. He swung his weight on the nearest and it gave, allowing to fall into both cage-cabins the flat cakes of nutrient which were the voyage supplies.

Both animals wolfed down the food while Farree examined the fastenings of the cages. Those had also been carefully installed, and, though the builders had not realized it, pressure on one side would allow those within to use a paw for escape. Though Bojor had been cautioned against far roaming in the ship.

Farree applied that pressure. Now the cages might look intact but their occupants were free as they wished or needed to be. There was a skittering sound and the hunchback swung around, groping for the heavy weight of the stunner.

It was Toggor who came sliding down, one set of claws hooked loosely about the woven metal rope which formed the bannister for the ladder. All the smux's eyes were up and open. From the small creature flooded excitement and fear, but excitement was the stronger of those two emotions.

"What happens—" Farree beamed the question which Yazz had earlier used to greet him.

Once more he was greeted with a fuzzy picture of the crewman in the control cabin. Now that hazy figure was pounding on one section of the wall, and from him, through the smux, there flooded a raging anger and frustration.

Whatever he had tried to do in that place, he had not been able to accomplish it, and he was in a murderous mood.

"The Lord-One?" Farree asked then, picturing for himself the best replica of the off-worlder he could hold in mind.

What returned to him was a door with a bar as firmly across it as the one he had found sealing in the Lady Maelen. Perhaps overcome by the narcotic in the airstream, Krip had been downed and then imprisoned.

There had been only one of the crewmen in the smux's sight. Where then was the other?

The rumble of the bartle's growl and a click-clack of fangs from Yazz suggested they, too, had picked up Toggor's report. But if both the other-worlders had been sealed within their cabins after being overcome, why and how had Farree escaped?

Unless, Farree guessed, he seemed so negligible an opponent to the crewmen that they saw no reason to fear him and he had been classed with the other of Maelen's little ones. Well. He breathed deeply, inching forward to the ladder. No, there was no taint of the gas here. He was free, as were Toggor and the other two when they needed to make a move.

He had gone through the ship with Toggor and he knew it. Each cabin, storage place, walkway, was impressed firmly on his mind. Now, the stunner lying across his knees, he turned once more to the smux who was surely the one of them best suited to moving about unseen.

"Other man—" He spoke that aloud in a low voice as well as mind beamed. "Other one—"

A bit of the frustration of that one in the control cabin remained with Farree now, even though his contact with the smux was so limited. It would seem that the creature gained something from his demand, for he returned to the ladder rope down which he had come and began to climb.

There was another point which Farree must keep in mind: undoubtedly both of the crewmen were armed, and probably with far more potent weapons than the one he handled so awkwardly. A force blade or a laser could end any confrontation before he began.

He—

With all the directness of a blow, touch came to his mind then—the Lord-One Krip!

"Maelen?" A questing call sounded through his head as if it had come to his ears as a great, rousing shout.

There was no answer. But Farree cut in: "Her cabin—it is barred. Is yours also? Toggor reports it so."

"Farree!"

"Yes. I am free and with Yazz and Bojor. Toggor goes

aloft. One of the men has been trying to do something in the control cabin but has failed. I do not know where the other is—"

"Sleep gas. And you?"

"'Must be too far beneath their notice," the hunchback answered wryly.

"A force bar," came back quickly. "It must be detached. Can you—"

Farree interrupted with what he saw as the truth. "I cannot move while I do not know where they are—"

"Wait!"

He felt that also—the searching thought—though it was not beamed at him. Once more Bojor growled and this time raked his claws down the inner side of the door. Farree held up a hand in a signal which apparently the large animal understood.

"They are both shielded now," the Lord-One Krip aimed at Farree again. "I cannot find them—"

"There is Toggor. He has gone to search above—"

Instantly the prisoner seized upon that. "Seek him. I will feed you—seek him!"

Farree's whole twisted body quivered at what happened. There flowed into his mind such power as he would not have believed he could hold—nor did he try to contain it. Instead he thought of the smux, picturing him tightly and allowing that additional force to scrape along the path of his own thought.

For the first time the picture he received in return was far less fuzzed. At an odd angle, for the smux must be at floor level and the others towered far over him, Toggor was again surveying the control cabin. One of the men knelt on the floor, and there were tools laid out. He was working on a panel, which seemed to resist any attempt to loosen it.

"That is persona locked!" There was relief in Lord-One

Krip's thought. "They can never open it without wrecking the tape there so that it cannot be used."

"What do they want?" Farree dared to ask. His head hurt so that he was rubbing his forehead with one hand. To provide a mind path for the Lord-One was like trying to contain a burning river.

Abruptly, as if the other sensed his pain, that flood ceased and he lost contact with the smux as quickly as if someone had snapped a barrier between them.

"The voyage tape," came the answer. "They wish to switch tapes. It can't be done. The lock answers only to—to Maelen!"

There was anxiety to be felt, as if the Lord-One Krip had seized upon a perilous answer. The Lady was a prisoner: they might be able to force her to do what they had not been able to accomplish. Farree wondered briefly why they had not already tried that method.

"Perhaps they fear—" Lord-One Krip beamed. "There are many tales of the powers of the Thassa, and she is a Moon Singer. Since her duel with evil on Sehkmet there are even more tales. Yet we cannot hope that rumor alone will keep them from her."

"Yazz has fangs, elder brother." For the first time one of the others interrupted.

Echoing that was another hot, half-formed thought—the hazy rendering of an attack by the bartle on a barely realized human figure.

"Not yet," Lord-One Krip answered with a direct order through mind probe.

Farree resumed touch with the smux, and now that creature was turning about in the control cabin. What the hunchback caught was not the man still laboring futilely with the paneled wall but another dimly projected picture of the second settled in what Farree had been earlier told was the astrogator's seat.

It was, he decided, as if that second one was only waiting the result of the first's labors to go into action on his own.

So they were both in the control cabin! He kept only a thin tendril of connection with Toggor and began to edge up the ladder, the stunner against his chest, one hand on the guide lines to draw him on.

He passed the level which held his own cabin, panting with the effort he must use to reach the next level, needing to depend on his sole handhold to aid in negotiating the steps. Unused to the weaker gravity and with no magnetic boots it was a harder climb for him.

Once more he fronted the Lady's cabin with that pressure bar in place. He laid his weapon down within hand's reach and strove to move the barrier. It was beyond his strength, as if it had been riveted in place. He tried mind touch, and this time he did not meet the blank nothingness—rather a hazy, fluctuating return which might have been that of someone coming out of a deep sleep.

"Wake!" He pressed his own thought to the utmost strength. "Wake!"

The return was stronger, the alert and forceful pattern which he had come to associate with the Lady Maelen. She had fully roused. Now her demand for information was nearly as sharp as that of the Lord-One. It was he who gave her first answers. Then she turned her mind send back full on Farree.

"The bar—how is it fixed?"

He squatted, stunner in hand, to study the locking barrier and project the picture of it. So—and so—and so.

"Locked by persona!" flashed back an answer when he had done. "Now—"

But what she might have added was interrupted by a flash from the smux.

Toggor had dropped away from the cabin, was coming back down the handhold. The two in the control cabin were on the move, apparently descending to the next level. Farree himself skittered down the ladder and took refuge temporarily by the door of his own cabin. If they came that far, he might duck inside.

The odor of the sleep gas was gone from the level of Lady Maelen's prison. Perhaps they had some way of filtering it out of the air.

"We come." The united mind touch of Bojor and Yazz reached the hunchback. Swiftly he countered their suggestion. Neither animal could make a swift and easy ascent of the ladder, and they both would be too easy for the crewmen to pick off with either stunners or the fatal laser beamers.

Farree listened with his ears as well as his mind. Toggor had not withdrawn to this level. Instead, those eyes on stalks were watching the ladder near a closed door, which might mark the cabin of the Lord-One. Would the crew members believe that Krip was the one who held the information they must have?

"Care—" A single word from the imprisoned man. Farree had a fleeting impression that the Lord-One suspected these two had in their power some way of judging or listening to mind speech. Farree swiftly closed that channel but he kept his thread of contact with Toggor. It might well be true that the enemy could sense a human thought exchange but would not suspect it between their prisoners and the animals.

He heard above the vibration in the ship's walls, which remained a steady hum, a metallic clatter, and then voices came down the well of the ladder.

"Don't try anything, Thassa. We have a mind lock. We also have these. Those hands of yours—how would you like a roasted finger? Or a charred ear—that should be enough to scramble your thoughts, wouldn't it. Come out and get up to the control cabin. We want that tape pocket opened—and right now!"

"Persona set." That was Quanhi. "Clever, aren't you?

But what has been set can be unset just as quickly. Get moving!''

They had the Lord-One with them—there followed the clip of magnetic boots on the ladder. But it was the Lady Maelen who had set that lock! How soon would they learn that and return for her—perhaps leaving the Lord-One maimed as the spacer had suggested?

Farree's anger burnt as it had before during his short life. Before he had had to stifle it—had been helpless against those who aroused it. Now—now there surely was something he could do! He had the weapon to hand and Toggor to run scout for him.

"And us. And us—"

That quick assurance came from below, surprising him again with the eager anger which moved Bojor and Yazz. The bartle—could the beast force the lock across the Lady's door, releasing her?

"I come." Bojor's only half-sensed message, which Farree had to strain his mind below the usual channel to intercept, was almost as angry as a vocal growl.

"Not yet." The bulk of the animal and its difficulty with the ladder might cause too much of a delay. Farree tapped his stunner against the step above where he crouched and tried to think.

Once more he made his way back to the level where the Lady Maelen's door was barred. Holding the stunner and continually glancing from ladder to door, Farree ran his hand across it at his chin level. It was easy to feel the thumb indentation of the persona lock was made to answer to one of the crew and him only.

He had closed his mind, nor would he try to open to the Lady lest they be checked upon by those others. Farree stationed himself near the upper ladderway, his attention for all that was above. Then he dared to give the signal to the impatient two below.

The passage of the thick-bodied bartle was a tight one and preceded by a number of grunts and half-voiced growls. Then the heavy shoulders and the tufted head appeared, and a moment later Farree retreated up a step, leaving full possession of that level to Bojor.

Long talons were unsheathed and wound about the bar. Farree watched the shoulders tense until their thick covering of bristly hair stood erect, and knew the animal was exerting its full strength.

At that same moment from overhead came an alert from the smux: "One comes!"

Perhaps the enemy had already learned that only the Lady had the true answer to their riddle and would bring her up to taste their method of coaxing. Farree clung to the ladder, wedging himself as best he could to the centermost part of it where the steps were the widest. He lifted the stunner with both his hands on the firing pin and waited.

Legs in dull gray spacer uniform appeared—then the rest of Pitor Dune. There was nothing of the disreputable Limits crawler about him now. Rather he swung down as if he were the master of the ship.

Farree fired. He had not aimed at the head, but for the center of the body, and a moment later the man folded in upon himself and tumbled forward before the hunchback could get out of the way. He heard the shout the half-paralyzed man gave even as the body knocked him flat, both of them landing against the shaggy flank of the bartle, who growled and showed fangs.

The hunchback wriggled out from under the bruising weight of the crewman and pushed him aside, farther along the floor, toward Bojor. The bartle used teeth now as well as talons to fight the stubborn hold of the bar.

A sudden thought caught Farree as he struggled away from the man screaming oaths at him. He fought to enter the bartle's mind with the plea to stand clear for a moment. Then he pushed and shoved the inert but cursing man to the position before the door and hooked up one of his hands to press the thumb in the hollow. There was a fifty-fifty chance of this one being the warden.

But the bar did not yield, and Bojor, irritated at being disturbed during his own efforts, swept both Farree and the crewman aside with a powerful blow. The helpless man slipped through the opening at the center of the ladder well and was gone before the hunchback could move to stop him.

There came a shout from aloft: "What's to do? Is the witch bitch out? Answer me, Dune." When there was no answer, the ray of a laser clipped into molten droplets part of the hand rope, seaming a line across the steps.

At the same time Farree tried to urge Bojor back out of the line of fire. The creature gave a last deep grunt and the stubborn bar loosened a fraction. Prying at that end, the bartle was able to pull it fully free and allow the door to open.

The Lady Maelen stood just within. She had a second stunner in one hand, and there was a look of grim purpose on her face. But she did not speak nor mind send an order—rather signed with one hand. The bartle rumbled deep in his throat once again and then moved cautiously back and onto the ladder, pushing his bulk through the level opening to descend. Farree, also obedient to that signal, set his crooked back to the wall and waited for orders, his own stunner ready.

"One of them is gone?" Her question came not mind to mind but in a whisper so faint that it barely reached him. He nodded and pointed down the ladder well.

"Listen, witch bitch," came a shout from above. "Do you want your fancy man here to fry?"

"Do you wish," she called back, "to planet where we have friends and then strive to explain where we are? Our voyage is already past the turn point. Whether you would or no, you are now bound by the ship's tape, and nothing save a destruction of the whole guide system will prevent it carrying out its instructions. Do you wish to die in a drifting derelict?''

''Friends waiting?'' The unseen captor above appeared to catch upon only one of her arguments. ''You have no friends, witch bitch. You were exiled by your own people and cannot return without breaking their laws again. Yes, see, I know you, wearer of other bodies! Now, do you yield or do I cook this fake Thassa of yours?''

''I swear to you by Molester, there is no way you can change the tape. We have gone too long and too far.'' She was standing very close to the upper ladderway, but out of sight of the one who must be above, perhaps just above, as the last call had sounded much closer.

''So it is Yiktor whether or no, that is what you would tell me? Well enough, there are those on Yiktor who can take charge of you as easily as I can cook this friend of yours. Wait and see—''

But the gloating voice stopped almost in mid word. Instead there followed a cry of disgust which became one of pain. Down the ladder thudded a squat-barreled, ugly-looking weapon which Farree knew was a laser. It hit against the edge of the lower well and flew into the air, falling straight out of sight.

There was a second scream of pain fast becoming agony. Then Farree saw Toggor swinging down the rope, his claws gleaming bright scarlet and dripping greenish droplets. It had been many days since the smux had been out of the hands of Russtif. His venom had not been forcibly drawn. It might not be enough to actually kill a man, but the pain from any smux wound was, as Farree knew, intolerable.

''All clear!'' There had been sounds of a brief struggle, and now the Lady Maelen leapt for the ladder and started up them, Farree following.

They found what they sought on the level below the pilot cabin. On the floor, one hand a brilliant scarlet as if it had been scalded, lay Quanhi. His eyes were shut and the rest of him limp. As first Maelen and then Farree came through, it was to see Lord-One Krip backed against the wall, rubbing one fist with the fingers of his other hand, and the knuckles of that hand were skinned. Maelen turned, and, without a word, played the stunner she carried straight upon the head of the already unconscious man.

"Let him sleep in peace," she said. "But first—" She knelt down and ran her fingers through the short dark hair of their prisoner. "No webbing shield. There must be"—she shook her own head as if she wanted to deny just what she said—"an implant of some kind."

"Maybe they were mind washed," Lord-One Krip suggested.

"This one was protected from the beginning. Pitor Dune was not—at least on the surface. On ship he was. I wonder where they wanted us to planet."

7.

"**N**ot, I think, on Yiktor," the Lord-One returned. "But they would expect us to land at the port and—"

She smiled a little then. "We shall surprise them. Into the Dry Waste we shall go, if the tape proves true and he who set it had no reason to lie. Also I scanned him as he took payment. What he might have done is relay our navigation points to another. That the arm—and ear—of the Guild are long is well known."

"Manus Hnold gave his word," her companion returned. "He is Free Trader—and they are used to keeping secret landfalls which might have future use."

"We are close now to turnover, little kin," she said to Farree. "Seek you now your own place, for with turnover comes ship shift. And these others—" She looked down at the man Lord-One Krip had silenced and beyond him to the ladder well. From below still arose the dulled sound of curses. "They must be put into stass also."

It was not easy, handling the limp bodies of the two crewmen, though the bartle had strength enough—had there been room—to toss them both easily about. But at length each was bound down with safety straps on his own bunk and Bojor and Yazz were back in their cages, taking their own precautions against the spill of turnover.

Toggor crept once more into the fore of Farree's robe and lay flat as the Lady and the Lord-One went into the control cabin and strapped down. The hunchback was in his own cabin, the stunner made fast to the straps which were his protection. He forced himself to relax and waited for the queasiness and giddiness of the reentry into normal space. As he lay there his mind was as busy as his body was inert.

The Guild. Its tentacles of power ran from star to star, perhaps magnified by rumor, or perhaps not even rumor could suggest the full tale of its controls. Where there was law, there was also the Guild—that was a matter of balance, and it had always been so as far as Farree knew. Each planet was supposed to police itself, the Patrol only in command where there was off-world interference or against independent worlds where the Guild had carved out niches of "safe ports" for itself. There were worlds where rumor said ships planeted and exchanged cargoes that were not of the usual kind and paid for in unknown ways. Wherever there was an unusual find also—there the Guild appeared sooner or later.

His present companions had spoken of Sehkmet—of a Free Trader forced by power failure to land on a supposedly dead planet only to chance upon a vast treasure of Forerunner artifacts and knowledge that was already being harvested by the Guild. That the Guild would not take kindly to having that operation broken up he could well believe. And Lord-One Krip and the Lady Maelen had had a hand in that breaking. He gave the small nod which was the only movement his present bonds allowed him. Yes, the Guild could well be after them.

He waited for the rise of fear within him. There was that and a shiver of excitement, for he knew well that, had he been given the same chance again, he would make the same choice. To Lord-One Krip and the Lady he was not the scum of the Limits, but one, Farree, to be trusted.

Turnover! He was pushed against the bunk, the padding within it seeming suddenly leaden, far from the soft surface on which he had rested a breath or two earlier. There was a sharp pain in his head, and then the giddiness and nausea hit together.

Later, the spasm past, he dared to loose the protecting belts and ties and climb up to the pilot cabin, wedging his small body into the seat of the com officer they lacked. Both the Lord-One Krip and the Lady Maelen were absorbed in watching a screen, where pinpoints of light were growing larger and larger as their ship bored on through normal space.

The Lady Maelen broke silence first. "We shall earth at night, I think. The code—" She reached forward and the fingers of her right hand sped across a board of buttons. "That will see us past any orbital guard. We must hope that that has not been changed."

Time passed, and then they were centering in on one of those balls of light. Farree wriggled forward in his seat to watch their goal come rushing toward them. They would orbit twice, he had understood from the plans earlier made, and then set down under mech-pilot on the spot to which their tape had pointed them across the star lanes.

It all seemed like a dream to him. The outer star-spangled space was cold and lonely, he thought. And how could a twist of ribbonlike metal bring them in without any action on their part? To trust in such was a little more than he could accept as the time grew short before they must set down.

At last he deliberately closed his eyes and turned his head into the bargain. He did not want to see a world come rushing up toward him. It seemed that he would spatter against it as a fos-beetle spatted against a screen, unable to waver in its flight to avoid the barrier.

A giant hand perhaps as large as the bartle's whole body

pressed him down. There was a pain which shot through his hump as if he had been slashed by a knife, and he tasted the salt-sweet of blood in his mouth. Then darkness and nothingness fell like the space between the star worlds.

"Farree," a voice called. Reluctantly he crawled back up out of the darkness in answer. He looked up into the face of the Lady Maelen. She passed a damp cloth over his nose and mouth, and it showed the dark red of blood. He felt an ache through his whole body, but he caught at the webbing of the seat, which had been loosened, and drew himself up.

"I am all right," he made quick answer, refusing to let them believe that he was merely a charge upon them, as if he were indeed one of the "little ones"—those to whom cages came as prisons.

He felt her probe and met it quickly. No, he wanted no care, only to be treated as she would treat one of her own straight-backed kind.

She drew back. "You *are* of our kind, Farree." She did not speak that mind to mind but with her lips, as if she acknowledged relationship by word instead of thought.

He did not try to answer her. One needed only to look at him to know that she spoke in pity only, and the notion of her pity brought a fierce surge of anger which he could not voice.

Lord-One Krip was still seated in the captain's swinging chair, and now his fingers played across the board which the Lady Maelen had earlier used. Farree became aware of something else: the vibration that had been a part of him while they were en route was gone. The ship was motionless and silent. On the looking screen there were tall rises of bare rock. They had indeed landed and, from the look of it, not at any port.

There was a greenish light upon those rocks. Lady Maelen took a step forward and touched the man's shoulder lightly.

Though no word or mind speech Farree could catch passed between them, the scene outside the ship changed.

Gone were the light-touched rocks with their deep indentations of shadow. Instead they saw a moon in a sky which was not dark. For around the globe of that gold-bright coin were two rings of light, stark and clear. Beyond them, a hazy surround of a third was yet but a palid shadow of the others.

The Lady Maelen flung her arms up as if she stood in the open reaching to touch that wonder.

"Three rings—not yet but soon!" Her voice held a triumphant sound as if she had won through some hard battle to reach this time and place.

"And where"—Lord-One Krip leaned back in his seat, his still hands resting upon the edge of that board of many buttons—"are we?"

"Sotrath will lend us light. If I only had long sight I would—"

But the three in the cabin of the ship were not to hear her words, for ringing into the mind of each of them came a challenge, so clear and sharp that Farree reeled and saw that even the Lord-One Krip had caught at the edge of the board, holding so tensely that his grazed knuckles stood out as white knobs.

"Who comes thus into the Quiet Places?"

For a long moment Farree thought that there would be no answer. Then the reply came from the Lady Maelen.

"I am she who was judged, she whose rod of power was taken from her. She who wore fur and fangs and—"

"And comes again in a new body! Whence got you that, Singer who was and now is not?"

"Thus." There was a tingle in Farree's mind; that was the only way he could describe it. No passage of thought, rather a high sweet sound as if someone sang without words. How long it continued he could not have afterwards said. It trailed up and up into notes he could not hear but which still fed that tingle in his mind.

Once more that other voice spoke. It came from nowhere but arrived with all the authority of a guard: "This is a thing which must be thought upon. Not lightly are the People answered by a flouting of their Law."

Lady Maelen bowed her head as if she stood before a speaker and surrendered her will to that other.

"Let it lie upon the Scale of Molester. For such a judgment I am ready. Those with me are guilty of naught save striving to help—"

"All those with you?" resounded the voice. "What of the two who lie prisoner in body within that ship?"

"They shall be delivered to the judgment of their own kind."

"They are trespassers by your aid into a place which is forbidden to all save the People and those they summon."

"Sotrath has summoned us. Three rings will shine and then that which is crooked can be made straight—"

That which is crooked—straight!

Farree took a single step forward. Surely she did not mean that! She and the Lord-One had picked him out of the Limits, cast off his casing of Dung, but there was no magic in the world—this or any other—that could straighten him, three rings around an unknown moon or not!

There was a bitter taste in his mouth as he swallowed, not born of his blood this time but from his thoughts. Yet he was given no time to sift those, for again the voice rang clear.

"Unto Molester shall it be, even as you have said, you who are not—"

There was a kind of echo in his mind, but the words were sharply cut off and Farree knew that the speaker had withdrawn. Once more the picture screen in the control cabin showed, not the sky, but towering cliffs about them. The bright light of the moon brought those sharply into focus, and the picture began slowly to move from right to left as if the ship itself was turning on some giant spindle. The cliffs ended. Before them now stretched a wide plain unbroken by any growth higher than a few thick patches of dead-seeming grass.

This was an empty land appearing only as a wasteland. Then once more cliffs arose to wall them in. Lord-One Krip leaned a little closer to the screen.

"This I have seen."

"He did well, that Hnold. We are within short distance to the meeting place," Lady Maelen returned. There was warm satisfaction in her voice. "Let me but go and all shall be readied."

"Wait!" His hand went up as if to back his command. "Look to the—"

He pressed thumb hard upon a button and the screen ceased its turn. Before them were still tall cliffs under the clear moonlight, but in the sky above the ragged edge of those cliffs something moved, striking fire now and then from the same moonlight.

"A flitter!"

The Lady Maelen's lips flattened against her teeth in a grimace. She, too, leaned closer to the screen. "But this is the Land of Beyond where only the Thassa move. And the lordlings of the inner lands have no sky flight!"

"Others do," he returned grimly. "Such as those we have on board."

"Wait and watch!" Her hand on his shoulder pushed him fully down into his seat again.

The airborne transport came on, fully into the moonlight, where the rocks seemed to reflect back the glory of the rings to show the clearer what passed either on earth or through the air. The craft had no riding lights, and yet it appeared to hold a course that would bring it to their own landing place.

Guild? But how could the two prisoners have summoned such support?

"They were waiting," said Lord-One Krip in a low voice.

"That they could not have been!" she protested. "The tape was unchanged and brought us—"

"Perhaps they expected their men might fail," he returned. "They had ready then a secondary plan."

"Which will not serve them either." Her fingers dug into his shoulder as she watched the oncoming flitter closely but with no expression of alarm. "See!"

The small craft boring through the moonlight had nearly reached the lip of the cliffs. Then it seemed to waver— almost as if the same wind which rippled the grass patches was strong enough to seize the flitter from the control of those on board. The craft sideslipped to the right, drew level with what Farree could believe was an effort, slipped again. It near-skimmed the top of the cliff, and then it made an abrupt turn and half circled to put itself back on the same course it had followed toward them.

Only no longer was its flight swift and sure; it slipped from one side to the other in jerky motion. The craft could have been a bird netted by a sure fling of a hunter, struggling for its freedom to no purpose.

So jerking and fighting the craft passed out of sight behind a taller pinnacle of the cliff rise and was gone.

"The Thassa have their own defenses," the Lady Maelen said. "None approach here unless they are of the blood or are summoned. This is the Old Place and here lies the heart—" She stopped suddenly and looked curiously abashed, as one who talks of hidden things and then realizes her words can be heard by those who have no right to listen.

"Will they crash?" Lord-One Krip asked in a level voice.

Now she frowned. "Not so. Our defenses are not to destroy—not even any evil which may come. They will be but diverted and also they will forget—"

"Not if they, too, are mind shielded."

She frowned. "I do not know. A shield is made to keep out thought thrusts. It is not intended to stand up to the force of the Elders acting together. We shall see how well any man-made thing may last against the full force of the Thassa."

"Let us hope," he said in the same level tone, "that the force is fully effective then. Do we go?"

"Not yet. With the dawn perhaps. Maybe then the summons will come. We cannot enter without that."

Farree lay once more curled on his own bunk with Toggor squatting beside him. This was a long way from the Limits yet. He rubbed his forehead. There was something—a pale shadow of a shadow of a memory that once he had lain within a ship before. Still, how could that be? His only clear memory came from the noisome sink of the Limits and that was all he thought he had ever known. He wondered—pushing away that shadow which made him uneasy and aching—what the dawn would bring. That Lord-One Krip was also uneasy this night, he sensed. However, if there was any crack in the confidence of the Lady Maelen he could not detect it. She was restless, yes, but not as one who awaited trouble, rather as one who would be out and doing—one who stood before a door, impatient that it be opened to her.

He wondered about the Thassa and that voice out of nowhere. Had it perhaps rung out also in the minds of those in the flitter, warning them off in a way they could not protest? Or had it taken charge of their bodies as he had heard tales of among the spacers, forcing them against their wills?

He thought and later he slept while, in his broken and fleeting dreams, he looked upon a three-ringed moon and felt power drawing him to—to—but to what he could not remember when he awakened.

It was Toggor tugging with a claw at one of the locks of his unruly hair that brought him out of that drowse. The smux radiated hunger, and Farree felt an answering emptiness in his own bent body. He slipped into the narrow slit of the fresher and allowed the mist there to wash him, coming out to a fresh robe and sandals. Then he went to the galley, smelling, even before he opened the door, the fine odors of food.

Lord-One Krip was at the table, an opened ration tin at hand, but he was not eating. When Toggor gave a squeal and leaped onto the table, he shoved the tin at the smux, who clacked claws over it and immediately began to eat.

Farree was a little daunted that the other had made no sign of seeing him nor given any greeting. But he got his own tin and crawled up on the empty seat opposite the man, waiting for him to break the silence between them.

"She is waiting still." Lord-One Krip might have been talking to himself, for he did not look in Farree's direction at all. "But what if . . ." He did not finish the question, and Farree dared now to do it for him. After all, he was a part of this company, too, and if trouble lay before them it was his right to know.

"What if the—the voice—says we must leave?"

For the first time the man looked at him. There was the crease of a frown between those upward-slanting brows.

"Then we go."

Greatly daring, Farree asked, "Where are we?"

"At the meeting place of the Thassa. You do not understand, little brother." He clasped his hands before him on the table. "I am not Thassa"—with the fingers on one hand he pinched the skin on the back of the other—"though I now wear a Thassa body."

"One does not wear bodies," Farree cut in sharply. "One *is* a body." For a wild moment the thought of another body— a straight, tall, humpless one—filled his mind. What if what he had just denied was the truth and he could change? There were many wonders on other worlds, but never had he heard such as that!

"The Thassa *wear* bodies." He could see that Lord-One Krip meant in truth what he said. "To become a Moon Singer, a one of power among them—they change bodies with animals, running wild on the land and learning from them other scents and desires. I was a crewman on a free trader, and here on Yiktor I was taken by a lordling who would have of me the secrets from off-world—or else use me to wring such from my captain. He gave my body to pain."

Farree hunched under the burden on his shoulders as if rolling himself into a ball. He knew what Lord-One Krip meant. Such had been his own portion.

"I was—damaged. Maelen was a Moon Singer and also the leader of a troop of little ones—animals who gave shows she devised. She saved me by singing me into a barsk."

Farree swallowed. "An animal?"

"An animal"—nodded the other—"one which was notably fierce and supposedly untameable. It was not one of hers but one which had been captured and badly treated, and which she was curing and trying to mind free. So did I live on Yiktor for a space. But then there was a Thassa body—a Kinsman to Maelen—a Thassa who had taken on animal form but been killed in that form. His body was empty of mind, for the animal transformed with him had gone mad. So—I became Thassa—for my own body was judged dead by my shipmates and spaced after they had taken off.

"For this act Maelen was condemned by the Thassa and her wand of power taken from her. When she left this world she, too, was an animal—and as such she traveled with me. Until Sehkmet. There—well, there were bodies, very ancient bodies, who could change at will. And one of them was a woman. She would have ruled, but Maelen invaded her, freed her captives and the inner core of evil which dominated her, so her body became Maelen as you see her now. We have returned to Yiktor with this ship—for it has long been Maelen's dream, as you know in a little—to become once more a Moon Singer and then to go out among the stars with her furred folk, proving to all that life is sacred and those considered the lesser may, in their own way, surprise those who see them as that.

"When Sotrath bears its three rings is a time of great power, and we have waited for that to return. But now, just as that flitter was guided from the inner land, so may we also be sent on our way."

"She does not believe that." Farree did not know how he knew that truth, but he was certain he did.

"She is—Maelen. Once a Singer under the moon, one cannot be stripped of such powers easily. And on Sehkmet she found a battle such as few even of her people must ever have faced. Thus she believes what she wishes to believe—"

"Belief is a comfort and a weapon, a wand of power, and a pointed laser." Maelen stood in the doorway of the cabin, her eyes alight. The long cascade of hair, which she usually kept tightly braided, flowed free around her shoulders, though locks of it wavered a little, as if stirred to rise by some magnet. Her drab ship's uniform was gone. Instead, she wore breeches and boots of a russet color close to that of her hair. Her shirt had a wide stiffened collar forming a tall fan behind her head, and she had a sleeveless jacket of some yellow wooly stuff which was not unlike fur.

Farree heard Lord-One Krip's breath come forth in a low sound of wonder. The Lady Maelen turned slowly around as if to allow them to view her. In the drabness of the ship she was almost like a flame glowing with warmth, for that eagerness Farree had earlier sensed in her was now a consuming fire.

"Come!" She beckoned to both of them. "The Thassa gather. Soon we shall be summoned also."

She swung up to the control cabin, Lord-One Krip on her

heels, Farree moving more slowly behind. The screen was on and they looked out into or onto a sun-drenched world. There was life—no flitter in the skies, but rather there came at a steady pace wagons with covered tops and huge earth-crushing wheels pulled by teams of shaggy-coated four-legged animals that plodded steadily onward at a ground-eating pace. Nor could Farree see that any held the reins, any walk beside them with a goad in hand. Rather the animals had the air of being about a necessary business of their own.

The wagons were brightly painted, colors vivid, against the dull gray countryside over which they plowed. Now he could see figures on the front seats of some of the wagons, though they were still too far away to be well viewed.

They were all headed for a break in the wall of the cliff, one so regular in size Farree could almost believe it had been squared off by some ancient intelligence. For as he looked upon that roadway he had a feeling of age—of age and forgotten story.

Then, once more, came that clear voice in his head: "The Thassa gather. Come you who would speak."

Maelen threw back her head. She did not reply in that wordless, voiceless sound but in a thought touch as firm and clear: "We hear and we come!"

8.

They stood out under the open sky, a wind rippling around them, pushing at their bodies, making a flaming banner of the Lady Maelen's hair. Behind them Yazz and Bojor snuffled and snorted, their pleasure at being free of the ship projecting a warmth reaching from mind to mind. The wagons went their way still, and it seemed that not one among them was interested enough in the ship even to look in their direction. Perhaps strict order drew them forward. But there were fewer of them now, a straggling end to the push of that company.

The Lady Maelen led her companions toward that same break in the cliff wall. And, as the sun slanted across the rock, Farree, holding his head at the best angle his deformity would allow, saw strange markings on the stone. As if once there had been carvings there, now so worn away by time that their ghosts alone still haunted the rock.

Beyond a narrow passage through the cliff lay another open space, and there the wagons had been staked out, the animals that had drawn them loosed to graze at will. Here were squared openings set in patterns as if the rock itself had

97

been mined for a city of dwellings. Again the ghostly markings ran across the yellowed stone. There were the people of this company also, and after each wagon had taken its place they headed toward one of the openings—larger, more wreathed with the patterns.

Farree heard Lord-One Krip draw a deep breath.

"The gathering," he said as if he spoke his thought aloud.

"The gathering!" echoed the Lady Maelen but there was a note of excitement in her voice, whereas Lord-One Krip appeared to be less eager to take the way toward that open doorway in the far wall of the cliff.

They were approached by some latecomers passing the same way, but to Farree's bewilderment and growing unease these Thassa ignored the party from the ship as if they did not exist. But neither did either of his companions try to exchange greetings or even glances with those whose pace now matched theirs.

So, of that company and yet apart, they came into a vast assembly place within the rock. The floor underfoot inclined gently to a center where was a dais, and on that stood four of the Thassa. Farree studied them eagerly, hoping to read something in their attitude which might token that the ship's party was not trespassing but was to be welcomed.

But, though the four stood watching, their eyes appeared to go above, beyond, or to either side, not toward the three from the ship. The last of the Thassa split into two small groups and took their stations on either side of the broad open aisle which led down to the dais itself.

Now the Lady Maelen stopped short and stood, with Lord-One Krip a little behind her and Farree still farther back, aloof in that crowd of strangers where he felt more than ever his crookedness.

It was not dark within this hall cave for there were globes of light suspended overhead to provide the same light as the moon had flung the night before across the outer world. Now around them there raised song without words, entering into one's very skin and bones, becoming a part of one.

It seemed to Farree that that song could put wings on the listener, lift him up and away from the body, freeing the innermost part of him to float and fly above all which tied him to the earth. He forgot time, and space, and himself, and was only what the song bore with it.

At last that died away in a slow sobbing as if the fading of a people or a life was now a part of it. Farree smeared his hand across his face and so wiped away tears—he who long ago had learned that weeping availed nothing. It was the dying of something great and wonderful, that last of the singing, beyond his small power to describe, and it wrung him, bringing with it all the feeling of alienness he had ever known.

There was a tearing in his chest, and a fierce aching awoke in his hump. He put his hands over his ears, trying to shut out that dying song. Then he saw that one of those on the dais had shifted the silver wand she bore in her hands. The end of that pointed now in his direction just as he was aware that she saw and knew him. Straightaway the sound ended—for him—though he still half crouched, too aware of the burden on his shoulders and the pain which held through that. But he was released from the sorrow borne in the song.

The wand swung, pointed now to Maelen.

"What now is your tale—in this time and place—exile?"

It was the same voice which had questioned their landing, ringing again in their heads.

Maelen moved forward. Lord-One Krip stepped up beside her. If she faced a foe, then he, too, would front that hostility. Not to be left behind, Farree followed, his head at a straining angle to watch that company of four.

"Standing words cannot be altered. As was said here once before to you who sang and then forfeited that right."

Farree thought that that came from one of the two men flanking the woman with the wand.

"The third ring waxes, the power rises." Maelen faced them proudly with such a bearing as might a warrior waiting for the first order to advance.

"It waxes—" That was the other woman. "Well, well— the Old Ways are not to be denied. Speech is yours, you who were once a Singer."

"I am Maelen."

"That is the truth. Yet you come wearing a new guise. Do you again meddle as you once did with changing?"

Maelen threw open her arms as if she was so loosing all shields she might hold against any of these.

"Read, Older Sister."

There was silence, so deep that it might have been that this hall was now deserted. Yet Farree felt a stirring in his mind at too high a level to follow. Thassa bespeaking Thassa, he guessed—not for such as he to hear.

They stood motionless, all in that company, as if caught in some twist of time unending, unchanging. Then the woman who had challenged Maelen broke her statuelike stance and turned her head, first right and then left. She might have been speaking soundlessly to those with her, sitting in judgment. But it was the other woman among the four who touched minds now.

"You have been along a strange path, Singer-that-was. There abides in you now that which we cannot assess—save that you have used it as you could for the good of those who trusted you. Singer, no. We cannot judge for you. You must name yourself. Are you asking such a naming?"

"The third ring waxes," Maelen returned slowly. "No, I ask not any power which does not come to me openly and is earned. But I am still Thassa, and this thing which started on another world and with another race is not yet ended. It will again be my debt on the Scales, and Molester shall judge in the end as all of us are judged.''

"On the Scales then let it lie. You do not judge—''

"Am I still exile?''

"You are what you are, by your choice. Thassa is not closed to you nor''—she now leveled the wand and pointed at Lord-One Krip—"to you, once stranger, who have worn our seeming well. Nor—''

Once more the wand centered on Farree. And he saw a look of vast surprise cross her face, the rod quivering in her hand.

"Go with Molester's Hand above you, small one,'' she said slowly. "His Scales shall weigh you and in the end it shall be the truth for you also.''

He wondered at the way she said those words, as if she pronounced some judgment. Yet one that was not a heavy one for him. Perhaps, he thought, with a stab of the bitterness that was always with him, her surprise was that such a one as he had ventured into this company. Dung of the Limits might have no place here. He dropped his head and looked downward to his clawlike hands with the greenish skin, his feet which were no better, looking too small and weak to support that burden on his back. Thus he saw Toggor's eyestalks looming out of the neck opening of his robe, turning this way and that as if the smux must acquaint himself with all this company and the moon-glow hall in which they were gathered.

"You have not yet come into your inheritance.'' That loud, clear voice rang in his head. "We are what Molester shapes, and for each shape there is a reason and a duty—''

It was the bitterness which made him brave enough to answer with the mind touch, "And if the shape is spoiled in the making, Lady?''

"There is nothing save that which is ordained. You will come into that which is yours at the proper time.''

He supposed she meant when he was dead, which was hardly an encouraging message. Then he remembered Lord-One Krip's own tale of how he had been, at a time of great need, transferred by Thassa power into the body of an animal and then into a man's form again. Could such work for him? For the first time Farree thought seriously of that part of the off-worlder's story. Would it be better to run like Yazz on four feet, or claw a way in Toggor's form, than to shamble as Dung? That was a thought to consider.

However, though the words of the Thassa Elder might promise change—what change and how? He breathed a little faster and then became aware that around him the people were starting to leave the hall within the cliff. Only Maelen and Lord-One Krip did not move, and, seeing that, he also stayed where he was.

The Elders did not leave the dais, but she of the wand made a small beckoning gesture, and Maelen and Krip moved toward her. Only Farree remained where he was, still bemused by that thought of another body, unburdened, four-footed perhaps. Though where was even a beast that would change places with such as he?

Those on the dais had come forward to face the two from the ship, and again there was a flow of thought too high and fast for Farree to catch. He dropped cross-legged on the stone where he was, and Toggor climbed out to hold the folds of his robe and project the feeling of hunger and impatience to be fed.

Then the smux suddenly loosed hold on Farree and with a leap reached the stone of the floor and caught a big-bodied insect that had swung from circling about one of the moon globes above, transferring the morsel to his mouth with a message that such prey hardly made up for the hunger in him.

"Come, Farree." Lord-One Krip looked back to him. "It is back to the ship for us now."

Yet the Lady Maelen remained still with those leaders of the Thassa as he rose to shamble after the off-worlder. No, not an off-worlder here where he wore a Thassa body, whatever might lie within that.

"What do we—you"—he caught himself quickly not to claim too such familiarity with the Lord-One—"do now?"

The man shrugged. "That remains with Maelen and the temper of the Thassa. This she had longed to do—to return here and be again a Singer, a companion to little ones with fur and feathers."

"But—" The question Farree might have asked was swallowed up by sound from the sky above them: the beat of a flitter coming low above the valley which led to the hall, swinging on toward the ship. Lord-One Krip began to run and Farree could not keep up, only trotted along as best he might. He noticed as he passed that none of those gathered by the wagons looked skyward.

There was something here to which he could not put name, but it made him feel that he was forcing his misshapen body through a turgid flood which sought to cover and stifle him.

The flitter swept on, and he fought to follow Lord-One Krip into the open where the ship stood. Was that strange wave of strength broadcast from the airborne craft, or was it some side issue of a protection summoned by the Thassa?

Farree stumbled around boulders, having twice to stop and draw enough panting breaths to send him on. He could see Lord-One Krip ahead but he, too, moved as if caught in some flood that would wash him back instead of forward, a current of power raised to keep him from his goal.

They reached the end of the valley, and there Krip halted, the whole tense posture of his body showing that it was not by his will. He was struggling still.

Farree felt a sudden push of new force against him, and he could not breast it for himself. Rather he clung to another boulder and stood as straight as he could, watching—almost certain now that this force came from the flitter and was not a protection raised by the Thassa.

The flitter set down not far from their ship. Men issued forth from the flitter. Two of them went toward the inclined way leading from the smoking land about the fins into the center of their ship, and two others took their places between that and the open mouth of the canyon, standing with feet slightly apart and weapons ready in their hands— That pressure kept Krip and Farree away from them, helpless against what they would do.

Once more his own shoulders' burden began to ache, weighing him down, as if the pressure against him had sought out his weakest portion of being and there centered upon him. Lord-One Krip no longer struggled but stood where he had been stopped, his arms folded across his chest. Farree could feel the thrust of thought he hurled toward those at the ship, though it was pure pressure in the mind, not coherent words and phrases.

They were not gone long, those two who had invaded the ship, and when they came back they had the former prisoners with them, walking easily, not hampered any longer by their bonds. Then, together, those from the flitter and the two others lined up before the ship's fins. One of those who had gone aboard had in his hand what looked like a square box which the downing sun caught and awoke into an eye-hurting burst of light. He placed this carefully on the ground and knelt beside it—

The current of power that had entrapped them within the canyon was in a single moment reversed. Farree gave a shout of sheer astonishment and fear as he was swiftly drawn forward in spite of his attempts to anchor himself to one or another of the boulders his small body scraped by.

If that force reft him from anchorage, it was not as successful with Lord-One Krip. Just as he had earlier striven to pass some unseen barrier into the open, now he fought fiercely, as

attested by all the movements of his body, to remain now
where he was.

Farree had not the personal strength of the other. He
scraped stone painfully, looked vainly into the face of Krip as
he was drawn past the man. The Lord-One's features were
stark with effort. He looked to Farree and a single thought
passed from him to the other.

"Hold—where and how you can."

Only, if Krip was able to hold, there was no hope in any
such battle on Farree's part. He was aware only of a movement at his breast. Toggor had leaped from his clawhold
there to seize upon the Lord-One's arm.

This desertion brought a new stab of fear. Farree never
knew how much the smux could guess or knew of the ways
of men. He had operated under Farree's urging in the ship
and back at the Limits. Now he might be acting on his own,
and his action brought home to Farree his own complete
helplessness.

In one last attempt to withstand that force, the hunchback
flung himself forward on his knees and caught with both
hands at a stunted scrub, striving to keep his hold, only to
have his fingers loose of themselves and make him scuttle
along on hands and feet like some unwieldy shell-encased
monster.

"One!" He heard that voice dimly and then a second.

"One, but the least of them!"

"Put it on alpha then—"

He had crawled until he could see their boots clearly.
Having once lost his feet, that treacherous wave of force kept
him low, so he came as a spirit-broken animal might slink to
Russtif at the crack of a whip.

"It is on alpha. I tell you we deal with the unknown.
And—"

There was a startled cry from one of Farree's captors. The
hunchback now sat within touching distance of that shining

box. He was soaked with sweat from his fight against the power, tasting blood in his mouth where he had bitten down on his lip in that agony of struggle. But Farree looked up to see he who knelt by the box, swaying back and forth, a look of torment on his face. One hand was going forward to the strange weapon, advancing plainly against his will.

One of the other men from the flitter gave a harsh exclamation and joined his fellow by the box, slicing a hand down with vicious suddenness so that it struck against the wrist of that groping one. There was a cry of pain and the first man nursed his wrist against his body.

"Take off! While we can!" It was Quanhi who yelled that. "They have strengths we don't know—"

"Nobody can withstand this." The one who attacked his fellow said that grimly.

"No? I see Krip Vorlund over there still. Did you think to bring him crawling to us like this?" The toe of a boot flashed out to catch Farree in the ribs, and the pain drowned out the pain he felt in his hump.

"There are Thassa here, and it is the cycle of the third ring. No one on Yiktor goes up against them—"

"So we just go?" demanded the other.

"So we go, but not empty-handed. We have this one, and perhaps he is less idiotic than he looks. Gompar knows what questions to ask and how. He'll spill out his insides easily enough."

It would seem that this speaker had command of the force, because they did turn toward the flitter. Farree was picked up and slung aboard, then a tangler was turned on him and before he could hope to move the sticky cords had netted him in.

He had already striven to reach the minds of those who had taken him—and came up against the blankness of shields. Now he was a small ball of misery and fear pushed to the back of the flitter where he lay, his hump rubbing painfully against the wall, as the small craft arose with an upward leap.

None of those aboard paid him any more attention. He made himself push aside panic and take stock of that company. Their former captives sat well to the back, crowded in not too far from him, and the four who had come to their rescue occupied the fore seats.

They were dressed uniformly, in space suits, and had their hair bristle short as did most crewmen. The leader seemed to be the man now at the controls of this small ship. It was never easy to guess ages, but Farree thought that he was younger than Quanhi. He had a seam of scar from one corner of his mouth to his jawline. Otherwise there was nothing about him to suggest that he was any different from any crewman Farree had seen off duty in the Limits.

The man by him was, in spite of his spacer clothing, a different type. Had Farree not seen him here, he would have thought him a wealthy tourist, the kind who sometimes ventured into the Limits for a thrill and then often complained of thievery or ill-usage. He was stout—almost enough so to appear bloated—and his features were of an unusual smallness, squeezed together at the forefront of his head, with a high, bulbous forehead and a neck which in the nape was marked by two rolls of fat. It was on his knees that the box of power rested, now fitted into a case. He kept running his pudgy hand about its surface as if he felt chilled and this kept warmth for him. His lips were pushed out in a petulant pout, and it was plain that he was far from satisfied with their just-past action, yet he made no protest in words.

There was no way that Farree could either see out of the flitter or even mark the time they spent in the air. His bonds allowed him no movement, and he could guess that what lay ahead was nothing to try to anticipate.

They came in at last for a landing, which jarred Farree again against the wall and would have brought a whimper of pain from him had he not once more bitten down upon his lip. To let any of these see that he was frightened would be the last thing he would do. He clung fiercely to that, and for a moment thought of how Lord-One Krip had told him of running in the body of something called a barsk—so fierce an animal that all feared it. What would happen if he could claim now the claws, the strength, the bulk of Bojor?

However, there was no chance of that. He would remain what he had always been: too weak and helpless a creature to stand against anything thrust upon him. Even now, one picked him up and slung him easily to another man waiting at the hatch. And as that one carried him he got his first look at what lay about him.

He was upon an open plain with no sign of the cliff which had broken the other one. Instead a mound arose, plainly not a natural one. On that was a broken, ragged heap of tumbled-down stone walls while a tower in its middle pointed a finger to sunset clouds. As much of a ruin as the place looked, there were dwellers within. He saw movement along the near-broken walls as he was carried up the incline to where the tower stood.

A courtyard with walls and half-destroyed buildings verging on all four sides surrounded the tower, but it was to the latter that he was carried. Then, being carelessly knocked against the wall, he was transported upward to be tossed like a bit of unwanted refuse into a narrow room with a wider arc of wall narrowing to nearly a point where the door now slammed into place, leaving him alone.

A window broke the arc of the far wall, but there was no furnishing here, only the bare stone that already had given him bruises. He had landed on his back and the pain in his hump awoke from an ache to a burning stab, until he managed to roll over on one side, facing that high window where all he could see was a narrow slit of sky.

For the first time since he had been taken, Farree had time

to think. It was plain that the Thassa part of Lord-One Krip
had managed to keep him from being swallowed up in the
same trap. But what could these who held him, Dung from
the Limits, hope to learn from him alone? He knew so little:
only that some time ago the Lord-One and the Lady Maelen
had helped to break up an operation of the Guild and could
still be in danger because the Guild could not allow its might
to be flouted easily, or because they had certain knowledge
which went beyond that particular action and which might
lead to another discovery.

Good enough reason for their capture and the attempts to
take over the ship. But Farree had not been with them during
that earlier exploit and certainly had no knowledge that could
be sifted out for the Guild's profit. Maybe they intended to
use him for a bargaining piece . . .

Farree's mouth twisted wryly. What was he to the two of
the Thassa that they should risk anything in his behalf? True,
they had taken him out of the morass of the Limits. However, they had a feeling for helpless animals as he had
learned from their talk. But one did not risk all for an animal
and certainly he, Farree, could not rate any higher than that.
It would seem that he was now as much on his own as he had
always been in the Limits and with far less to help him here.

9.

It would seem that none were in a hurry to make what use they could of him, for he continued to lie alone, wrapped by the near-strangling cords of the tangler, in the tower room. Hunger awoke in him and thirst, both of which he had known too many times before to yield to now. He lay and watched the scrap of sky, which was edged by the high window, and he slept for a while or at least had no memory of the passing time. It was dusk beyond the window when the door was at last opened. Quanhi came in to stir him with one boot toe.

The spaceman pointed a laser on lowest beam at one stretch of the tangler cords, and those straightaway began to shrivel up until the ashy remnants fell away and Farree was free of bonds. His whole body ached dully as the boot reached out once more to prod at him.

"On your feet, Dung. You are needed."

His arms and legs were so numb from his bonds that he found it almost more than he could do to get to his feet. But a stubbornness in him would not let him crawl, and he made it, though he wavered toward the wall of the room and had to steady himself there.

"Move—or do you want a touch of this?" The spacer twirled his laser, and Farree lurched forward. Though there was the pain of returning full circulation and the ever-present aching in his hump, he managed to keep his feet and go on.

Though the curve of a stair which hugged the wall, cracked and worn as to steps, nearly defeated him, Farree at last reached the ground level of the tower and was herded on into another section of the ruin. His glimpse of the open before entering the other building gave him a chance only to see that there was indeed a force here—men coming and going, all of them wearing space clothing.

However, the room he was now herded into might have been lifted out of some Lord's holding back on Grant's World. Hangings of a blue-copper cross-spinning covered the ancient walls, and there was actually a matching carpet under his feet. He was brought to a halt before a table of silvery wood. Behind it were two folding chairs of tapestry and precious gonder wood. The table itself had been recently used for what Farree would have thought a feast, but the soiled plates and cups had been pushed to the far end, and now there were several boxes set out before the two men seated there.

One was the overfleshed man from the flitter, and his hands still caressed that box he had brought from the scene of Farree's undoing, stroking it as if he so pleasured a pet animal. His companion at the table was of a different pattern. There was in his look, his every movement, an air of command that led Farree to believe he was fronting the leader of this outlaw company. Though the face before him bore no disfiguring scar nor was he high-nosed in manner like one of the upper city Lords, Farree, after one meeting with those eyes, shivered and longed to draw himself into a ball as Toggor did when threatened.

It was the fat man who spoke first: "This is the one which was drawn . . ."

Had there or had there not been a thread of uneasiness in that? Farree thought he distinguished a suggestion that the fat one was not as pleased with his capture as he might have been.

"And the others?" the leader asked quietly, even mildly, as if he lacked much interest in the proceedings.

For a moment the fat man was silent, and even his pudgy hands ceased their gentling of the box. He pursed his lips as if he searched for a proper word or would get one out of his captive if he dared.

"The others?" the leader repeated in the same quiet tone.

"They withstood . . ." The admission was dragged from his companion, and Farree saw those hands tense on the box.

"Yes. The Thassa . . ." The leader could have been merely beginning an observation, but Farree was aware, by his own feelings of tension and fear, that the fat man changed position a fraction, nearly as if he winced.

"They are reputed to have more than one skill," the leader continued after a pause. "How do you think they have continued to exist for centuries of planet time with the Lords of Yiktor both jealous and afraid?"

"We had none to test," the fat man said with a note of defense in his voice. "Our material—"

"Was such as this?" the leader gestured toward Farree.

"He was with them the whole time." It was Quanhi who volunteered that.

"They gather strange life forms for the showing, do they not? What could they find more strange than this lump of offal? You"—his hard eyes caught Farree's and held them captive—"what were you to these Thassa?"

Farree had to moisten his lips with tongue tip twice before he could find answer. "I helped with the animals, Lord-One," he said in a hoarse whisper.

"Helped with? Or were one? Do you not know by now that these Thassa consider themselves above the rest of us?"

"Commander." Again it was Quanhi who dared to interrupt. "This one helped in taking back the ship—"

The leader gave a single bark of laughter that was more like a burst of oath. "A mighty opponent indeed. I wonder that you acknowledge his part in that."

"Commander." The man refused to be silenced. "He speaks with thoughts like those others."

"Yes, as you have said before several times. Well, Dung, can you read my thoughts now in your twisted head?"

"You are protected, Lord-One," Farree answered with the truth.

"Just so—protected. But so were the two aboard that ship and yet they fell into a Thassa trap. However, as you are not Thassa, we need not take the precaution of silencing you. In fact it is better not. Seek your friends—your masters—whatever those witch people are to you, and beg for their help. I will wager that such a call will bring nothing, but one can always hope, and these Thassa are ridiculously mindful of their own—even their animals. Now"—he leaned a little farther across the table—"let us get to the matter of what Dung knows about his betters. Why did Vorlund and the woman come here?"

"I do not know." Farree barely got the words out of his mouth when a heavy-handed blow from Quanhi sent him forward to come up against the table edge with bruising force.

"Let me fry a finger from him, Commander. Such a reminder—"

The man at the table held up a hand which instantly silenced the other. Farree might not now be able to read minds but he could feel the emotions heating in this room and that from Quanhi was a tinge of fear.

"Dung, do you know what these Thassa do with those they take?" inquired the same low and level voice. "They change people—men—into animals and animals into men.

Do you wish to find all that is you behind the hide and fleas of, say, a zinder?''

He spoke of a mound of foul oozelike flesh which fed and crawled and was an abomination in the eyes of all unfortunate enough to meet it. Farree shivered. Not that he believed that he—that anyone—would be so treated by those he had met wearing the name of Thassa, but the picture of the creature in his mind made him ill.

Apparently his shiver informed them that such a fear did lie deep in him. But how wrong they were. To be an animal—a swift, beautiful runner such as Yazz, a mound of strength and courage like Bojor—to him who was Dung—what could be a more welcome change?

"I see you understand me. Did you not know that they would not keep such an abomination as you with them? You would find yourself furred or feathered or caged soon enough. Now, let us ask again: Why did Vorlund and the woman come here? The Thassa have no ships, and that one which brought you is too small to carry many. But only a few recruits and they could cause us a problem—a small problem. Did they ever mention the planet Sehkmet to you, humpback?''

Farree considered quickly. He could well pretend that the fear of the animal transformation governed any answer. And what did he have, in truth, to say? He was not sure why they had come to Yiktor—save that the Lady Maelen was moved by a pressing desire to set down here when the three-ringed moon swung in the sky and that that had something to do with her powers. He was having to think faster than he had ever been pressed to do before, weighing one fact against a supposition and a guess against a fact.

"They said only that there had been a great find there and that they had something to do with it. It was a matter in the past which they spoke little of.''

"A matter of the past reaching well into the future—which is now. Yes, something was found on Sehkmet, and they had

a hand in it—those two.'' Though there was no change in the
Commander's set expression of half boredom and flagging
interest, still there was a note in his voice which suggested
that he might not be broadcasting fear now but rather anger.

"You read minds, I am told.'' He leaned forward a fraction to look down into Farree's face only inches above the
top of the table. "Therefore you could know what they did
not say as well as what they said. Now what of that?''

The hunchback shook his head. "Lord-One, those can cut
off their thought by will even as you are shielded. I could
read only what they willed me to—the small things that they
thought it needful for me to know.''

For a very long moment the other simply observed him.
The dark eyes were expressionless and there seemed to be no
surface life in them. It was as if the Guild leader could
shutter them at will.

"That could almost be the truth, Dung. Only I cannot be
sure, can I? We shall do some probing when Isfaltan gets
here with the reader. There is nothing human which can hide
a thought from that. So you will share our hospitality for a
time. If you wish to bespeak your friends—''

Farree had already made a decision, the best he could
summon in the here and now.

"Lord-One, when that summoned''—he pointed at the
box the fat man still so jealousy guarded—''did I not come?
They did not, but saved themselves by their own ways.
Therefore why should I believe that they care now what
happens to such as me?''

"The truth again. The Thassa do not fight, nor war even
when they are attacked, but always withdraw. They will be in
no haste to rescue one who is as you—a misshapen thing out
from the slime, which they might have taken merely for an
experiment.''

Perhaps that was the truth. Now that he was not near the
Lady Maelen or the Lord-One Krip, how could he be sure

that it was not? He need only look down at what he could see of himself and think a bitter truth or two. On Grant's World he had had some value. What was he here but some refuse swept up during their escape—of less worth than Yazz or Bojor?

"I see that I have given you something to think about. Consider it carefully. Return him into keeping."

Return him to the tower room they did, though they shoved into his hands a roll of nearly stone-hard ration crisp and a canteen of water. He ate slowly, chewing at the hard stuff with caution lest he break a tooth. It would have been easier to put some drug in that scant ration of water than in the roll of hardened nutrient. There could be no sleep gas here, but neither had they rebound him. It might be well that they thought him so safely caged that they need take no such precautions anymore.

He could not put his back against the wall; his hump was still tender. Now he sat cross-legged in a corner of the room farthest from the door and tried to think.

What he had gained when Lord-One Krip had told him of the past and other hints garnered along the way—even what his present captors had said—all linked together. There had been a find—doubtless a big Forerunner one (such could make the finder wealthy beyond dreams) on a world named Sehkmet. The Guild had been busied with looting it when in some way Krip Vorlund and the Lady Maelen had spoiled their action. Now the Guild (and he did not doubt that the Commander here was truly a Guild Veep of some standing) had a double reason for wanting to lay hands on the two Thassa again: once for retribution and once to learn if there were more such finds to be uncovered.

Nor did he doubt that the Guild controlled that which would win their desires—first from him and then from the Thassa. It was a well-known fact that the Guild was ever on the search for new weapons—or old ones of lost and forgot-

ten races—which could be used with effect. This one which
had brought him into their hands was surely such. Yet Lord-
One Krip had been able to withstand its demanding call.

Thankfully there was little they could get out of him. He
was very glad that he had not been deep in any plans the
Thassa might have made. Certainly he could fight and he
would, testing his will to the uttermost. But in the end they
would wring him dry as one wrings a washing rag. That they
could and would use him as trap bait—that he also supposed
to be the truth. But he had no idea that any Thassa would
venture into the heart of enemy territory to have him out.
They had treated him well, near as if he were standing tall
and fully human. But . . .

He slowly turned his large head from side to side. Put that
shadow of hope out of mind. He had no chance of being
plucked out of the hands of the Guild. It was all he could do
to fight down the waves of dark fear that rolled over him
until he was breathing in small throat-hurting gasps and the
sweat rolled down his cheeks like tears.

There was no weapon. He had no Toggor this time to even
give him a hazy picture of what lay outside. His hands, thin
and long as they were, were only collections of brittle bones
that could be easily snapped by a single kick or blow. And
they had mentioned laser burns . . .

Farree's head fell forward until it rested on his drawn-up
knees. He wound his arms about his legs until he was near a
ball of distorted flesh and bone open to any attack which
might come. But his mind . . . ? Feeling very open to evil he
sent forth a questioning tendril of thought.

Time and time again that came against the blankness which
he knew marked a shielded man. There was no chance at all
of contacting any of them. Then he found a spark of thought—
not coherent but rather all emotion, and that emotion was
mainly hunger underlaid with wary fear.

An animal of some sort, perhaps the same type of vermin

as might be drawn to an inhabited building in the Limits. It was a very limited mind, but it was not shielded. He saw so little by its aid—only a dark run which he guessed was within the walls. But he rode with it, beginning by very slow sendings to build up the sensation of hunger which should bring the creature he had netted out into the open.

Hunger—the kind of hunger he himself had known only too often in the past. It was easy to think hunger—impress it on the hurrying creature in the wall. There was thin light in the haze of the run; the hunter must be approaching some exit to the outside. Hunger! With the same pressure he had used with Toggor he fed that need—hunger!

The creature was out of the wall into full light. But the picture was so hazy he could not be sure just where it was—within one of the buildings or clear in the open. Hunger—food—feed! He bore down upon that order which the minute brain of the hunter could hold.

There was a sudden leap which caught Farree by surprise. And now—food—he could pick up every nuance of that feeding, the tearing, the gulping—then—

There was a sudden sense of spinning, of falling, and at the end—Farree withdrew touch in a hurry. That creature he had "ridden" was nearly dead. He filled his lungs deeply, clasped his hands upon his arms with a nail-cutting grip. Almost he had gone into death! He could only believe that the forager had been caught and killed. Yet—insofar as he was success-ful—there was or had been one mind within these walls which had not been shielded. He had not only found it but made use of it after a fashion. Where there was one there might be more.

Also—and this was something new he had gained—he had not had to focus on a clear mental picture in order to make contact, as he always had or thought he had had to do with Toggor. Now, his eyes closed, his body still in that tense ball, he began another search.

From the single window in the wall so far above his head there was framed the sky. What life, other than Guild men in flitters, rode that sky? Awkwardly at first and with little success he thought of sky, and vaguely of a winged creature which rode the winds there. He knew little or nothing of birds. Their like did not abound in the Limits, save a few lice-covered eaters of carrion haunting some of the darker ways.

There was something about the—

A trace of thought! Farree poured all his strength into touching that, wrapping about it, finding its source. This was an air dweller, a flyer—and again it was hunger and the lust for a hunt that moved the unknown. He strove to see, but the difference in their sight organs was too much or—

It was as if someone had pressed a button. He could see: the earth spread below him like a great floor. The buildings on the knoll were a gray-black stain with flickers of light here and there. He could—

"Who?"

The hunger and the desire to hunt had been cut off as sharply as the change in vision had come to him. There was—another!

"Thassa?" He thought that.

"Thassa." There was no mistaking the sharp assent which came to his single-word question. "Who?"

Farree strove to mind picture himself in all his misshapenness. He could not be sure if the other were to follow him as he had followed the trace of the flying thing.

"Here!" That was no bird thought; rather it spoke in his own mind even as he strove to contact it a second time.

"No!" He had respect for the Guild. Mind shielded they might be, but in dealing with the Thassa they might also have alarms that could betray such an entrance as much as if an enemy of his captors rode into the gate.

"Not so." The answer came so firm and loud that Farree

uncoiled and looked sharply at the door, almost sure that had
been uttered aloud rather than by mind speech. "You are—"

There came no other word for a long breath or two. Then
with the same clear sharpness that mind voice said: "We are
on a level not well known—not known." There seemed to be
almost an aura of surprise in that. "They have their safeguards, but those are for minds such as theirs. They will not
know. What has happened?"

"Thassa you are," Farree thought back slowly. There was
no mistaking the kinship of this voice to the one which had
come to them earlier in the ship. "Why?"

"Why? Because you are open to us and all else is closed
save vermin of the walls and that which flies. Who are these
and what is their purpose?"

He was sure now that this was one of the four who had
stood in judgment over Maelen at the gathering. Perhaps the
one who had sealed his ears to that intolerable dirge that the
people had sung back in the audience chamber.

Though he would have wished the Lady Maelen that was
his own wish—though the Thassa meant hardly more to him
than a name, yet what was threatened touched those he knew.
He ordered his thoughts quickly and strove to relive in his
mind that meeting with the Commander.

"So." The mind voice had but that comment. "And they
think to perhaps use you as bait in some trap?"

"Which will not work," he answered quickly. "What am
I that any should venture for me here? But they bring other
machines—"

"Machines!" The other voice made that sound like an
oath. "Already they have profaned the Old Place with their
flyers, and now they would seek to use other things. But
have hope yourself, little one. I say this and it is never a
thing lightly promised, though you do not know us well
enough to understand that. The Song has been sung in your
hearing. Now you are under the wands of the Singers and

what comes to you also touches us. You are not forgotten. Think you on that and be steady as you have been!''

Abruptly, as with the flying thing, the voice was gone, and he had a strange sensation as if in some manner it had drawn that which was the inner part of him a short way after it. But no, that was no escape. He was still crouched here—Dung of the Limits. He could not see that there was any hope of escape. Were he on his home world, a number of things would come to mind; here was nothing.

He wondered over that promise, if promise it had been. From Maelen, he might have believed in it and taken heart again. But from one he did not know—the many sorrows of the past made him doubt. They might wish to help him, he allowed that. But that they could do anything he did not believe.

Thus it was his own fight. He thought of that creature that had run in the walls—if there were many of them and if they could all be aroused to attack some food supply. What might he gain from such a skirmish? He had no idea but he filed that possibility away. There was at least one flying thing he had touched—though it might be wholly under the control of the Thassa and might not be within reach again. If only he had Bojor!

Though even if he could summon that giant to him he doubted that he would. A laser would bring the bartle quick and painful death and avail him nothing. Once more he rolled himself into a ball and tried to shut out the thoughts from his mind to sleep.

At first he thought that sleep was impossible. His mind kept repeating that interview with the Commander and his helplessness as a prisoner. But many times before he had carried fears and torments into sleep, and this time it was also so.

However, he dreamed—not one of those broken and distorted series of pictures that had been his uneasy nightmares in the past. This was as clear as a mind picture and very vivid, so that he saw it all sharply and knew also that this was no dream but a fragment of sleep-unlocked memory of a time which seemed to him utterly far in the past.

He was crouched upon a bundle of dirty carpets watching two men. One of them, wearing a crumpled and much stained spacer's coverall, was—

"Lanti." The other man spoke the name even as it had come to the dreaming Farree's mind and reached across the stained table to catch a fistful of Lanti's shirt at the neck to jerk up the head which rolled loosely on the man's shoulders.

Lanti's mouth was slack with a drool of spittle from one corner, and his eyes turned up in his head. He breathed noisily. The one who held him struck a sharp slap on each side of the face.

"You blasted fool—answer me! Where did you planet then?"

But the man who was Lanti only puffed his lips and then snored. With a grunt of obscenities, the other let go of him and allowed Lanti's head to fall forward onto the table. He pounded a fist on that dirty board before him and then reached within his own jerkin and pulled out a piece of cloth. From its wrapping he shook out a scrap of something which glittered and welcomed the light in the place.

Seeing that, the dream Farree made a small movement forward and the man was instantly alert, turning to look at him. Such was the expression of demand upon his hairy face that the very small Farree gave a tiny whimpering cry and waited helplessly for a blow to follow.

10.

The man in one lumbering movement came to stand over him, scowling down at the small figure. He still held that glittering scrap between two fingers but Farree did not look at it.

"Dung." The big man slapped his face, even as he had done to Lanti, rocking him over so he lay nearly facedown on the filthy carpets. "What do you know about this? He has dragged you about with him so you must have some value. Is it that you know?"

He could sense the cruelty rising in the other. In one of those huge hands his brittle bones would snap easily; he could be turned into dead rubbish to be flung into the street.

"Far—" Almost he said the name which he must not. Lanti would beat him again if he did. If this bravo did not slay him first. "I—I know nothing, Lord-One." His voice was a harsh croak hardly above a whisper.

The second blow fell, only this bully mistook his strength and sent Farree speedily into unconsciousness. When he awoke once more he was sore, so stiff and sore that the slightest movement was a torment.

There was the gray light of morning around, but Lanti still sprawled across the table, his face turned away. Of the other man there was no sign. For several long moments, while feeling came back to his legs and arms, Farree waited.

Outside this hut he could hear the normal sounds of morning: the groans and oaths of men on their way back to ships, and the rattle of pots and pans in those eating places which sold first meals. But the hut inside was utterly silent.

At last Farree moved, humping himself off the carpets, daring to approach the table. That his first known enemy was unaware was a gift of fortune he would not throw away. He stood as tall as he might to survey Lanti. The bloated face was a grayish color, the pouting lips blue.

Greatly daring, ready to dodge if the man awoke, Farree put forth one hand to touch the other's dangling hand.

Slept? His flesh was cold. With even greater daring Farree tried to sense the other. There was nothing there—none of the faint traces of identity which one carried even into the deepest of sleeps. Lanti was—dead!

If he were now found here! Farree scuttled to his noisome carpet nest and brought out a square of cloth he had earlier garnered. He moved around the table, his small hunched form not unlike that of one of the sus-spiders, gathering up a half-gnawed slab of bread, the tail end of a flat eel, not pausing to eat, though his empty stomach yearned to be filled, but ready to take the food with him. A weapon? No—the two sheaths at Lanti's belt were empty. He had already been plundered of both his force knife and his stunner. Farree's only chance would lie in flight and hiding. He did not know why the other man had abandoned him—but perhaps he had discovered Lanti's death and had prudently put a distance between them. All this end of the Limits knew that Farree was Lanti's captive and the hunt might be up for him now.

Clutching to him with one hand the bundle he had made of

the food, he slipped in the dawn light out of the hut and sought the shadows, speeding at his best hobbling pace away from the only place he had known on this world.

Before this world, before Lanti, what had there been? He turned to that over and over again. Always to meet with dark as if a part of his mind slept endlessly—or was reft from him by some form of small death. Almost, once, he had remembered—when he had seen that scrap of glittering stuff in the bully's hand. But even then there had been a barrier.

He had always guessed that he must have come from off-world, and he could not understand why Lanti had thought to bring such a miserable creature with him. Farree must have had some value beyond his own misshapen body. Some value beyond—

Farree awoke. For a moment or two he was disoriented. These chill stone walls about him—they were not of the Limits—then, even as he blinked his eyes, all which had happened came flooding back. The promise which had been made that the Thassa would help. How much dared he count on that?

He tried to school himself to forget it. Those to whom he was now captive could bring to their aid things he was sure the Thassa, with all their might of minds, had never thought of. No, he dared not depend on promises.

By the window so far above him, he thought the sky was that of morning. And he was very hungry and athirst. To ask—to beat on that door hoping someone would hear him— No, better to go without than perhaps make them remember that they had him to hand.

He had just made this woeful decision when the door did open and a man in a spacer's clothing, but one he had not seen before, came in. In his left hand he carried one of those cans of rations made for emergencies and in his right was a stunner. He said nothing but gestured with the weapon. Farree withdrew to the far wall and watched the other set down his burden and go out again. There was an audible thud which he believed signalled a bar on the other side of the door.

The ration was meant to be both food and drink. It was a tasteless semiliquid, but he knew that it would strengthen and revive him, and he devoured it to the last drop. That done, he turned the container over and over in his hands. Now, were this only some wild tale such as men told in their cups he could put the can to good use as a weapon of sorts and break out of his prison. Only this was no tale, it was the truth, and he thought the only time he would see beyond that door was when the Commander had some use for him. At least they intended to keep him alive; the food proved that.

Bait for a trap?

Slowly, as carefully as if life itself depended upon it (which might indeed be so), Farree sent out a mind touch, not aiming it at anything human but keeping to the lowest level he could reach. Within moments he found another of the wall-living vermin. The creature was sleeping, and it was easy enough to take over.

He slipped in and the thing awoke, felt the hunger Farree carefully suggested, and whipped into one of the runs in the thick wall. What he received was hazy, very limited impressions of, first, those tunnels familiar to his guide, and then a sudden open space in which he could distinguish little, just enough for him to identify furniture, some part of a room.

The craving for food was tempered by the animal's native caution. As it made short rushes from one cover to the next, Farree fought the other's alien field of vision for something he could identify. There came a sensation of heat and he believed that his scout was close to a fire, undoubtedly one intended for cooking. Then the hazy glimpses which he could not identify fully steadied and remained the same and he believed that the creature crouched in some sheltered hiding place.

Fear—a vigorous stab of it, filling all that small alien mind—a smaller mind than Toggor's and of a different pattern. Toggor! If he had only been able to bring the smux with him into this captivity! All the mind touch which they had used in the past would have given him a better chance to work with this other-world creature whose very form was unknown to him so that he could not build up a mind picture that might clarify his probing. He wondered where the smux was now. And somehow that loosed his hold on the vermin from the walls and before he knew it he had sent out a thought tendril which he knew would not be taken. Only—

It was!

Farree was not able to smother the sudden ejaculation of astonishment as the familiar pattern of the smux was there. It was very tenuous, to be sure, yet once touched it could not be mistaken.

The Thassa—or the Lady Maelen or the Lord-One Krip— must be very close for him to have picked up Toggor's send, closer than was safe. As he had done with the bird, he reached forth and strove to use Toggor for a connecting link.

If the Thassa or his late companions were there he could not make the connection—there was only the smux. Still, Toggor was growing clearer all the time as if he were approaching the ruins where the enemy had set up headquarters.

That the smux had made such a journey on his own Farree could not believe. How ever long that trip in the flitter had been, surely the Thassa had no comparable form of transportation which would bring Toggor. Still, there was no mistaking the smux's mind and—

It was backed—strengthened—carried—not by any one mental thrust but by a uniting. Farree had not the training nor perhaps even the gift to sort out the will and the power that projected the smux's own small range of thought. Nor could he reach behind Toggor as he had with the skydweller. Yet there was a new warmth rising in him. It was plain that Toggor was approaching, and that he would have a better ally here than the native things which he could not picture and so could not actually possess.

Farree closed down his mental link. He could not help but believe it might just be possible that those who held him could somehow sense such communication. Let Toggor get within the right distance, and he could trace Farree by his own gift without revealing his presence to those who held this ruin as their own.

Now it was a matter of waiting. Farree found that impatience was a hard goad to elude. He wanted so much to use Toggor for eyes, to see what the smux would see, to feel—

He sat as upright as he could, his back awakening into the same ache as had kept him company for the past few days, as he strove to get to his feet under that window which was too high for him to see from. Toggor—Toggor was suddenly afraid.

He was—he was above ground, with no strong hold on anything—being whirled through the air in a manner over which he had no control—and he was crying out to Farree for help and comfort—to be released.

Had he been picked up by someone of the Guild guard? No, this severe fear came not from being handled but rather from being not handled, swung along in an open space where there were no good clawholds for safety's sake.

In the air? Had he been tossed? No, Farree could not feel that he was so helpless as he would have been had he been flung, say, over one of the ruinous walls. In the air, yet not thrown.

There was a whirling of hazy sight and then—

Above in that single window there was a shadowing. A bird—or at least a flying thing with feathers—had lighted on the stone sill. It carried a squirming object fastened to a cord about its neck and now it dipped its head and that cord slipped off. Farree was beneath the window, his hands upraised, and with a desperate snatch he caught the smux as it fell toward him.

There was a net about Toggor which Farree swiftly peeled away. Once free, the smux caught his shirt front and swiftly made his way to his favorite perch, inside the collar, his stalk eyes extended to their farthest level for sight.

Farree tried to reach the smux with thought send but all he received was a breathless, sickening sensation of being swung through the air. Toggor had not yet recovered from his journey. But there must have been some overwhelming reason for the smux to have been sent to this prison, and Farree knew that it might hinge upon a space of time, something to be done as soon as possible.

There was no way out of here except the window, and the flying creature, having delivered its burden, was gone.

The hunchback squatted down again in the corner of the room from which he had best seen the door, and carefully detached Toggor's hold, lifting the smux on his two palms so that the eyes swung and arose on level with his own. Once more he attempted to establish mind contact.

And this time he achieved a hazy impression of the Lady Maelen. Also something else—that Toggor was rebelling against some task which had been laid upon him. Exploration of this place? Perhaps the rough stone outside the window would provide clawholds either up or down. Farree thought carefully and then pictured the vermin of the walls which he had contacted earlier.

Immediately Toggor's attention was caught and riveted upon that suggestion. As he had routed out his prey back at the inn in the Limits, so was he ready to try the same here. But Farree was loath to let the smux go. Though he had touched minds—or rather scratched minds—with that runner in the wallways, he had no idea of its size or natural armament. It might prove too much for the smux.

It was plain at once that the smux did not agree with him.

A hunter's lust for the game welled up to possess most of Toggor's mind.

Once more Farree crawled over to stand beneath the window, but the smux did not loose his hold on the shirt. It was plain that he had no thought of taking that way again. Then how? There were no cracks in the walls of this tower wide enough to take the smux, and the door fitted tightly to the floor so that every time it was opened it rasped harshly in protest.

Just as Farree thought of that, the portal to his cell did open and once more the guard appeared, but did not venture any farther than the threshold. Toggor moved with the flashing speed he could show upon occasion and was into the shirt, well hidden, before the door was wide open.

Though the man held a stunner he had brought no food, only beckoned to Farree to come to him, and the hunchback obeyed. He foresaw another interview with the Commander and perhaps worse to come. Somewhere along their path to that questioning he must loose the smux. Thus he shambled slowly, his head bent forward as one who had been broken in spirit and planned nothing.

The guard waved him on to descend the crumbling stair, and down this he went. He was only too aware of the scrambling Toggor was doing in the shirt and hoped with all his might that his guard would not see the movement.

Luckily the inside of this place was dusky enough to be full of shadows, which just now were comforting and promising. He felt the smux thrusting its way into his sleeve and allowed his arm to dangle, refusing to wince as the clawed feet dug into his flesh for the other's descent.

They had reached the ground floor, and the guard said in trader tongue, "Wait, you!"

As if he were weak and tired, Farree leaned back against the wall, holding the smux-supporting arm straight down. The claws moved from one hold to another. Farree could only hope that there was no trace of venom leakage from any of those sharp tips. Then he felt Toggor loose all contact and felt a soft plop against his leg in the shadows—the smux was on the move.

Farree dare not watch that quick scuttle into the greater dark. His guard was raising his free wrist to his lips and reporting in code into a disc banded there. A moment later he waved the hunchback on again and Farree had to go, leaving Toggor to follow his own desires, not even having any chance to impress on the smux what was necessary. But perhaps those who had sent him had already done that.

Out of the door they went. The sunlight was so great a burst of glare in this parched land that Farree had to shade his eyes after the murk of the tower room.

"On with you, Dung." The barrel of the stunner struck the hump hard and Farree had to bite his lips to keep from screaming. The tenderness of the lump which burdened him had been growing more with each day. He wondered if that meant some ill he did not understand. Now he staggered a step or two before he could control the wave of pain and walk as best he might in the direction the guard pointed him.

The tower stood alone, not connected with the other ruins about it. Most of the buildings were roofless, had even lost half a story to time and wind and storm. Only the one he had visited before was intact. There were some men lounging by its door. Five he counted. But there was no way for him to assess the full number of the enemy sheltering here.

"Here comes the luck piece, Jat!" Two of the lounging men were playing pitch and toss with black and white counters. He who spoke leaned forward as Farree approached, holding out a stiff finger.

The hunchback longed to dodge that touch now but knew deep within him that it would be best to keep hidden the fact that his back burden was so tender. They might well make a torturous use of such knowledge. So he suffered the slap of those fingers stoically and tried not to show any pain.

"Luck for all of us if we need it," one of the onlookers commented. "And need it we might."

"Your lips are too loose, Deit," commented Farree's guard. "Better not let the Veep hear you."

"I signed on for service, not sitting around in rock piles—we all did."

"We all did," agreed the guard, "and you don't go back on a sign-up. Not with him in there—" He gestured with an outstretched thumb at the door just behind him.

"Get on with you!" Once more that punishing jab, but this time high on his arm, and that was as nothing. Farree went inside the building. Again he was surprised at the carpeting, the hangings on the wall, the various bits of a less austere life which the Veep of this company had carried for his own comfort.

For the second time there were the two at the table: the man in uniform and he who was so fat he bulged in sections out of his chair. He was intent upon a small picture com; the Commander was more at ease, smoking a spice stick, the scented air of which fought with the mustiness of the ancient room.

Neither of the men paid any attention to the entrance of Farree. He and his guard stood together back by the wall until the fat man gave an impatient push to the viewer before him.

"There is no silencer according to the reading, but this will not reach into that valley."

"Nor will it ever," commented his companion. "These Thassa have their own protections—"

The fat man pouted petulantly. "What kind of learning can defeat a far viewer?" He put thumb and forefinger together and clicked them against the silent screen.

"An efficient one it would seem." The Commander drew

deeply on the spice stick and then expelled a puff of bluish smoke. "Is that not so, DUNG!" His voice lost all its calm laziness and snapped as a leader might snap an order and expect to be instantly obeyed.

Farree fought to remain steady. He had feared and hated Russtif but that was nothing to the emotion this man raised in him. He could feel the threat behind those words as if a whip had been snapped in his direction and flaked a scrap of skin from his cheek.

"I do not know what the Thassa can do." He offered the truth but was afraid that it would not be accepted.

"Yet you have traveled with them, you have gone into their forbidden valley. And they do not allow that to any they do not believe is one with them. Or are you so weak and poor a specimen of living thing that they treat you as they would one of their 'little ones'—those beasts they gather about them, changing places with them? Which are you, Dung, man or beast? Perhaps they have already worked their will upon you and in truth you might have claws and fangs. Yet I do not believe that—not yet."

The fat man pushed aside the viewer with one hand and looked also at Farree.

"Get to the truth," he said sulkily. "Verify him!"

Farree knew what he meant, and he had the greatest need of holding on to himself, not to shiver and cry out. They meant to use upon him one of the enforcing machines which spacers told so many tales about. Within the influence of that he could hold back nothing that these two wanted. They need only ask their questions, and the machine would at once betray and subvert any desire of his to keep information hidden.

"Very well. It will be illuminating at least. Why do the Thassa want you, Dung? You are a sorry specimen. But perhaps for those who deal intimately with animals your ugliness does not matter. We shall see."

The Veep made a gesture with one hand, and before Farree could move the guard beside him grabbed a handhold on his shirt where it hunched across his tender hump, bringing, in spite of all effort, a murmur at the pain. He was so swung to the right and pushed down on the seat of a chair which another of the spacer guards had jerked forward.

One of them held his head cruelly at a backward angle while another one forced a silvery band well down on his forehead and into his tangle of black hair. Wires ran from this up into the space overhead. He could not tilt his head far enough back to see where they ended. But now he was a prisoner to a power he feared more and more as his helplessness became so clear.

"What is your name?"

The fat man was the questioner.

"Farree."

"Farree?" There was a slight frown on the Commander's face as if he were trying to capture a small thread of memory.

"What are you?"

"A hunchback." He made a true answer, trying to see if he could so limit their knowledge gained from him.

"And what else?" The Commander leaned a little forward on the table. He pointed his smoke stick straight at Farree as if he could use it at his wish as a laser to send the other into smoking refuse.

"Farree." That was also true. He held to the thought that if he limited any answer to the exact question he might not be so great a traitor after all.

"You were born in the Limits?"

"I do not know." Again the truth, and they could not reach behind that for something he did not know himself.

"A man knows where he is born, unless he is an idiot," puffed the fat man. "We do not believe you are an idiot."

"Why do you say you do not know?" The Commander showed none of the irritation of the other, but he was the more dangerous of the two and Farree had known that from the beginning.

"I cannot remember."

"You were wiped?" The Commander no longer stared at him so intently, but was looking over his head at whatever there betrayed his speech as true or false.

Wiped—a memory erased for some reason. Was that the truth which he had not faced during all the seasons in the Limits?

"I do not know."

"What do you first remember?" The Commander had back his gentle, ruthless voice.

Because he dared not try any tricks with the truth this time, Farree spoke of that which had been in his dream—the death of Lanti and his own escape into the jungle of the Limits.

11.

"**L**anti." Again the questioner repeated the name. He looked to the fat man who was still running his fingers around the edge of the visa-screen. That other shrugged.

"Who knows of the actions of one man among millions?"

"He had a purpose—"

"Do not we all unless we are being wiped into nothings? A kidnapping?"

"How could this"—the Commander indicated Farree—"be supposed to be anything worth the worry or a copper nick in any market, Sulve? Unless he knows something. This bit of something which was taken from Lanti—or which at least he knew about—what was it?"

"I do not know."

"You do not know!" parroted Sulve in his high voice. "There seems to be very little that you *do* know, doesn't there? Why did Vorlund and the woman take you with them?"

Why had they? Because he had touched minds with the smux? But he must keep Toggor out of this if it were possible.

139

"Russtif dealt in wild creatures, they were hunting such, and they discovered I could mind touch with some of them."

"Thassa reason right enough—perhaps." The Commander scratched a thumbnail across his chin. "It is known that the woman once showed trained beasts—and doubtless changed bodies with them from time to time as she did on Sehkmet."

Sulve's fat hands were suddenly still. "This one?" he jerked his fat-rolled chin toward Farree.

"No, the inquirer would have recorded that. Did they promise you a new body, a furred one, Dung?"

"No."

"But you dealt with the animals, that is so? And still you are human to the eighth—" The Commander's eyes had traveled from Farree's face to a point hanging above him—perhaps the indicator of this truth machine.

Human to the eighth point, Farree heard that clearly enough. Not human to the tenth and full! He looked down at his claw-thin hands and the greenish skin which covered them. Was he then no freak of human kind, but something else—something which was perhaps to all of these as Yazz and Toggor were to him? He considered that and shivered. Perhaps he was not so different from Yazz and Bojor as far as the Thassa were concerned after all.

He tried to straighten a little and the burden on his shoulders flashed a thrill of pain through him. Now the very question they had asked him became all important: Who *WAS* he?

"Why did they return to Yiktor? Was not the woman in exile?" Sulve took up the questioning.

"I do not know." The truth, always the truth. The Lord-One Krip had told him, but he had not yet heard it from the Lady herself.

Both of the men were staring at the point above his head now and a slight frown had returned to the Commander's face.

"What said they of Sehkmet then?" he asked abruptly.

"That they had helped to find a place of the Forerunners—a great treasure—and there were Guild men there who were defeated."

"Nothing more?"

"Nothing." Farree made quick reply.

"Ah." The Commander picked up a tube lying on the table before him, setting aside the smoke stick. He pointed it at Farree and the hunchback gave a cry he could not smother as a pain like a flow of skin-burning acid struck him full on.

"What said they of Sehkmet and this time the truth—"

"Only that the Lady Maelen is now wearing a body found there—that she defeated something strange and not of flesh and blood to claim it." Farree could not see that that was of any importance, but it was the rest of the truth about the past—something which these two might well know and so be able to check his word.

"You see, you can remember when you are prodded," the Commander commented. "Play no more games with me. Did this Maelen and Vorlund return here to gather a force to search elsewhere, hoping or knowing that such luck would continue?"

"I do not know. There were three rings and power—"

"We all know of the blathering about the three rings, Dung. And the Thassa have their own power. But this Maelen possesses something else, does she not?"

He was turning that rod of torment around in his fingers, playing with it as he divided his glances between Farree and what was overhead.

"I do not know." Farree tried to brace himself for another blast of that body-shaking pain. The frown was plainer on the Commander's face.

"What you know, it seems, is very little if at all what is needed. Let us take up the matter of Lanti."

For a moment it looked as if Sulve was going to protest,

but if he was not in accord with his partner he did not voice any objection.

"Who was Lanti?"

Once more Farree told the story of his first memory—of the spacer who had died over a spilled drink and given him freedom of a sort.

The Commander stubbed out his smoke stick. "In other words, Dung, you know little or nothing which is of service to us. Why should we keep you alive?"

Farree made no attempt to answer that. He had in him still that core of belief which had not let him whine in the Limits and which, even in spite of the pain, kept him from crying out here. Human to the eight point only was he? Then he would prove that his stock, whatever it might be, had some rags of courage.

Sulve tapped those rolls of fat which were his fingers on the edge of the viewer. "He is not worth two copper units—not even one of inguaw wood."

"Perhaps not in himself. But as bait—yes, as bait. They have been sending over those flying eyes of theirs. There may be some merit in keeping him a while longer."

He clicked his fingers, and the same guard who had forced the head circlet on Farree came to yank it off, his hair pulled painfully in the process.

"The tower again," the Commander ordered. "And the viewer for you, Sulve. If they come ahunting this misshapen blotch, we can at least know it once when they are beyond that impenetrable wall of theirs. They will not remain there forever."

"Time—" began the fat man.

"Time governs itself. We cannot thrust it forward nor draw it back. They depend upon the third ring of that moon of theirs. It may be only superstition, but I am inclined to believe that it is more than that as far as the Thassa are concerned. Remember, they were an old stock before the first lordling arose here to take land for himself.''

''Worn out—''

''No!'' The Commander shook his head firmly. ''Do not make the mistake of the untraveled, Sulve; you should know better. Because a people does not huddle in cities, is not tempted by trade goods, it need not be primitive. I have heard much of the Thassa—and I do not believe that they are in decline, but rather have passed into a new way of life by their own virile choice.''

A hard grip on Farree's arm dragged him near off his feet so he had to scurry to keep up as he was led from the room and across the broken pavement in the courtyard. They had learned nothing from him about the Thassa, and what good his memory of Lanti might serve he did not know. He dared not try a cast for Toggor—Sulve might be able to pick that up. Farree had heard many tales of the superior equipment the Guild was supposed to use. And what good would the smux do free in this place when the hunchback could not communicate with him?

He was soon back in that room at the top of the tower, flung into a corner and the door slammed against him, trying still to keep his mind clear of any thought of Toggor. That the small creature could unbar the door was impossible and there was no willing bartle to be summoned this time.

Once more he hunkered down, his arms around his knees, and allowed himself to think—not of the Thassa or the Lord-One Krip or the Lady Maelen—but rather of his vivid dream the night before and of Lanti and of who or what he himself might be.

Points on the human-man-alien scale had been decided long ago. There were creatures near the alien end of that scale who possessed attributes that even a higher ''man'' could not understand. Thus—

Eight points—and what did those points consist of? Somewhat for his body form: he had two legs, two arms, a head, and a humanoid body. He could be a crippled "man" as well as an alien. His skin was greenish in tint, but that was nothing, for the Thassa were white of skin and hair, and these two who had just questioned him were space-browned and had dark hair. He had seen "men" with two pairs of arms, with the scaled skin of the Zacanthans and their lizardlike neck frills, with the soft fur pelts of the Salarki and their feline features. All came and went through space and no one remarked at their differences.

But in all his seasons in the Limits he had never seen one so bowed of body as himself. Why had Lanti had him? He was sure he had come from off-world with that one and that he had had some importance in Lanti's plans before the spacer became so soaked in var juice that his mind was not far from a mush. Therefore, if Farree had had importance once—

And he had revealed that to the Guild!

Farree sat up, murmured at the pain of his back. But that was not harsh enough to drive out of him the thought that he had indeed revealed much to his interrogators. Not perhaps the information which they had sought, but concerning himself. The Guild was noted for the thoroughness of any hunt which might claim a profit. What had Lanti stumbled on which had produced that incandescent rag of stuff which his questioner had also shown to Farree?

That a report of all he had said would be referenced to the Veep in charge of this sector he was sure. Then maybe they would come for him again. They might have a way of breaking a mind seal—though that could also mean his death. What had he done, save make the truth perhaps more dangerous than he imagined?

Never had he felt, even in the worst times in the Limits, so helpless. Then he had had some chance at mobility, been able to run, to hide. Now he was trapped, and even though

Toggor had come to him through the aid of the Thassa, that
meant little or nothing. Dared he try to touch minds now with
the smux, or did the Commander and Sulve have a blanket
over this place which would pick up any telepathic activity?
Since they were all shielded against that themselves, it would
seem that they were prepared to face such.

They could be reading him now as one would read some
message in a viewer, using a machine which he himself could
not detect. If so, they would expect—what?

Thassa first surely. Since they had reft him away from
those mind controllers, they would believe that he would try
to reach his late companions for aid. So—not Toggor! Rather
the Thassa in particular—build up a series of thoughts about
some imaginary feat being planned by *those* under their
three-ringed moon!

He had never tried such a thing before—that of false
thinking, of imagining that which was not so in such a way
that it could be taken for the truth. If it were possible about
the Thassa, why, so it could be with Lanti.

First, the Thassa. Yes. Some order to his thinking. Slowly
and tentatively he began to build up a mind picture of Lady
Maelen—of her commanding a body of beasts—and into that
he pushed all he knew of beasts, not only of Bojor who had
served them so well on board the ship but also others—some
such as he had seen in Russtif's cages and some which were
entirely imaginary but as monstrous as he could make them.
He thought of the Lady taking council with both Thassa and
the beasts.

So—Maelen was taking council with her furred and
feathered—and scaled—troops. They would come with the
night—surely with the night. He had been squatting with
eyes closed and putting all his effort into that mental picture
of what he was supposed to expect. But a sound cut through
his absorption, and he looked up to see a waving claw reach
within the window above and hook onto the inner stone.

Fiercely he strove to keep all thought of Toggor away—of the Toggor that was—but suppose that Toggor was twenty, a hundred times his present size; such with huge envisioned claws would make an opponent worth reckoning with. Thus Toggor might be used to menace this whole Guild operation—as long as the subterfuge remained unbroken.

Now he opened his mind to Toggor and the usual hazy in-and-out messages passed between them. The smux had explored the lower reaches of the tower as well as what lay above: a flat roof surrounded by a parapet, which had seemed gigantic to Toggor but which Farree thought might be perhaps only as high as a man's waist. If he had some way of reaching the window, of climbing aloft, he might find himself a hiding place which would defeat them all—if he could sink his thoughts into nothingness. But there was the distance between him and that window. Could he only defeat that, he was certain he could squeeze his body, in spite of the hump, through.

Thinking carefully of a smux as large as Bojor on the march to rescue him, Farree arose to run his thin fingers across the surface of the wall. There were no holds between the old stones. In this part of the ruins there was nothing that he might climb to raise him to that door on the outer world.

He flexed his hands vainly and stared upward, defeated. The door, barred and probably guarded, was the only way out of here. He wheeled to face that and projected a picture of the giant smux without, ready to break him free even as the bartle had dealt with such a problem on the ship.

Toggor leaped from the wall to Farree's shoulder, bringing an answering pain from his tender hump. The eyestalks of the smux were all extended and he was staring at the door as if expecting something from that direction.

There was! Farree heard the grate of the bar being drawn. Then he moved. Gathering Toggor in both hands, he tossed the smux through the air, and he landed, even as Farree had planned, on the niched stone which formed the top of the door opening.

The smux reversed himself quickly and hung by two claws at the very edge of that shallow shelf, eyestalks retracted, ready to drop. Farree hunkered down again like one without hope, but he twisted his head around so he could see the smux in action. There was already a greenish bead forming on the foremost claw; the venom was coming.

A man slammed into the room, weapon in hand, and swung that toward Farree just as Toggor loosed his hold on the stone above and leaped for the back of the guard. There was a flash of claws at the man's throat, almost too fast for Farree to catch.

With a sharp cry only half uttered, the man staggered, dropped his stunner to reach for his neck with both hands as he wove back and forth on his feet, his face a grimace of pain and fear. It was Farree's turn to jump, and he caught up the stunner as the guard staggered on past, to bring up against the far wall and fall to his knees, his hand still clutching at the back of his neck. Toggor was already off that struggling body. Farree swung the stunner around and pressed the button. The writhing man straightened with another muffled cry and lay still, while Farree stumbled out of the door, the smux clinging to him, and slammed that shut, thick and heavy though it was.

He thrust the stunner through his belt and reached down for the bar which was almost too much for him to manage. However, at this time he could have accomplished miracles he was sure, as he thrust it home in the slots awaiting it.

Now—

He crouched at the head of the stair looking down. Without knowing how many Guild men were here and where they were stationed, to descend that stair, even armed, was more than he dare try. Down? If there only was a way up!

A dim picture cut into his mind: a section of vaguely outlined wall and on it—

Farree swung around. The smux had left him, was at the foot of that stretch of wall, reaching with its claws for something. Spikes—there were spikes in the wall itself. Not stairs but surely a way to mount the wall. As shadowed as that was Farree thought he could sight the outline of an opening, closed by a trapdoor, perhaps, but if barred it could only be from this side.

The smux was already halfway up the wall, swinging from one clawhold to the next. Farree set about following. He tested each of the rust-covered holds before he put his weight upon it, and, though the rust flaked off on his hands, there was enough solid metal within to support his weight.

Then he was clinging with one hand and both feet as he set his palm against the closed trapdoor in a push. The old wood resisted. Farree, gritting his teeth, tried a second time and felt a fraction of give. That was enough to encourage him. Now he held on with his hands, arching his body so that it pressed against the door. His hump was instantly aflame with pain, but he refused to slack his attack, and at last the barrier lifted enough for him to get one arm and shoulder through the slit. It took but a moment or two then for him to crawl forward and lie in the open air, the smux pulling gently at the long locks of his hair and uttering cheeping noises. His back was bound by a band of agony so that he had to use every fraction of determination to move again and allow the door to fall into place behind him. The top of the tower was covered by a mass of brush and dried grass, and he saw huge bird droppings. It was a nest which might have been well used for more than one season. There were bones too, cracked and splintered, some quite large, which made him wonder about the size of the nest builders if they used such animals as their prey.

A skull rolled under his hand as he got unsteadily to his

feet and hoisted himself a little against the parapet to peer
down at the main body of the ruins. Below the outer wall
were two flitters, doubtless the air transport for those in
residence here. He saw two men making their way toward the
still-roofed building where he had been taken for interviews.
But, for the rest, there was nothing to show that the ruins
were at all occupied.

It was a dull day with no direct sunlight, yet he could sight
a shadow to the east which suggested that there lay the hills
and cliffs the Thassa claimed as their ancient territory. Dry
clumps of grass, with here and there a wind-twisted bush,
were gray instead of green, and there were a number of
outcrops of rock, some large and standing as if to suggest the
ruin he was in had had much older neighbors of which only a
few wind-chiseled remnants remained.

Temporarily he was safe, but lacking food and water he
could not remain where he was indefinitely. Nor could he
expect any help—in spite of all his brave imagining of an
hour earlier. Toggor scuttled back and forth through the
noisome remains of the big nest, the long-dead fronds and
branches cracking under his weight, small as that was. Farree
caught a flash among the fronds which gleamed even under
the dead gray of the sky and pulled out a knife with a
stone-set hilt. His find was still in a scabbard—rusted there,
perhaps, through long exposure to the weather. He worked at
it determinedly until he could draw it, and to his great
surprise found the blade dull but still only speckled here and
there by corrosion.

This lucky find sent him kicking aside the rest of the mess
and searching through what had sunk to the bottom of the
nest. There were more bones: three skulls which suggested
they had once served animals perhaps the size of Yazz. But
there were other things, too: a time-tattered strip of skin on
which were set medallions centered with blacked metal and
dust-layered stones—perhaps once a belt. There was a goblet

of tarnished metal which he thought might be silver. A part
of a sword, only the hilt intact, the blade a lace of erosion.
He had heard of birds who sought bright things and laid them
in their nests, and this seemed to be such a hoard. Among the
objects also was a box wedged shut past his opening until he
hammered at it with the sword hilt and pried with the point of
the knife.

It came open at last, but what Farree found himself looking
at was a heaping of thick black powder. If that were the
remains of some treasure he could give no name to what it
had once been, and threw the box aside in disgust. Some of
the powder curled up in a puff to sprinkle over the matted
stuff of the nest which he had clawed away in his hunt.

There was an odd scent in the air, and then a tendril of
smoke arose from one of the besprinkled branches. A touch
of flame followed. Farree jumped back, realizing that the fire
would include all of the nest stuff unless he moved quickly.
He pushed the branches away as fast as he could from the
door which led downwards, knowing that if the worst followed he could retreat. Probably right into the hands of his
captors, since surely this mounting fire on the roof of the
tower would be sighted by someone!

The stuff was tinder dry and crackled from branch to
branch with the running of flame. Where the powder had
fallen from the box there were larger bursts of glare—not red
or yellow, but violently green—and from this thick coils of
greenish smoke began to arise.

Farree squatted by the trapdoor. If he could stand the reflected heat from the burning nest he would be safer there
than down in the tower itself. He had pulled aside a number
of dried bones while rooting in the mass and these he piled
now beside him, breaking them into brittle slivers and short,
pointed pieces. If he did not have to withdraw he had ammu-
nition of sorts to pin the hands of those reaching for him, just
as he had still the stunner he had taken from the guard.

Thinking of that brief encounter he summoned Toggor to him and induced the smux to run envenomed claws along the points of his longer weapons, poisoning them as an added weapon against any storming his place of refuge.

The heat of the fire was hard to face. Toggor crawled within the breast of Farree's shirt and clung as if this youth's body, hunched together as it now was, plus the distance of the fire, would keep him from the shriveling scorch of the flames.

That green smoke still shot skyward, though a breeze at a higher level caught it and fashioned it into what looked like a giant finger pointing toward the distant cliff land. If the Thassa did have any sentries or scouts, they must be wondering at what activity now topped the ruins.

There was shouting from below. Farree fingered the stunner and pulled closer to hand his collection of poisoned darts. He now heard the pounding of feet on the stair within. The magnetic-soled shoes of a spacer were not easy to mistake. He could not count how many were in that storming party. Could they even know that he was responsible? He had felt no mind touch since he had been here aloft and now, in another vain attempt to make a stand, he pictured Thassa— Thassa and giant beasts on the march—even winged monsters here aloft.

12.

The green smoke did not dissipate as a breeze swept over his tower perch. Instead it appeared to grow thicker, though it still slanted toward the distant cliffs. There were louder sounds from below. Those who garrisoned this outpost were gathering. He could see men running across the courtyard toward the tower. Even Sulve appeared in the doorway of the headquarters, his head turned up from his beefy shoulders to watch the phenomenon above.

Farree waited beside the trapdoor. He even dared for a moment to loose mind control, but all he encountered was a low emission from Toggor and those holes in space which marked the brain-shielded Guild men.

Now there was a puff like a small explosion, and Farree saw that the fire had reached the box and was feeding greedily on what was therein. Surely if any of the Thassa were on sentry duty they could sight this pillar of rolling puffs. Though what good that would do him, Farree had no notion.

Beside him the trapdoor heaved. He caught up one of the envenomed splinters of bone and readied himself. The door swung up and back from a mighty shove, and the barrel of a laser appeared in a hand. The one who held it remained as far out of sight as he could, only, in order to keep his perch on that ladder of spikes, he had to balance himself with one outstretched hand against the frame of the door.

Farree struck and his blow went straight. There was a yell of surprise and pain from below and both laser and hand disappeared, the latter with the splinter still standing up in flesh aquiver from the strength the hunchback had summoned to plant it home.

The brilliant white of a laser beam lanced up into the air but Farree had already taken refuge behind the upthrust door, his only shelter. He thrust once more from behind that, aiming blindly downward. Once more a longer bone spear he had chosen went home.

Fire from the laser ignited more of the debris of the nest. But though it glowed it seemed to be quickly extinguished by the flames of green which were already consuming what was left of the dried stuff.

Farree put his shoulder to the door and slammed it down. They could easily burn their way through that, he knew. He had no way of latching it from this side. So he squatted on its surface, making himself the only possible lock. The poisoned bone splinters had hit twice and the one or ones who had been struck by them would have something to think about.

The fire in the nest was near burnt out, so strong had been the gust from its first lighting. How long would he have before they could force the door that even now trembled under him? He knew that someone was pushing at it. Only the awkward stance that must be held by anyone climbing up those spikes of the ladder was in his favor.

Toggor crept out of his shirt and crouched on his shoulder.

"Farree?"

His name, not called aloud, but as clearly uttered in his mind as if it had been shouted. Thassa—not only Thassa but Lady Maelen herself! He took a deep breath. It sounded as loud as if she stood before him, but he was sure that she could not be out on the open land between this perch and the cliffs—the Guild would keep too close a guard for that.

"Here." He made answer, suddenly reckless enough to do that clearly, not caring at this moment whether any equipment of the Guild was able to pick up his call. Then he added, since his place of refuge was already known: "On the tower."

"Who holds?"

She was keeping her questions to a minimum of revelation and he would do the same: "Guild."

Though the fire was fast dying, the smoke showed no sign of abating. Its green finger reached farther out and out over the level land beyond the outer wall of the ruin. It was curiously thick, not diffusing in the air even though he felt a breeze against his cheek, an upspringing of wind which should have torn it asunder.

"Where?" That demand was ever clearer.

"On the tower," he answered, once again.

"Stand ready."

Ready for what? he wondered. Surely the Thassa, weaponless as he had seen them, could not hope to overrun the ruin and pluck him forth. But it was the behavior of the smoke which astounded him.

The reaching finger suddenly curled back upon itself. As it did, so it thickened, took on an almost solid quality. He felt as if he could reach out and grasp a tangible handful of it.

Back it came toward the tower. He swallowed. There was something ominous as well as unnatural about that return. He had no desire to be caught by the rolling folds of the stuff. But he could not retreat down the ladder. He still heard a muffled clamor from below, and he might well meet a laser head-on if he were to try even opening the door a crack. The grayish sky overhead had darkened, but the smoke was very plain against it. When it reached back as far as the outer walls of the ruin, the questing tip of that finger—or tongue—began to settle, seeking the lower stories of the battered buildings. At least it was not headed toward his own perch; none of it had sprayed out in his direction.

He dared to get to his knees, still holding in both hands his bone weapons, not crawling off the door, yet allowing himself a wider view of the smoke as it dipped down near to ground level. The nest had been consumed, and the end of the smoke before him had become only ragged tails which arose to follow the body of it, as if they had been summoned by order.

From below came shouts, and the pressure on the door beneath him was gone. He got to his feet, ready to drop his full weight upon it if the need again arose, and looked down.

The smoke did not touch the ground, but hung above it at about the height of a man's knees. And it was not dissipating. Rather it was like some shapeless animal hunting, ready to engulf anything that moved. He saw Sulve draw back and slam the door in the faces of two of the guards who cursed and then ran for the dubious shelter of one of the roofless buildings. No one ventured forth from the tower.

Now there was a heaving mass covering all the open space of what had once been the courtyard. A sound brought Farree's head up—made him look beyond the ruins to the reaches of the land outside.

There was movement about the flitters which had been parked there; he thought he saw a body being tossed to one side, and strained to watch more carefully, though he was held by the need for staying where he was, making a barrier of the trapdoor.

Suddenly there was a sound which no one from the Limits could ever mistake. The flitter was preparing to take to the air. Farree squatted down once more. He had no idea what that off-world ship might carry which could scoop him up prisoner. Transferring his bone splinters to one hand he took out the knife he had found in the debris, determined to do what he could to defend himself.

The small craft spiraled upward into the evening sky. Already the outer of the three moon rings was partly visible. Farree wished that he had faith in it enough to believe that he was going to come out of this unscathed. He waited, cold with more than the rising winds of dusk, winds which made no impression as yet on the smoke below but which grew more and more chill and lashing here above.

From the sky the flitter was descending, and then from it came the unmistakable mind send of the Lord-One Krip.

"Stand ready!"

Farree was sure that this was no trick of the Guild. A man's voice might easily be imitated but he had never heard that a thought pattern could be concealed. That was Krip Vorlund overhead and he—he was to stand ready!

It was not too dark to see now that a rope ladder had fallen from the belly of the flitter. Farree thrust his bone splinters and the knife into his belt, settled Toggor with almost rough haste within his shirt, and waited.

To climb a swinging ladder in the air—his mind flinched from even imagining such a feat. But this was the way out he had longed to find that until now there had been no hope of discovering. The flitter hovered overhead, and he was able to grasp the ropes in his hands. There was a third, he suddenly discovered, one equipped with a hook, and he clasped that into his belt before he started the dizzy ascent into the evening sky.

"Hold tight!" As he clung desperately to the ladder the flitter lifted and swung him on, through the air, toward the outer wall and away from the trapdoor and whoever might try to reach him now. The ropes cut his hands, so tight was his grasp, and he dared not look down. Then he heard another order: "Climb!"

At first Farree thought that he could never loosen his grip, never reach for the next hold bobbing above him. Somehow his body obeyed, while his mind remained frozen by such fear as he had never known before. Only climb he did.

There was a surge of power from the flitter, and now the wind tore at him. A brilliant white beam cut through the air where he had dangled only moments earlier. Someone was alert, free of the ruins, and aiming a laser.

A hand reached down to him from the opening in the belly of the flitter, promising safety. He was not even aware he had climbed far enough for the hand to reach him. But fingers gripped tightly at the cloth across his hump. The flesh beneath answered with white-hot flashes of pain, but he was dragged on up and into the flitter. He looked up into the face of the Lady Maelen. She reached over his prone body and pressed a lever which closed the opening as he remained where he was, too weak with relief to move.

The small craft was shaking, and Farree guessed that it was being driven to the full extent of its power away from the ruined keep. Whether they were bound back into the Thassa country of the high cliffs he could not tell.

For the moment he was content to lie where he was, breathing heavily. Toggor crawled out of his shirt and squatted on the deck beside his head, all eyestalks erect and turned toward him as if the smux knew concern.

"We are descending now," the Lady Maelen said in trade tongue. "We cannot enter the inner places in this off-world craft."

The inner places? Had it taken so short a time to reach the heart of the Thassa country? Apparently the swift flight of the flitter had been even more speedy than he had imagined. For they were setting down. As they bumped to a halt, which jarred Farree's body and brought an answering thrill of pain from his hump, the Lady Maelen moved to open the cockpit door. But the Lord-One Krip did not rise from the pilot's seat.

Instead he was leaning over the panel before him, drawing his stunner. Reversing the weapon and making of it a club, Lord-One Krip calmly hammered at the dials on the panel of controls, splintering their protective covering, and then the dials themselves, until he had bared a network of wiring which he proceeded to tear loose and twist out of shape.

"It will be a long day—several of them—before this ever flies again," he commented when he was done. "It is better that we be on our way."

Once outside, they looked up. Evening was fast becoming night but the sky was alive with the glory of the third ring, and Farree saw the Lady Maelen gazing up at it, her hand raising to gesture in the air as if she truly gathered that light and brought inward a portion of it clasped between her palm and fingers.

Before them was the entrance to the place of the hall. There were heavy ruts in the soil, from the regiment of carts that had passed that way before them. Lord-One Krip's touch on his shoulder headed Farree in that direction.

Once more he came into that place where the cliffs themselves were honeycombed with the very ancient doorways and the hand of time lay heavy on the half-arid land. But they did not go to the hall again, rather made their way to a lesser opening that was hardly higher than the heads of the two who escorted Farree. Within the entrance to which there was no bar or door shone a pale light which might be a portion of the third ring blazoned proudly across the evening sky.

They were waiting there, the four who had stood on the dais of the hall, though they were not standing in judgment now. There was a subtle difference that Farree could sense without being able to set name to it, but he thought that whatever difference the Lady Maelen had had with these, the leaders of her people, had either been resolved or postponed to handle a more immediate problem.

"Welcome, little one." The voice he knew. It had cut into

his thoughts too many times since this venture on Yiktor had begun for him to mistake it, or the speaker: the woman who stood a step before the other three.

"What have you learned that you could awake the Eor-fog?"

"The Eor-fog?" he repeated aloud in the trade tongue. All at once fatigue hit him hard. He wanted nothing so much as to curl up in sleep, a sleep without dreams, and remain unwaking for a long, long time.

The mental picture which flashed into his mind in answer to that question was of the thick green smoke which had issued from the powder in the box. He replied speedily with the truth, that he had found the box and that its contents had had no meaning for him.

"A nesting place of the grok. But those have been gone from here for many seasons. Fortune stands at your shoulder, little one, that such a thing could have happened."

He thought that he could well echo her statement. Looking back now, he could see that luck which had abided with him in the time he had been captive to the Guild. Perhaps the old superstition was the truth and his hump was a mark of luck—though one he would do without if he could.

"They thought to use me for bait." He brought out his only explanation for his remaining alive and in good condition.

"Yet the trap sprang on *them*," the Thassa leader said.

"They have lasers." He would not have her believe that perhaps they had seen the last of that company in the ruins. Whatever else the Thassa could mount in the way of offensive weapons, he could not tell.

"They could well have great weapons," Lord-One Krip spoke across his head in warning. "If they believe that we control some major find—"

"They may have what they please," the woman returned shortly. "Thassa control is now sealed to them."

Farree dared then to raise his voice in his own warning. "They may have patience, too. And can your land"—he thought of the arid country about—"give sustenance to all your people indefinitely?"

"Perhaps not. But there are other places to hunt for olden weapons besides a grok nest, little one."

He thought she was entirely too confident. As if she were the Commander and her forces set to harry a people who seemed, as far as he could determine, ready to depend upon intangibles for defense. Though he remembered how the flitter had been forced into another flight pattern the first time it had flown a scouting mission near the Thassa valley.

"You are tired, little one. Rest safe and know that you sleep within such a setting of sentries as those without have never met before."

It was a dismissal, and he went willingly enough but certainly not with a quiet mind. After his venture with the smoke he could believe that there were unusual weapons possible but that they might in the end triumph. He had lived too many years in the Limits under the ever-abiding shadow of the Guild where the indwellers spoke with awe and dread of what that organization could do and had done in the past. He still believed that the Thassa leaders were too confident.

But he went willingly with the Lord-One Krip to another of the cave rooms and there ate of dried fruit and strips of something which might be meat but which he believed was not, drank his fill of a sparkling fluid which was more than water but not a wine. Then he curled on a pile of mats with Toggor still beside him and waited for the sleep he craved. It was late in coming.

The Guild had wanted him for bait, yes. Almost the trap might have sprung. He realized suddenly that he had never really believed that the Lady Maelen and the Lord-One Krip would come searching for him. Perhaps it was a matter of duty for them, the same feeling of responsibility as he had for Toggor—that they could not leave him in enemy hands. That was the only reason he could accept.

Had he been anything else to the Guild? Though he had closed his eyes for sleep, what he saw again was out of his vivid dream: Lanti sprawled across the table and that other shaking him by the shoulder, drawing back in frustration and disgust when he realized the former spacer was dead. That scrap of stuff which the other had held—Farree tried to fasten his memory on that, sift it for its value.

Only what he saw now in the wink of an eye, the draught of a breath, was not the filthy hut of the Limits but somewhere else—

It was as if he were aloft again, swinging on the ladder, only there was no fear in this essay into open space, flight was something right and brought no fear. He looked down as if he rode on the back of a bird, not in any flitter, for the free air was all about him and he knew that he was here by *his* will and not because he had no choice.

He was looking down upon a rippling land of brilliant green: groves of trees whose leaves were clasped lightly about gems of eye-pleasing color which he knew were flowers or fruit. For the first time Farree could remember, he was truly alive, feeling no telling weight upon his shoulders, able to move his head freely. He was straight of body; without touching his shoulders he knew this. This again must be a dream, but one he clung to fiercely. If he never awakened from it, then he was repaid for all the ills of the past.

He descended through the air, lightly, easily, depending now he knew upon nothing but his own will and body. Grass rose shoulder high about him and there was the sweet smell of—

It was the scent which broke the dream, pulled him back into the grim reality of his own world. Yet it was a pleasant scent, one which he knew. He opened his eyes and the Lady Maelen was kneeling beside him.

There was a small furred creature on her shoulder, bobbing

its small head against her throat. Behind her Yazz stood, tasseled tail aswing.

"Farree . . . who is Lanti?"

Before he had time to truly align his thoughts, he answered. "I was with him. I think he brought me from another world to the Limits—me and something else that was worth more."

"Tell me," she urged.

He felt himself scowling. To have been awakened out of that dream in order to recall bitter memories was—hurtful.

"How did you know of Lanti?" he demanded.

"I saw him."

Farree hunched his body together as he felt a flow of anger beginning far inside him. "You were in my dream!" he accused her. He had met them mind to mind, yes, but he had never given them the right to monitor him without his knowledge. What more had she read from him that he knew nothing of? He felt as defenseless as he had in the hands of the Commander. At least then they had used a machine and had given him reason to know that he was about to be invaded.

"You cried out," the Lady Maelen said slowly. "It was a cry of hurt. I would have given you peace—that is all."

Perhaps she was right and had meant him only good, that he would again feel at ease.

"No!" There was deep concern in her voice, and she put out her hand as if she would gentle him as she might an animal that had been ruthlessly abused.

Only he was no animal! He was as much a man as a Thassa, even if he only held relationship by human standards to the eighth point! Perhaps the Thassa themselves, for all their humanoid appearance, were farther apart from the off-worlders who used that scale than he knew.

"Please." He was not aware that he had shrunk from her touch but maybe he had, for her hand fell to her knee.

"Please." She spoke the trade speech aloud; perhaps she knew that to mind touch now was more than he would allow. "Bad memories can lighten if they are shared."

"I have nothing to share." He pulled up and faced her almost as if she had been sent by the Commander to win out of him some last scrap of truth. "You know it all. I was with Lanti in the Limits—beyond that there is no memory."

"You were erased?" She was studying him so intently that he longed to be able to enter the wall of the stone chamber to hide. There was a new alertness in her eyes.

"I do not know. I do not care." He said that with all the fierce firmness he could summon. He saw that she would accept it.

"It can be reversed, you know. If you should want—"

"I do not!"

She raised both hands so her fingertips touched her forehead in the way of an oddly formal salute.

"Your pardon, Farree. Know that all will respect your barriers until you give them permission to do otherwise."

"It—is—well . . ." He stumbled a little over that. And remained sitting until she was gone out of the chamber. There was a small chittering noise and he saw that Toggor was climbing upon his knee. He drew one finger down the back of the bristly shell which was the outer plating of the smux. Did Toggor also know resentment at times when Farree strove to catch his thoughts? What did the animals which the Lady Maelen loved and companioned with—what did they think of that companionship? He knew that Yazz and Bojor welcomed her effusively after they had been separated for a space—that they perhaps companioned with her by choice. Perhaps they welcomed the fact that another life form could communicate with them and that they were not frustrated by a lack of touch. He was no trainer nor owner of animals. Only Toggor.

Now he put out his cupped hands and the smux climbed

into the hollow. He raised them so that he could meet him stalked eye to skull-enclosed one on a level.

"How is it, Toggor?" Tentatively Farree tried the mind touch. "How is this for you? Do you feel that I am forcing that on you which you would find freedom from? I am not Russtif to hold you captive, either body or mind."

He received no thought no matter how hazy, only a feeling of peace and contentment as the smux rocked a little from one set of claws to another in his hands.

13.

Farree ate, he drank, he slept deeply and dreamlessly. If those of the Guild made any foray into the country of the Thassa, he knew nothing of it. When he at last awoke it was to see a band of clear and clean moonlight across his short legs, feel about him an ingathering of spirit. Had it been the latter which had drawn him out of that deep sleep?

No thoughts touched him directly. Perhaps the Lady Maelen had set a barrier to stop those, as she had promised that he would not be asked more than he wished to give. But, even though none had been sent to arouse him, he was as one hearing distant and summoning music. For just a moment there was a troubling deep in his mind as if something stirred there which might flower if he let it. But instantly that same barrier which he had striven to raise against the Thassa fell into place and he was free.

There was a basin of water in a small side crevice of the cave room and handsful of moss for towels. He shed his sweat-dank clothing and washed the whole of his crooked body. His hump was still unduly tender to the touch, it also itched, as if his pain had abraded the thick, corrugated

167

skin, and he was careful in his drying as far as he could reach.

His shirt was so grimed he hated to re-cover his now clean body with it. But he did not have to. Near the crevice he found a small pair of breeches in the same pattern as those the Thassa wore and a shirt, wide across the shoulders, which gave room for his deformity. A chirping sound broke the silence of the cave and he saw the smux, throwing a grotesque shadow across the beam of moonlight as he came toward him, eyestalks erect.

Once more Farree sensed the aura of well-being and contentment which Toggor broadcast as he came. It would seem that the smux was well pleased with these lodgings, bare as they were. Farree reached for his belt to draw in the generous folds of that shirt when sound rang about him.

It was like the deep note of a huge gong, and his body vibrated with it. The boom did not seem to come from any one place, rather as if it were truly born of the very air about him. Three times it sounded, and he found himself moving out of the cave room as one who had been summoned and had no will except to obey.

He crossed the end of the valley, avoiding the sleeping beasts. Above him stretched a sky, which he twisted his small neck to see the more. There was the full circle of the third ring, and when one looked at it from here it was no true moonlight cast apart by some natural process of Sotrath itself, but rather a rainbow-touched encasement of the lowering moon. His flesh tingled, he felt alive to the last hair on his overlarge head, to the smallest tip of nail on his claw hands. It was as if the body he wore drank the radiance of that light as he would drink, after a long thirst, water from a clear fresh-flowing well.

The light appeared to draw the remainder of the ache from his hump, though the itching of his skin under the shirt grew worse until he longed to draw off the garment and use his nails on his own skin. In spite of that discomfort, his sense of well-being was acute.

There were none of the Thassa in sight. But he could hear again their song, issuing from the hall ahead. Only this time it was not a tale of loss and of long ages, but rather a cry of welcome to something which gave life anew.

Almost he expected to be turned back as he drew into the shadow of the long-eroded doorway. But there were no gate-keepers nor sentries here. The way was open and he passed on, drawn by the cadence of that song for which there were no words he could understand, only the rising melody.

Then he saw that through some ingenious means the light of the third ring was here also, banding across both the four Thassa who stood on the dais and the others who had come to gather below. In the glow their white hair held rainbow sheen; they were each enshrined in an envelope of light which made their bodies look almost tenuous, as if they were now only shadows. No, shadows were of the dark—rather wisps of iridescence.

He saw a Lady Maelen who was different. Her bright hair stirred about her as if each lock had a vibrant spirit of its own. The glow wrapped her round as it did all the others.

Farree halted inside the door and stood watching. Perhaps, in spite of the drawing he had felt within him, he was not one of these—perhaps it was better to keep his distance as a stranger.

The itching on his back grew stronger. He found himself rising on his toes, which were bare against the ancient stone, almost as if he were reaching again for some skyborne aid which would swing him out across that company, lift him even farther into the banded light. He flung his arms wide and lifted his head as far as he could from his crooked shoulders so that the moonglow touched his face. It was more than light now—it was welcoming warmth, like the soft pressure of a friend's hand sweeping aside the tangled hair on his forehead.

His feet moved—rocking back and forth. He began to feel the imprisonment in his misshapen body as a punishment, something that kept him chained to crookedness and sorrow when just ahead of him, inches beyond his reach, was all he had longed for and never thought to have.

The song was dying away—the desire in him died with it. He stood quiet now, and he could have wept that what had been promised or offered he had not been able to take. He was only Dung after all. There was bitterness in that which came welling up inside him as part of that sensation of irreparable loss.

There was silence now, and he stepped back under the very arch of the doorway. What if he had blundered on a secret thing and they were to find him here? He wanted to give no offense.

"Welcome."

Clear in his head, as clear as that voice had ever been, came the single word that Farree knew was to make him free of that company. He did not know why, but again he was drawn forward and now he walked slowly down toward the dais. That which had emitted the glow of the ring was fading; also, shadows gathered and lengthened. The Thassa no longer stood each and every one robed in glory.

However, it had not been his presence which had broken the spell. He knew that as he came hobbling forward. She who stood behind and above the Lady Maelen was holding out her wand. As if that had been one of the laser weapons of the Guild there was a glow at its tip, and he truly thought that he could trace a dim line of light straight from it centering upon him.

Welcome he was. There was no chance to misunderstand the wave of good wishing which arose from all that company. Then it broke as individuals and couples passed him heading for the door. Yet he was still held and summoned.

The Lady Maelen and the Lord-One Krip had made no move to leave. As Farree came level with them they fell in, one to right, one to left of him, all three facing the four Elders on the dais. She who had drawn him lifted her wand, and he felt that drawing vanish. Yet he also knew that he was not so excused from her presence.

"There is much in you, little one." Her thought speech was pure and somehow musical as if some lost tone of the night song still held in it. "Sotrath draws you even as it draws those who are sons and daughters of this earth. Yet you are of different stock and have yet to come into your heritage."

Out of all his bewilderment and unhappiness he dared to ask her then: "Who am I—what am I, Great Lady?"

She shook her head a fraction and there was a twinkling of the small crystalline gems which headed the pins holding her mass of hair.

"Who are you? Ask that of yourself, little one—for your like we have not seen before. What are you? That you must also learn for yourself."

"I am—Dung!" Again something had seemed just within his grasp and had eluded him.

"You are what you wish to be. Are you truly what you have named yourself?" Her mind touch was quiet, like a soothing hand laid across a child unhappy from a nightmare.

"I am—Farree!" He defied that other part of him which was sourly bitter.

He saw the jewels glitter again as she gave the smallest of nods.

"You are even more, as you shall know when the time comes, little one. We have some of the farseeing, but we are pledged not to use it for ourselves. We must not be led into making choices, only face those clearly and alone of mind.

But this I tell you, Farree—the time will come when you shall truly know what you are and who. And it will not be an ill time—but a good!''

Some of the warmth which had been among the song's notes and had flowed from the great third ring caressed him softly again. He tried to bow, though with his twisted body it was an awkward salute.

''For such farseeing as you give me—thanks, Lady.''

''One does not give thanks for the truth. But there is another matter for us now. Come!''

The other three who shared the dais turned as one and started away, and he fell in behind while Maelen and Lord-One Krip followed, Farree still between them. So they came into a side passage of the hall and at last into a room which was not all austere and comfortless stone but had around two sides a bench padded with woven lengths. More such hung across the bare stone of the walls. Again by some trick of the long-ago builders there was an opening in the roof through which fed the light of the third ring to give radiance to the room, for there were crystals or gems set in patterns on the flooring now flashing rays from one to another. Farree watched them in wonder, hardly daring to step out upon such a carpeting, as they winked in subtle patterns almost like the lights upon the control board of a ship. Yet these were rocks and gems, and they were far from any off-worlder thing.

The four Elders settled themselves on one bench and motioned the other three to take that nearer the door. He settled down there between the Lady Maelen and Lord-One Krip. Then one of the male Elders pointed with his rod to a portion of the wall and it opened, coming forth from it, on a tray transported as if by wings, a tall goblet which glistened with life in the moonlight.

That was borne to Maelen. She accepted it and drank a single mouthful; then she passed the cup to Farree and nodded encouragingly. He drank and passed it on to Lord-One

Krip. Once he, too, had accepted and drank, the goblet turned and was away again.

"It seems that these off-worlders who follow the lower path are here well housed and intend to stay until they have accomplished their purpose." He who looked to be the eldest of the Elders broke the silence first.

"Perhaps it is we who have drawn this trouble upon our people—" The Lady Maelen spoke in answer. "That we did on another world in fear for our lives, and more than just our lives, has sent ripples to Yiktor."

"They were here before," the woman who had spoken to Farree said. "I know not what they seek, but we have our own barriers and guards and they have not penetrated those—"

"Save when they sought to draw us forth." Lord-One Krip spoke sharply. "Those machines were tuned to one persona pattern, thus only Farree was forced to answer. Somewhere they had prepared to so cage us."

All four of the Elders inclined their heads in agreement.

"Therefore the quicker we go, the less the threat—" he continued. But the woman held up a hand in a gesture that silenced him.

"We are the Thassa and the years lie many and heavy behind us. Nor are we the less now because we have discarded much which the off-world holds in high regard. We cannot be hunted by their hounds—"

"Perhaps not, but you can be destroyed. And do not think that such a thing is beyond the minds of those who try to hold the gateway of your land. What they cannot take, they remove."

The faces of all four of the Elders were set sternly, and she who seemed their first speaker slowly shook her head from side to side.

"Let them try." There was such confidence in her words that Farree did not know whether to accept them and be content or whether to wonder at the disbelief of those who had never been off-world and did not understand the spreading and iron-handed power of the Guild.

"Their presence here can be reported." It was Lord-One Krip who offered that. "The Patrol—"

Again her head moved right and then left. "They move against the Thassa in their own lands. These come brazenly to do what they will. We are not so far from our sources even in these days that we cannot defend our own. Do you think that these would retreat even if the three of you were taken and laid at their feet?"

Lord-One Krip's mouth set and his shoulders squared as if he were about to reach for a weapon.

"The tales concerning the Guild are many and black. I cannot believe that any bargain they made would be honored. But there is this—time may be against them. This is not yet a world they control. Their nest in that ruin is the largest consolidation now of their power here—else we would have heard. Therefore a pact with them would buy—"

"Nothing!" Her word had the force of an aroused one's oath. "We do not treat with such as these. However, they may force us back into a path we forswore long ago—that we would meet open force with open force. When we chose what lies here"—she touched her forehead with the tip of her finger and then spread out her hand level and empty between them—"against what we might carry thus, the balance shifted and the Scales of Molester were set anew. It is our thought that these invaders will not be easily turned aside, bemused by illusion. You say they are mind guarded— thus our first defense is negated. Very well, if illusion cannot grip them, then we shall summon the power. These are the hours of the third ring when the power ascends, and during the height of it we must make our move. No—"

She looked straight at Farree and under that regard he felt like a small crouched animal without any burrow in which to hide, as if all he was was spread out before the four for their reading.

"Picture," she ordered, "what you know of these men."

He began with that force which had drawn him forth from shelter, compelling him to deliver himself to the enemy. He continued with his trip in the flitter, his coming to the ruins, and his imprisonment in the tower—then his meeting with the Commander and Sulve. Then, for the first time he was interrupted by a raised hand of one of the men.

"This Sulve has been heard of. He is outwardly a merchant whose ship is in port for repairs."

"I believe him Guild," Farree answered. "They are supposed to have their men in many places—mostly unknown."

"True enough," Lord-One Krip agreed.

"It matters not what he seems to be." The woman sounded impatient now. "Let us know the rest."

So he told the story of his two interrogations, one under a machine which would prove the truth or falsity of his answers. There was a shade of another expression on the face of the Elder, one Farree could not read.

"So they depend always on machines. They have no trained Deliverer with them," she commented. "This machine"—she spoke now to the Lord-One Krip—"such are in use off-world?"

"The Patrol are said to have them, and they are used by the law on several worlds. But what is known to the law sooner or later comes into Guild hands."

"I do not think," the Lady Maelen said, "that they could read Thassa."

"They will not get a chance!" Again the male Elder flashed with some heat.

"Can you," Farree began slowly, one part of him struggling against the other which was all sober reason, "equip one who is not Thassa with false information and plant him to be retaken?"

For a long moment that seemed to stretch and stretch there

was quiet in the room. He wanted to cry out he did not mean
what he had said, that there was no way he was going to be
trapped into returning into the hands of the Commander. For
there would be no games played then—his very mind might
be peeled and segmented so that the false would be made
plain enough to those whose powers he had feared and held
in awe all his life.

"I think . . . not!" That was Maelen. "There is Yiktor
itself to work for us."

"Perhaps." The woman made a dismissing gesture with
her hand. "But the full story is not yet told. What happened
then, little one?"

He told of the coming of the bird with Toggor, of how by
the smux's help he had set up the trap for the guard. Toggor,
as if he knew well he was being discussed, came out of
Farree's shirt to sit upon one of those knobby knees, his
eyestalks well up and all turned in the direction of the Elders.

For the rest Farree hurried over his climb to the tower top
and the nest there. When he spoke of finding the small box,
the man among the Elders who had not yet spoken leaned
forward and demanded: "There were symbols on this box—
you could read them?"

Farree shook his head. "It was very old—"

"That it was!" the man agreed. "We knew not that such
still existed. But if it was there, what else may still be ready
to hand?"

"How did you know how to use it?" again he asked
Farree.

"I did not. It was very old and worn. I forced it open, and
the powder in it touched the dried nest stuff and aflamed."

"So. The Scales dipped in your favor then. This is something to be thought on. Only yet your story has no end—give
us that, little one."

Farree spoke of his improvised weapons of bone and the
assault on his perch, of the strange cloud of smoke which,

instead of being wafted away by the wind, had sunk into the courtyard. Then he ended with the message of hope and the coming of the flitter to bear him away.

"Well enough," the Elder who had questioned him about the box said when he finished. "You gave them the truth and it did not serve them; you have escaped them, therefore their wrath, or that of their leader, will be great. I know that we may look forward to some new attack on their part. And since you are not Thassa and so vulnerable to what they may launch in the form of controls . . ." He hesitated.

Farree moved a little on his seat. Uneasiness and wariness arose within him. He had half offered, in spite of all good reason, to be bait, even as the Guild had thought to use him. But they had not accepted that from him. Now—now he must make them understand.

"What if they set some control on me and I prove a key to open your fortress?"

"Forewarned is forearmed," Lord-One Krip made answer. His hand closed about Farree's upper arm and he kept a grip there as if he feared that the hunchback was about to take off forthwith to tempt the Commander and his men into the open.

"There are none that can touch you here now." The Thassa Elder spoke with such conviction that Farree was compelled to believe her. "We have a defense which has not grown any the lesser through the years but stronger, as we have learned more and more concerning our own powers of self."

"They will not give up," Lord-One Krip said slowly. "Even if we see them evacuate the ruins and seemingly depart, we may be sure they have not given up."

"Nor shall we. There will be eyes aloft and eyes afield. Those who go on two wings and those who trot on all fours will keep them ever under eye."

Farree drew a deep breath. The bird which had brought Toggor, Yazz, other animals either linked by mind to—or

even exchanged with—a Thassa. What if all the Thassa
became one with the birds and the animals of this world?
How could those still in human guise know or prepare to
defend themselves against such an overthrow of all which
was natural by their own thinking? Hand clutched on hand
before him. What would it be like to have a fine, well-shaped
body like Yazz—to be free of the miserable itching burden
always on his back? Could this be done for him? His life as a
humanoid had not been such that he would not willingly
relinquish it for this other and freer guise.

"Not so!" She had read him, this Thassa Elder. "It is not
given for all to make great change. Even the Thassa cannot
do that as they please. Would you condemn Yazz to your
body then?"

Farree set teeth on his lip and bit hard. All his thoughts
had been for himself, that was the truth. No, he could not ask
that any—animal or man—take on the burden that he wore.

"You must be a Singer." The Lady Maelen must also
have caught those thoughts. "And there must also be to hand
one furred or feathered who needs the strength of man—one
hurt in mind or greatly beloved to the Singer. It is not an easy
thing like putting off one kind of clothing and assuming
another." She was kind, but he did not need her kindness, he
thought sourly for that moment.

"I have been thinking upon this matter of the Eor-fog,"
the other Thassa man spoke. "That such a weapon was left in
a grok nest is a mystery beyond all mysteries. It has been so
many tens of tens of tens of seasons since the last of the
weapons was destroyed. Certainly these ruins were built even
later as an outpost for the Lord Janger's land. Where did the
grok find that? There was nothing else?" He looked to
Farree.

"This"—the hunchback drew the knife from his belt
—"and a sword—I think it was a sword—which was rusted

past use. Some scraps of leather which might once have been a belt. And bones—many bones.''

"If Janger had come across any such arms," the woman Elder commented, "he would not have been overrun during the march of the clans. But there remains no record of usage. Who knows where the grok came upon it? They are easily attracted to all bright and shiny things. The cock brings them to the nest to attract a hen to what he has built for her.''

"The grok do not range too widely," answered her companion. "This was a better hunting land then. And the nest was old. It might well have been built in the first year Lord Janger set his own masons to work. These lordlings look for omens and fortune favors. The Lord Janger's war sign was a screaming grok—he would have never had such driven from his own inner keep. No, the box came from somewhere near.''

"You are saying?''

"Saying that perhaps there are other supplies here in the heart of Thassa holdings—only waiting to be found!''

"There was the surrender of all!'' the woman Elder protested.

"Something might have been overlooked. I would advise that, instead of setting all the seers upon actions of the enemy, we put some to hunt those places where we have not walked hereabouts—to see what time itself may have hidden for future finding.''

14.

Moonglow was gone with the deepening of the dawn. Farree stood in the valley of the Thassa watching a mustering of the clans and then an outspreading of men, women, and even children—each small group heading toward one of the carven doorways in the cliffs. But he remained with Lord-One Krip and the Lady Maelen and their place was apart: up the throat of that canyon which led to the valley and to the edge of the plain on which still stood the ship that had brought them. By them danced Yazz on impatient feet, ready to be gone; while Bojor hunched from side to side, swinging his heavy head aloft as far as nature would allow it to reach, the nostrils wide above the tooth-fringed muzzle as the creature tested the air.

That the Guild would have reason to explore their ship was something they all agreed upon. Though there was nothing within it that could possibly give any service to the Commander's force—not now. Star maps, yes, but Yiktor had been their true goal and on Yiktor they had landed. Whatever other voyage tapes were in stock within would lead only to false trails, and so perhaps would serve better now than weapons to confuse the enemy.

They did not enter the ship itself as that could prove a trap, but took places behind the fallen rocks which lapped about the foundations of the cliffs and so set themselves to wait and watch. This waiting and watching left the mind open to thought, and thought now plagued Farree. He kept returning to that dream-released memory—the one of Lanti. Who was *he*, and how had he come into the hands of that discredited and disgraced spacer? For, thinking back, it was plain that Lanti had had some reason to keep apart from the others of his kind who came to enjoy the tawdry pleasures of the Limits. The hunchback fought hard to fix on some point further back in time than the spacer's confrontation with the big man, striving to picture better that glittering scrap of something which had brought that one to hunt out Lanti and his captive. For he was certain that he, Farree, had not been with the spacer of his own will.

Only, when he struggled so to remember, he came always to a dark wall. What was sealed thereby he had no way of telling. Perhaps it was best that he did not know. Yet, no matter how many times he told himself that, the same number of reasons for remembering followed. Until he became aware of something else.

From behind the rock which he had chosen for his vantage point he could see the Lady Maelen and crouched behind her, his jaws moving rhythmically as if he chewed upon cud, was Bojor. There was a stir—not from them, rather in the warmth of the desert air itself.

Down from the sky wheeled a flying thing which was wide-pinioned and descended in a spiral, with only a few flaps of wings to keep it on course. It was black, yet the light struck rainbow points of color from the sleek fur on its body and along its wings, which appeared clad in skin and hair instead of feather wreathed.

It landed on the very rock behind which the Lady had taken refuge, and he could see that its head had no bill, rather a sharp muzzle with a show of teeth to suggest that it was a hunter and a formidable one. It was very large, perhaps its head would near top Farree's were they to stand side by side. It's second pair of limbs, which had been folded tightly across the upper section of its body, unfolded and reached out, naked claws showing, as if to menace the woman it now faced.

There was a shrill chittering sound and the wings flapped noisily as if the creature wished to take off and was compelled against its will to remain. Maelen's hands moved as had the claws. Not reaching for the winged one but in a kind of pounce and retreat pattern as if she played with some prey in a cruel fashion.

There was mind send—but of such a pattern as Farree could not follow. The thing took tiny steps that with the beat of the wings raised it a fraction from the rock only to let it drop again to its perch. Large eyes gleamed a brilliant gem-flash green and the overlarge ears twitched back and forth.

At length one of those uneasy jumps did take it into the air, and it beat its way up, to hang overhead, a wild flutter of wings keeping it steady above the rock on which it had perched. The Lady Maelen's right hand moved in a half circle and the thing wheeled out, circling about the silent tower of the star ship, once, twice, thrice before it was gone, soaring up until it was only a speck in the sky, a speck which headed toward the distant ruins if Farree could judge aright. He believed that so another pair of eyes had been added to their own scouting mission.

It was hot and grew hotter as the sun arose. This was a barren land, where even the patches of bleached grass looked dead on the root and fought a retreat against sand, gravel, and rock. Toggor had early made plain his opinion of their station by retreating into Farree's shirt, drawing in his eyestalks and apparently going to sleep. The hunchback also discovered that watching monotonously while nothing happened was a base for drowsiness. Since the departure of the winged one there had been no movement beyond the cliffs of the Thassa.

Thus it was almost with relief that he did see a dot in the sky—the creature the Lady Maelen had dispatched? No—there was no mistaking the sound. There was a flitter on the wing.

Surely the spaceship and flitter would draw any attention, whether it was the Guild who came now or some other cruiser—perhaps even a local planet guard. He knew very little of Yiktor save what he had learned from the Thassa, but they were only a small handful now and kept to their own barren land.

The flitter did not approach the downed ship straight, but circled. Though, Farree noted, it kept its circle from invading the air over the cliffs.

"C-2 double 3: Reply. Are you in trouble?"

It was not the clear mental call of the Thassa, but rather an actual voice out of the air overhead. Surely a Guild detachment would not use that approach! This flitter must serve some local form of the law.

Farree looked questioningly to the Lady Maelen. She had not moved. When he turned his head cautiously, he could see no trace of motion in the Lord-One Krip. Whoever these newcomers were, the Thassa wanted no contact with them.

"C-2 double 3: This is port command. Are you in trouble?"

The newcomers, lower now, could certainly see that the downed ship's landing ramps were out.

"This is a type four planet. C-2 double 3—landing is allowed at the control port only. What is your difficulty?"

That encircling approach the flitter had made was very much closer to the ship now. The smaller craft was preparing to set down. Farree saw movement ahead, a small body flitting from one tangled growth of grass or standing stone to the next, working its way purposefully toward the silent ship and the newcomer. Too small for Yazz—and besides, that prancing champion could not have made such a stealthy advance. It must be some other one of the animals the Lady Maelen could and did command. It squatted finally not far from the ramp of the spaceship, and when it was still it melted so into the background that Farree could not distinguish it at all.

The flitter set down and a figure got out, a stunner, plain by the length of its barrel, in hand.

"We are coming in. This is control from Central Port."

The voice rang loudly. Farree thought that it came from the flitter rather than the man who had landed, and was magnified to a shout by some instrument on board.

There were two aground now. They did not advance toward the ramp together but separated, weapons in full sight. One remained at the foot of the entrance ramp while the other climbed inside. There was a wait—the intruder must be investigating the ship with caution. In time he returned and gestured with an outflung arm so that his companion started back to the flitter.

He did not make a straight track but swung in and out across his first path, apparently in search of some track that might have been left on the ground. Though it would take an expert tracker, Farree was sure, to find any such.

The searcher halted and beckoned. His fellow ran down the ramp to join him. Farree felt that as long as the control men were present there was to be no attempt to attack the Thassa. The Guild would lie low. Oddly enough, he felt no confidence from this belief. Part of him wanted to front the Guild again, to have done with the suspense.

The strangers inspected the ground thoroughly, one of them even getting down on hands and knees as if he possessed Yazz's sense of smell and would hunt along their last

trail—day old as it was. Finally the two gave up and returned
to the flitter, which took off—but not soon enough to miss
the return of the flying creature Maelen had sent out earlier.
The thing saw them and shied to the north, sailing to a
greater height, apparently making for cover.

It need not have feared. The flitter arose easily and turned
to go back the way it had come. Farree realized the gravity of
the craft's visit. Any ship that did not planet at the port
probably was, in their eyes, outside the law. They might
continue to fly patrols in this direction, waiting for the crew
of the deserted spaceship to return. Thus the Guild would
not move, nor could the Thassa show outside their valley for
fear of questioning. And all knew that the Thassa had nothing
to do with off-world ships. Not all the Thassa—

Farree wondered. Who knew about Lord-One Krip, who
had been a Free Trader? And what of the Lady Maelen?
Surely their story had caused talk on this portion of Yiktor.
But just as surely they had nothing to fear from the laws of
this or any other world. It was the Guild who must go
underground.

"Perhaps—" Lord-One Krip's mind touch came almost as
clearly as had the voice from the flitter. "Yes, my story is
known—probably to far too many here. Also what happened
on Sehkmet. The Guild have their own ties with the law. We
are better without allies."

As the flitter disappeared in the distance the Lady Maelen
straightened in her hiding place and Bojor moved back to
give her room. She leaned against the rock that sheltered her,
both palms against its rough surface, her head turned to the
north where the creature of the skies had disappeared.

Scrambling over the smaller rock came the furred one
Farree had only glimpsed when it had gone forward to scout
the landed flitter. It leaped for the Lady Maelen and she
caught it in her arms, cradling it against her breast as if it
were the child whose size it matched. Again Farree caught

only broken words of whatever message it delivered, as its sending range was far above his own thread of mind exchange.

"It is true—" Now came her own send verifying. "Ista 'read' them. Those were not Guild, nor do they even know that this is the heart of Thassa territory."

"What *do* they know?" Lord-One Krip broke out sharply.

"What they shall learn by their path of return flight." She was smoothing the dark fur gently. "Ista put it in their minds to swing northwest a little."

"The ruins—the Guild." Farree voiced what Lord-One Krip must also be thinking. "They will see—"

"All which is open," Lady Maelen agreed.

"Which may be nothing," he returned. "The Guild will have their own precautions and hidey-holes."

"Perhaps. I would like to know how swiftly they can take to cover and whether they now have their flitters in hiding. There is little place there to conceal those. This may well bring another player into the game."

It would seem, however, that the visit and retreat of the guard flitter was not to end their own attending to the empty ship, for neither the Lady nor Lord-One Krip moved to withdraw. And waiting without any prospect of someone coming was a tedious thing, Farree discovered.

Toggor crawled out of his shirt and made raids where he could crook a claw under a stone and turn it over, scooping up grubs and insects so exposed. Farree ate his own rations and drank sparingly from his water flask.

It was the coming of the winged one for the second time that broke the dullness of the afternoon. Circling down, it perched on a rock which brought it eye-to-eye in height with the woman. This time Farree was not even able to catch the faintest wave of whatever message passed between them. The creature bobbed its head twice and a moment later took to the air again.

Then came the Lady Maelen's send: "There has not been

grok here for as long as the memories of the jarn exist—
which means during at least one of our generations. But there
is a height in the north where they had a second nesting
place. Near that are caves. Also"—now she spoke slowly,
almost as if she were thinking her way through a problem—
"those in the ruins have been seen twice scouting in that
direction, and what they must so seek is—"

"A storage place!" Lord-One Krip was quick to answer.

"There are none—or so I would have sworn. The Thassa
destroyed all that existed when they turned their backs on the
old knowledge and took to the roads and open places."

"A man would have said that Sehkmet was an empty
world also—until raiders and the Guild proved that untrue,"
Lord-One Krip replied. "They have access to machines which
can give them readings. They may even have a sensitive
among them."

"A sensitive?" Farree broke in.

"One who can release energy in such a way as to spot,
either on a map or on the ground itself, objects which are
foreign to the land—things that have been handled and used
by some intelligent creature."

"Would not such a one have found the box?" Farree
ventured.

"Of a certainty he or she would—had they been searching.
But the ruins were of the plains people, and they depended
only on steel in their own two hands. Thus one of their old
holds would not have been explored. These—to them the
Thassa are a puzzle, a puzzle and a threat because they have
never been able to understand us. Thus they would go nosing
as closely as they could about the edges of our home place,
breaking the peace as they will discover."

The furred one the Lady Maelen had been nursing in her
arms suddenly came to life again, and she sat it down on the
rock where recently the jarn had perched. It leaped once
more into the nearest clump of spike-armed bush and began

working its way back to the ship. Bojor sniffed and moved a fraction from where he had been crouched upon his haunches.

Once more there was a distant dot in the sky, and the far-off troubling of the air. A flitter—was it the same one? —was returning. Farree caught Toggor and stuffed him again inside his shirt so he would not lose track of the smux during any quick move.

That craft made a wide circle about the sky-pointing ship, but this time there came no shouted message from the sky. It circled twice, and Farree could see that it bore no insignia. This flitter must be from the Guild, though the boldness of such an enterprise in the open light of day bothered him. It argued confidence on the part of those inside, and confidence on the part of the Guild meant arms and men ready to withstand any attack.

The third circling was much closer in, and finally the flitter set down at almost the same place that the guard ship had earlier chosen. Three men descended from the cabin. All were armed and moved cautiously, retreating toward the ramp of the ship backwards, facing the cliffs as intently as if they already knew that there were three sentries on duty there. Three? No, more if one counted Yazz, who still crouched in shelter with Lord-One Krip, and Bojor—as well as the furred one in hiding now.

Once reaching the ramp one of the men darted up it, his two fellows keeping guard. Then the second, and finally the third. Were they there to search the ship as the guards had done, or were they ready to raise?

Neither of the Thassa had moved. Farree, feeling more and more like a child or one of the animals who could be roused by command but did not have a voice in any plan, twisted from one side to the other trying to keep those two in sight.

Farree could not tell the time as it passed. He expected every moment to see the ramp rise, the ship take off. Surely that was what had brought this party here. But there was no change. At last movement showed at the side lock and down ran the three men, sprinting for the flitter as if pursued by the bartle or some even more threatening beast.

"They have discovered the persona." Lord-One Krip's message came with a faint suggestion of laughter. "It would require a full production yard to breach that control lock."

"It would seem that they have also seen more than they like," Lady Maelen answered. "Sadi projected well even when there were mind locks against her. She showed them one five times her own size and all teeth and talons at ready! She makes an excellent guard. And if they used those weapons of theirs, it was to no account."

Illusion? Farree wondered and was instantly answered.

"Illusion and not from one of us. Sadi projected what would frighten *her*, and she did it on a mental length which apparently their shields are not set to handle. See!"

The last of the men had barely reached the ground with a flying leap from the ramp when there appeared behind them, filling the full of the hatch door, a beast such as Farree had never seen before. It was larger, leaner in bulk than the bartle. Its head was split halfway along with a mouth which sprouted two rows of fangs, spittle dripping from them as if in anticipation of sinking home in frail flesh. The forefeet which projected now onto the ramp were taloned with great claws that looked as if they might rend apart the very envelope of the ship's hull.

All three of the men were firing lasers, but the shaggy coat of the apparition absorbed the worst of that attack easily and took no hurt from one of the most formidable weapons known to the space ways. One of the men broke and ran faster, quickly followed by he who had stood beside him. Only the third retreated in good order, still firing uselessly as he went.

The huge menacing form at the head of the ramp pulled back so that only the head with that murderous threat of fangs still protruded. There was a wait which Farree ticked off to himself—twenty-five in whispered counting. Then the flitter arose and began circling the pillar of the ship once again as if seeking another way in. Farree almost believed that they might, should there be some opening, drop a man even as he had been hoisted up from the top of the tower in the ruins.

But it would seem that there was no other way of penetrating the ship, and the flitter was not armed with anything other than the weapons that had already been used to no purpose.

Finally it winged away eastward. The massive head winked out of being. Then the small furred creature Maelen had earlier held and caressed came racing down the ramp and across the land toward the Lady's rock.

"Well done!" Lord-One Krip called that aloud as if the small beast could hear and understand. The Lady Maelen stooped and caught the guard up in her arms for a second holding and caressing.

She set the animal down on the rock before her, stroking its upraised head.

"Sadi will watch with Yazz," she said, "and with the old one here." She reached over to scratch behind Bojor's ears. The big animal stretched his neck to the farthest so that she could reach behind his jaw also. "I think that we had better take thought to what lies northward—to that which has drawn the interest of those others so much that they have already made three trips in search of it." Her hand swung to point in the direction where the jarn had first appeared. "Nor do we know what brought the Guild here in the first place. That we ourselves have returned to Yiktor could not have been foreseen when they settled in. For that was done at a much earlier time than our coming. Thassa memory is long—but is it long enough when there was also a will to do away with something that was future danger? The Elders of another day may have even memory-wiped our stock lest some be tempted to return and use something which was not right for us.''

That they considered the animals guard enough for the ship seemed strange to Farree, but nothing or very little which the Thassa did could he compare with the actions of those he knew from the Limits days. He trudged back through the canyon to where the temporary settlement of the rest of these aliens was— Aliens? He was the alien here, even more divided from the rest than he had been from most of the Limits dwellers.

Yet he discovered, though he could not see that he contributed anything to their aid or defense, both the Lord-One Krip and the Lady Maelen took it as a matter of course that he was to be one of the party pointed north. They began the journey at moonrise, with the glow of the third ring making the plain almost day bright.

With them went a third Thassa, one Maskay, who, Farree gathered, had roamed much in that direction and had contact with the wildlife thereabouts. It was difficult to tell age with these people, but Farree thought him perhaps a generation older than his other two companions. And the Lady Maelen appeared to look to him to set the direction and the pace.

They halted before the rings were quite faded by the coming of the grayish predawn light to encamp on the top of a small rise where a trio of wind-twisted trees gave shelter. There was a seep of water at the bottom of that knoll, though it quickly funneled away in this arid land. This seemed to be one of the landmarks Maskay knew well.

He stood under the downswing of one of the wide branches and pointed on northward.

''It is another night's journey if we take to plains pace, and then come the hills. That is a dry land and the spring at Two Prong is of bitter water. Only the jarn can live in those heights.''

"Yet you have been there, Kinsman," the Lady Maelen said.

"When I was young and foolish, I went many places that were strange. And little or nothing did I learn from such wayfaring," he returned with a smile.

"Yet the jarn live there and like all living things they must have food and water—and—"

"Hush! And under cover. Down with you!" Lord-One Krip swung out his arm and caught Maelen's waist, pulling her down, while Maskay jerked back under the tree.

It was very plain to hear now—the thrum of the flitter. Through the last haze of the third ring it bore across the sky. Farree waited for it to hover above them, to sense by some off-worlder equipment that they were here. But it passed overhead well up in the sky and kept on to the north, exactly as if the pilot had a definite goal in view.

"Guild!"

"Are you sure?" demanded Lady Maelen of Lord-One Krip.

"There is a difference in the beat. That craft is not made for short patrols but is a long-range flitter—for exploration."

"It flies"—Maskay put into words Farree's thought—"as if those aboard it know where they would land and also as if they must be there in a hurry."

"True. I wonder if they have found what they seek. If so it is best we make the same discovery and as soon as possible."

Farree tried to stretch his head a little and then stopped, warned by the pain in his back. His whole body ached from the pace they had kept and he was not sure he could go on—not without more rest. Yet he was also sure he was not going to be left behind.

15.

Once more Farree lay in hiding above a machine that was not of Yiktor: a flitter at rest on a ledge thrust forward from a mountainside like a great shelf. He could see the shadow of a head within the bubble of the top cover, but the door was also open, and he knew others had gone forth.

Through the ring-lighted air above dived and soared at least two of the jarn, providing eyes for the Lady Maelen, who lay full length on the lip of a second ledge across the narrow valley. So aptly balanced were those two outcroppings that one could well believe them the work of some intelligence, taming the mountain ways by a bridge that had long since vanished.

There was a noticeable trail upward on the opposite side, beginning not far away from the flitter, angling along the side of the cliff toward its high summit. They had sighted nothing moving up that path, but the jarns had reported that earlier those from the flitter had taken that way.

There was a similar trail on this side of the gulf also, and they had explored it via the jarns—to pace it themselves would have been to offer the flitter a clear sight of them. It did not reach clear to the full heights on this side but ended abruptly in a straight cliff wall that had no sign of any opening. And Maskay had set out a half day ago to hunt farther to the westward, setting the length of a night for his explorations.

Farree found himself drowsing in spite of the need for sentry go. They had hurried after the sky craft when it had been sighted yesterday, but he had found it hard going with his shorter legs and the weight of his hump. Though he would not have voiced any complaint even if they tried to wring it out of him, now his body was one ache, and he felt as if he could not force himself to any further effort at all.

The barren lands which surrounded the heart of the Thassa country had given way to coarse grass and woods scattered here and there. Here in the mountains was growth also, wind-gnarled trees for the most part, growing in pockets. Far above there was the bluish-white shadow of snow early fallen or late thawed—it could be either.

One of the jarns drifted across the gap between them and the flitter to hunker down on the rocks that concealed the Lady Maelen. That the creature was reporting, perhaps from Maskay, Farree was sure, and a moment later the mind touch aroused him.

"There is nothing above save a road which is now encased in ice. It seems that those look in the wrong direction for their treasure. It may well lie on this side." She passed along the report and her own interpretation.

"But the way here leads nowhere—only to barren rock," he dared to protest wearily.

"What seems barren rock," she corrected.

Illusions again? He would not deny that the ancients of her race might have set such to cover their trail. But how to make sure of that?

"I go, before those others and Maskay return." It was Lord-One Krip who answered.

"You could be seen—"

"If I walk, yes. But if I creep . . ."

Farree had hunched around to face that trail. Perhaps it had originally been cut into the stone on purpose to give fair footing, perhaps it had been so worn below the surface about it by countless feet over a period of uncountable years, but it was plain that it was now a trough. The hunchback looked to Lord-One Krip. His body was slender, but even if he moved on hands and knees he certainly would show up to any watching this side of the cliff. Though he shrank from what he was impulsively agreeing to do, Farree cut in: "To creep is what I have done most of my life. Dust me well with the soil." He was already scraping up his own handfuls and smearing it across the backs of his legs and across his hips, leaving the tenderness of his hump to the last. "I can make it best."

The Lady Maelen turned her head and looked at him as one who is weighing one thought against the other. Then slowly she nodded.

"There is something in what you say, Farree."

He had so wanted her to refuse instead of accept that once more that old cord of bitterness awoke in him. They were willing to use him even as they used the jarn, the bartle, any and all of the life on this world. The rainbow of the rising third ring swept over him and it seemed to bring with it a soothing. Even his painful hump felt a touch of coolness— which could not be the truth, as since when had a radiance of light had substance?

Farree shucked off his belt bag and tossed some more of the gravelly soil on his back, biting his lip against the tenderness of the hump, the small flashes of pain he felt when anything touched it now.

He crawled on his belly until the upward slope of that path faced him. Then he asked the question that he should have voiced earlier.

"If there is illusion, how may it be broken?"

"Try to pierce it," she answered him. "Illusion can distort sight but not touch—unless the one who tries to break it is totally under control."

Fair enough, he thought. His deluded eyes would at least serve him until he reached the solid wall at the top—or the wall that only appeared solid. He began to crawl, the rock harsh against his hands, panting a little with the effort of keeping as flat as he could in the depression of the way.

He went slowly, with many pauses, hoping that if the one with the flitter had any long-seeing glass trained on this side it would show only a portion of his hump—a rock bedded against rocks.

Sotrath climbed above the horizon and the three rings were clearly defined, the elusive third spreading glory over all the land. Flecks of glitter answered from the stone under him, the wall ahead.

On and on he went and then froze and flattened himself to the stone as a warning reached him from below.

"The others are returning."

He was tempted to look for himself, but there remained the matter of time. The Guild men could well try this side of the cliff now, having been baffled on the other. So he strove to speed up his crawl and yet not reveal that anything moved there. He lay during one of his periods of stillness, his pointed chin resting on his crooked arm as he looked ahead. To his relief it seemed that the wall was not too far above. Now he felt the pinch of claw on his shoulder and remembered that Toggor had not been left behind. Could the smux be sent ahead to prospect for an opening? Did an illusion fashioned to deceive the eyes of his species also confuse animals? He did not know, but the knowledge that the smux was still with him was a warming one.

The path up which he hunched his way was leveling out. Yes, he could see the wall before him. The path, if path it really was, ended abruptly at its foot. He was out on a level space. Putting up a hand he chirped to Toggor, and the smux obediently climbed into his palm and turned toward the stone. He lowered it.

On Farree inched until he was within touching distance of the wall. For a moment he hesitated. To his eyes it was so firm a barrier that he could not believe it was illusion only.

He put out his hand and his palm met solid substance. But it would be necessary for him to test it fully from one border of the sunken roadway to the other.

Edging along, he began at the outer side, Toggor clawing along beside his hand. Not here—nor here—nor— He stopped with a gasp of astonishment and fear. Before he touched the fourth time, Toggor was gone. One moment he had been there brushing the side of Farree's hand and the next he had disappeared!

Frantically the hunchback struck the wall at the same point where he was sure the smux had vanished. There was a solid surface right enough, but there was also a crack through which he could feel a slight stir of cold air. Quickly he traced that crack. It ran only for a short distance, but where it ended there was a second crack, this ascending vertically. He returned and felt his way back, found another vertical crack. There was certainly a sealed opening, perhaps a door. He thumped it, hoping for some give in it. There was none. Perhaps he was too near the ground to move it, or perhaps it *was* sealed past any of their forcing!

He lay with his head close to the crack and tried to search out Toggor with the mind touch. The return was very faint, as if the smux answered from some great distance, but at least he was alive and within, though Farree would not have believed that crack wide enough to admit him.

Still lying with his head against the wall, he mind sent his discovery to the Lady Maelen. The rainbow of the third ring washed over him, brightening those flecks of glitter in the rock. In fact, as he glanced up the wall against which he now lay, he could see that the speckles were drawing together to form a dim pattern, or perhaps awaking one which had been deliberately set there generations ago.

"I come." That was the Lady Maelen.

Farree turned his head a little and saw her, lying belly fast to the stone, as he had, and pulling herself forward a few inches at a time. Even so, it was not long until she took his place by the unseen door as he edged back to give her room.

Her hands went out in a wider sweep than his could equal and then she nodded.

"It is true. There is a door here and—" She lay now on her back and looked up at the surface of the wall where those particles appeared to move together and outline to form shapes of their own. "There is here an illusion set. But, by the Third Ring, O Sotrath, to Thee thanks of heart and mind! By this Third Ring of Thine we can see!"

She began to hum, so faint a sound that it was hardly as loud as the clatter of Toggor's claws on the rock. Farree once more felt the power of that singing.

The glittering bits waxed brighter—taking on the rainbow hues of the ring itself, now red, now blue, now green, now yellow—or a swirling mixture of them all together. But as they gathered to make lines and curves on the surface of the wall, Lord-One Krip sent a thrusting thought.

"They are aboard the flitter—and it is rising in this direction!"

That warning from below was as sharply clear as if it had been shouted aloud. Yet the Lady Maelen did not move, nor was there a falter in the low sound which issued from her lips. More and more did the pattern clear on the door in the rainbow sparks of light. And that light now outlined the portal itself. It promised an opening of a size to let the three of them enter abreast.

Now the noise of the flitter was loud enough to drown out

the sound of her song even though he lay beside her as flat as he could push his body. He did not turn his head to watch the enemy—not yet—for the wonder of that design of lights held him entranced.

"They come."

The second quick warning was not needed, for the drone of the flitter rolled above the cliff and echoed and reechoed from the rocks thereabout. Now Farree did lever himself up and face about in time to see the forward, upward sweep of the craft. It might well be that the two of them had already been sighted and were easy game for those on board. He waited, shrinking inside, for the flash of a laser beam to cut out at them.

The light of the third ring was a mist growing ever stronger. Perhaps in that they were not as good targets as Farree feared. He was aware of movement beside him, of the Lady Maelen getting to her knees and then her feet, still facing the closed door in the cliff as if she had all the time in the world to deduce its secret and need fear no interruption in that task.

He scrambled up in turn, his back now to her and the door, facing outward. Small as he was, he could not protect her whole body with his, but he would do the best he could.

The flitter was heading straight for them, as if it meant to crash against the cliff and crush the both of them. But at the last possible moment it swerved in an almost perpendicular climb that carried it up to the mountaintop beyond.

Surely they had been sighted! Farree could not understand why they had not been cut down, at least with a stunner. Perhaps those thought to let Maelen open the way for them and then take them.

He glanced back at the woman. Her arms spread wide, she was touching with the tips of her fingers this and then that of the circling patterns of color her singing had brought forth. But there was no answer. At last her mind send, as strong as Lord-One Krip's warning, rang out.

"Come! This is Thassa sealed and in this body it will not answer to me. Come!"

He sprinted up the road which had been such a laborious climb for the other two and faced the doorway between Maelen and the stones. She set her own hands upon the backs of his and moved them from place to place in a swinging pattern. At that moment Farree had little hope that Maelen's suggestion would bring any success. He turned his head upward as far as he might to see where the flitter had vanished in that last upward swoop.

The sound of the craft still echoed loudly in his ears, and he could only hear at intervals the hum of song that Maelen still wrought to open the door.

Back and forth Lord-One Krip's hands moved under her control. Then—at last—there was a grating. The sound of stone scraping stone—of something long held moving again. A crack appeared, not as the thin line the ring outlined but as a darker space. Forward moved that layer of wall and Maelen pulled Lord-One Krip to the right side, Farree taking three steps to their one to join them. Outward it moved but not far, as if the disuse of centuries had so frozen it that there could be no real release. But there was an area of dark. The Lady Maelen, dropping her hold on her companion, squeezed through it, Krip following closely on her heels, and after them Farree.

His hump scraped the stone in spite of his turning sidewise and the pain of it made him gasp and stumble. Then he was in the dark where only a pale radiance of the ring reached in from the outer world.

Maelen had swung about, and Lord-One Krip reached out a long arm and jerked Farree to stand beside him as the hum broke into words—a chant which sealed the entrance to this place of darkness, leaving them in a lightless place of age-old stone.

Then there was the gleam of light again. Far softer, and more limited as to reach, then the radiance without. However, they could soon see after a fashion by the small globe balanced on the Lady Maelen's palm. Farree felt a clutch on his breeches and reached down to scoop up Toggor.

The Lady Maelen tossed the globe of light and Lord-One Krip caught it deftly. She was breathing in small, fast gasps as if she had been running, and there were beads of sweat trickling down her face like tears.

Lord-One Krip held out the globe and swept it from side to side, but all they could see were rock walls shading off into clouding shadow and a dark opening before them where perhaps the road they followed continued on into the heart of the mountain.

"They may have a distort with them," Lord-One Krip said. "If so, it will not take them long to—"

"Ah, but we shall not wait!" There was purpose and power in her answer, even though she stumbled when she took a step forward. Farree caught one of her dangling hands, set it upon his shoulder in spite of the ache of his hump, and stood ready to be her support. To his satisfaction she accepted his aid, and he felt her lean against him as they moved on, Lord-One Krip with the globe of light going ahead.

Perhaps it was because the third ring's beam did not reach here, or because that which had been awakened by its gleam had been only on the outer door, but here there were no glittering bits on the walls to add to that limited light. The stone, though it showed the marks of tools here and there, was otherwise bare.

Their road ran straight for a space and then began an upward slope. At first the incline was not enough to cause them any difficulty as to footing. Even as he climbed, taking what he could of Maelen's weight, Farree was listening.

If those hunting them did have a distort, they could open this way as easily as an innkeeper could slash open a melon.

Then a sweep ahead with stunner or laser would bring the three all into Guild hands. He was glad of that upward slope for that very reason.

As they went that became more pronounced. Until Lord-One Krip, crowding against the right-hand wall, lit pockets chiseled there, meant surely for fingergrips. Farree steered the Lady Maelen until she laced fingers in the nearest. He could no longer support her and climb, as he had to stretch nearly tiptoe to set his hand in any of the holds, for these were hacked nearly shoulder-height for Thassa.

Their retreat slowed nearly to the same crawl which had sent him up the outer road. The Lady Maelen, nearly drained of strength by her singing, shifted from one hold to the next with obvious difficulty, though she made no complaint. Finally Lord-One Krip stopped short and said: "Take this and the lead, Farree. I will see to Maelen."

He obediently crowded past the other two, obliged to hold to them before he could accept the globe and use his other hand for the wall. Steeper still grew the road. So far they moved in a silence broken only by the sound of heavy breathing or the faint swish of some article of clothing against the wall.

Toggor climbed to Farree's shoulder and extended all eye-stalks, staring ahead as if he could either pierce the dark so or was trying to. It was a chitter from him that brought Farree to a stop. The smux saw or scented something ahead.

"Stay!" For the first time he took it upon himself to order those two who had commanded his life since they had met in the Limits. "There is something ahead." It was Lord-One Krip's strength the Lady Maelen needed now, and not his lesser aid.

Farree pulled himself forward at the same slow speed with which he had climbed the road without, expecting any moment to see the way before him once more walled, and he wondered if the Lady Maelen could sing again an open door.

What the limited light of the globe showed him moments later was a stair leading up. Only down the side of this trickled moisture which had stained the stone with encrustations and given life to some strange and ominous-looking growths pallidly yellow and dankly gray in the globe light. There was movement in one such growth as the light fell across it. A thing of thin spotted wings flew up nearly in Farree's face.

"There is a stair," he called behind. "But it is wet here, and the footing may be even worse—there is water. . . ."

"We come," was the only answer Lord-One Krip made. Farree realized that, in truth, they had no choice but to go forward.

He waited by the foot of that stair and only when the other two reached him did he take the first step, grimacing with disgust as his fingers found the next handgrip half full of a growth which gave forth a putrid smell as he could not help but crush it.

So they went, slow step by step. Luckily the treads were wide and gave them room to stop now and again for a breather. There seemed to be no end to that upward climb. However, after a space the seepage ceased and they were free of the fetid growths and those slimy things which lived among them, eyeless hunters of the dark.

Again it was Toggor who gave warning of a change in their road, chittering in Farree's ear. He passed a warning to the other two. It had seemed to him that the Lady Maelen, instead of gaining strength as she was aided along, was slowly failing even more. Now here was a major test for them all.

A crevice rent the road before them, leaving only a small space where the three huddled together as they looked ahead. There provision had been made for travelers but it was not one which Farree wanted to try.

Reaching out into the dark, in the center of the way, was a

span just wide enough for one person at a time to walk. That stretched into a dark where the globe, no matter how far Farree tried to reach with it, did not show them a far side.

He had taken command of their going since the climb began, but dare he lead them over that narrow strip of rock above a chasm? He was not sure. Yet neither could he give the Lady Maelen any help—it must be he to go first.

Already he felt top-heavy and weak of leg. Could he better crawl than try to shamble at his usual pace across? He fumbled with the globe and then plucked Toggor from his position on the hunched shoulder. Tucking the globe into the front of his shirt, Farree placed the smux beside it, giving one clear order. He felt the movement of the foreclaws against his skin and knew that the smux had grasped the ball of light, would hold it with all the safety Farree was able to devise.

Dropping to all fours, the hunchback ventured out on that bridge. He arose again to a sitting position, his feet stuck far out on either side, his fingers gripping the stone with a grasp which scraped his skin painfully. So he pulled himself along with nothing but the very muffled light to show mere inches before him.

As it had in his trip up the sunken road, time seemed to reach forever. There was no end to his scraping advance. His hands were cut and sore, his body ached from the stretching he must do. Yet there was something stirring far back in his mind. Not a feeling that he had done such a journey before— not a distinct memory—but rather that there was a far better way of accomplishing such a journey if he could only remember how. That blocked recall was something which weighed him down now when it was most necessary that he keep a clear mind.

There was an end to the bridge at last. He edged forward, wiping his bleeding hands against his shirt, to make a scrambling half-fall onto a wide space which was indeed the lip of the rift and seemed solid before him.

He ripped the globe out of his shirt with a speed that brought Toggor with it. The smux dropped to the stone while Farree used the globe, getting to his feet and walking a bit forward, hardly daring to believe there was this solid flooring beneath his feet.

He did not go far, but swung around and did which it took all his strength of will to accomplish, squatted once more to make a return journey, with the light again at the fore of his shirt—Toggor ordered to keep it so as he himself lurched, handhold by handhold, out into the open on the narrow span.

He met them near halfway across, Lady Maelen seated and hitching herself along in the same position he had chosen, Lord-One Krip behind to steady her. Now Farree was forced to go backwards, so offering them what light he could and holding fast only to his contact with Toggor, urging the smux to give all possible assistance with the light.

16.

Even the third ring's spectacular radiance did not reach this far down into the gloom. They had gone through the mountain upward, across that dangerous open of bridge, to come out upon another ledge perch. The bulk of a second peak overtopped them so they were deep in the shadows here. They made the full round of the ledge and found only one place where there seemed to be a promise for descent, though that way was by a narrowed thread of footpath nearly as daunting as the bridge they had mastered in the caverns behind.

What lay in the dark depths of the rift into which they might descend they had no idea. Had they indeed come to the end of any road of escape? Lord-One Krip took up the fading globe of light and made for that dubious path to explore the possibility of their getting into the depths.

Lady Maelen sat with her back against the wall, her eyes closed as if she had not yet recovered the strength she had expended in the opening of the door. Farree prowled up and down the perch they shared in a vain attempt to forget his back. Something, perhaps it was his journey across the bridge,

had started in his hump, not only the fierce ache which he
felt all through his body, but also an intolerable itching, so
that he wished to shuck off his shirt and score his own flesh
with his broken nails. He could not sit still and endure this.

Toggor clacked claws across the stone and bent all eyestalks to survey the path ahead. When Farree passed near him
he gave one of his flying leaps and caught hold of the
hunchback's arm, climbing quickly to his shoulder.

Farree could no longer see even the faint gleam of the
globe on the path. Either that roadway had taken a turn—or
perhaps the light had at last failed and Lord-One Krip was
feeling his way step by step down the slope. To remain
where they were if the pursuit was up behind them was
folly. To be caught on that perilous way was perhaps even
more, yet the uneasiness which filled Farree made him consider that the less of dangers.

"Lady"—he approached Maelen—"can you walk or
descend?"

She turned her head slowly and eyed him as if he had
recalled her from some long journey.

"They come?"

He attempted to send a probe back through the roadway of
the mountain but picked up nothing—not even the deadening
defense which marked those wearing their protection against
mind send.

"I read nothing. But the longer we stay here—"

"Yes." Even her voice sounded as if it came out of the
dregs of fatigue. "I will try."

He lingered beside her as she crept to the head of that
narrow downward path. She did not attempt to get to her
feet. Farree leaned forward to catch, as tightly as he could, a
hold upon her belt.

So linked, they made their way after the vanished Krip at a
slow pace, with frequent halts. Farree kept one hand locked
upon her belt and the other feeling for handholds along the

walls. To his great thankfulness he discovered that there were such, perhaps chiseled by the same makers who had left the similar aids within the inner passages.

The strain on his shoulders brought the fiery pain back again but it was better than just to sit or stand waiting—for what he had no idea.

They came to a place where the trail they crept along doubled back upon itself in a risky curve around which they crept or scraped a painful way. It was there that disaster struck.

The Lady Maelen must have trusted a loose stone for anchorage. She cried out and slid toward the edge. Farree braced himself, not knowing whether he could hold or not. She was kicking her legs, striving to find some purchase as he anchored himself desperately. His left fingers were deep in one of the handholds—those of his right hand laced to her belt. However, he had to stand and take the strain of the increasing weight of her body, made worse by her frenzied attempts to find a hold for herself.

The pain across his twisted shoulders was so intense he might have been caught in the full beam of a flamer, unable to help himself, unable to hold her long.

There was a sensation of being torn in two—of agony. He felt as if the skin over his hump had parted. Still he held. And, through what seemed to be his blood drumming in his ears, he heard a cry.

"All right—I have her."

He was clamped into the linkage he had set himself. To free his fingers from the hold on her belt was more than he could do at that moment. There was liquid running down his back, spattering into a pool between his legs. He could not let go even if he would.

Then the weight which was the Lady Maelen no longer pulled him sidewise. Other fingers plucked at his fingers on her belt, prying them loose one by one. He had fallen to all fours when that strain had gone. Now he toppled forward, to lie face down, his shirt wet through, though there was no longer pain in his back.

He was hardly aware when there was a grip on his hand which now dangled over the edge of the path. The night air bit with a chill tooth at his back through what seemed to be rents in his shirt. But before he lapsed into semiconsciousness he felt a hold on first his wrist and then the upper part of his arm, drawing him away from the rim of the depths. For a moment he fought that, but the strength had gone out of him and he had to loose his hold to that grip and the sideward pull.

Then he was down from the path, on a surface which might be another ledge or at least was much wider than the way he had taken with the Lady Maelen. That pain which had centered so in his hump was gone—instead there was a furious itching. He twisted out of the hold upon him and got to his knees, stretching backward with both arms to claw at the burden on his shoulder. At first he thought it was the shirt which tore beneath his raking nails and then he knew it was skin, thin tatters of skin!

There was pain, but it was nothing compared to what he had felt earlier. More and more he raked at that loosened skin, felt it rip and fall away from his body. There was under it something which moved, arose—as if for all these years he had carried some other living entity on his back.

The thin light of the globe was before him. He did not look up, only pulled and tore until that which he had carried for so long was released. It moved seemingly of its own accord. He raised his head now, could raise it higher than he ever remembered doing. Muscles he had no knowledge of moved, seemingly by instinct. That on his back was unfolding—stretching—no longer in more than a few quirks of cramped pain—reaching outward.

"Winged!" He heard Lord-One Krip's voice with a strong note of awe in it. "He is winged!"

Muscles moved again, stretching in a new way. He felt a sweep of air about his small body and he dared to reach back again with one hand. What he touched was like the softest of down laid over taut skin.

Winged? Was he? How could such a thing be? Somehow he stumbled up to his feet. That which had weighed upon him all his remembered life was gone. He cautiously thought of wings and tried to move such if it were true that he had them.

There was a wide sweep through the air behind him. A small smart of pain as if something had scraped on an edge of rock. Now he longed to see!

Before him lay the globe of light. Across it he could see the faces of those he had followed—and there was awe on both. Again he raised one hand—then the other—and explored by touch. There were extensions from his body right enough. They felt slightly damp, and he had the sensation that they must be fanned in the air to take moisture from them. How did wings feel—if they sprouted from one's own body?

Who—WHAT was he now? Oh, what was he?

He edged halfway around so that those others might see the better.

"Is it true?" he demanded, wondering rather if he were unconscious from some fall back on the trail and this was all the result of feverish imagination.

"It is true!" the Lady Maelen assured him. "Your hump held wings—they are growing larger—"

"But—I am not a bird!" There were also flying reptiles and perhaps even weirder things on the many worlds from star to star. But his was a man's body—or at least humanoid. And in all his years of listening to travelers' tales in the Limits (and very strange some of those had been) he had never heard of a winged man.

Once more he fanned those straightening wings (they must, he decided, have been closely cramped within that hump) and felt his whole body lift a little. Frightened, he clapped them together. He had no idea of flight, and he thought that that must be learned. Yet in him now moved the wish to take to the air—to spiral out into the dusk, up into the circle of the third ring which was a glory now far overhead.

Even his neck felt odd, and he had to rub at it. He was able to lift it high, to hold it straight as he never had before. No more peering out on the world from a painful angle.

Then, as if a hand had reached forth and touched him on the shoulder in warning, he remembered what they fled and where they were.

"Down"—he looked to Lord-One Krip—"we must get down."

"We are down," the other answered. "This is the bottom of the gulf. And—but come and see for yourself."

A few steps on and Farree discovered he must keep the wings furled if he would walk, and he dared not try to fly, not yet. They were once more on a road or else a smooth stretch which was flanked here and there by stones fallen from the heights around. There were in walls about them the same kind of doorways chiseled into the stuff of the cliffs on either side as he had seen in the Valley of the Thassa, though this did not widen but was a narrow way between two chiseled walls.

Their small light could show them no more than those openings were too regular to be natural and they seemed to go on and on. In the darkness ahead, where the light from the globe could not penetrate, anything might be waiting, and Farree forced his mind to turn from what now was on his shoulders to search out any hint of a living thing before them.

He picked up small anonymous stirrings that were certainly animal or bird and were too far from the general thought pattern for him to follow. But of anything stronger, more threatening, there was not a hint now. Lord-One Krip, the globe half-muffled in his hand, led again, but Lady Maelen clung to his belt rather than accept Farree's assistance and the winged man was alone. Cautiously as he went he fanned the wings slightly, not daring to trust to them but sure that they needed that stretching and drying. He had peeled the rest of the rags of the shirt from his body and used those to sop up the runnels of moisture which dripped down his shoulders across his chest, which was no longer squeezed forward but was slowly coming into line with his shoulder points.

Winged! What was he then: some species so far removed from those with whom he now traveled that they would find him utterly unnatural? He watched the two moving through the dark, outlined only by the feeble glow of the light, and wondered what would happen to him now. In some ways he longed once more for the familiar weight on his back, the old knowledge that he was handicapped by something that could be understood.

Now he needs must keep those new appendages clipped close lest they scrape against the stones between which many times they had to squeeze a narrow passage. Yet they went so slowly, perhaps because of the Lady Maelen's deep fatigue, that his awkwardness had time to disappear. With each step he took there was a new confidence rising in him.

The fact that this rift among the heights must once have had meaning grew more and more evident the farther they went. The dark openings on either side were so cleanly cut that he knew them to be of the same fashioning as those in the valley where the Thassa had their meeting place. What lay within those portals the two he followed apparently had no desire to see, for their path was ever on.

They came at last to a place where the narrow slit widened out into something which was a sky-roofed valley. Yet not one like unto that of the Thassa meeting ground, for here the desert aridity was lacking.

Above the radiance of Sotrath and the third ring was once more open, and the land before them was brightly illuminated. There was the glisten of moon rings on water, for the whole center of this basin appeared to be a lake. That body of liquid was buttressed about by a thick cloak of vegetation such as Farree had seen nowhere else on this world.

Large growths of trees which supported looping and tight vines made a wall about the lake. Farree, without ever thinking of what he did, eager only to see ahead, used his wings for the first time—fanning the air and leaving the ground.

He immediately discovered that flying was an art that must be practiced, as any other exercise. His initial soaring was too abrupt and carried him up too far, the rhythmic beat of his newborn wings was something he had not mastered, and he made leaps in the air rather than sustained flight.

Still, those leaps had been enough to show him that the lake encircled an island that was so centrally placed that it might have been the pupil in a great unblinking eye. On that island there were walls and a tower not too unlike that from which the flitter had lifted him days earlier.

His two companions made no attempt to force a path into the thickly cloaking growth but had collapsed rather than seated themselves on the last space of open ground before that dense stem and branch began. The Lady Maelen sat with her head turned up to the sky, her eyes fixed upon the glory of the third ring, her mouth a little open as if she now drank sip by sip from the brilliance. As Farree watched, perching a little above the two on a last outcropping of fallen rock, she stretched wide her arms as one waiting to embrace something or someone before her.

Lord-One Krip sat with upturned face also, but his eyes were not on the glory in the sky but on Farree, as the winged one realized. And there was wonder in his face which was slowly overcome by an expression of purpose.

"What lies beyond?" he spoke rather than thought. Per-

haps he feared that thought send might interrupt what the
Lady Maelen was doing.

"A lake and on an isle, in a ruin, a tower." Farree
answered promptly.

"Can you reach it over that?" Lord-One Krip motioned
toward the thick intertwining of the growth. It was only too
plain that without some form of cutting tool they could not
hope to blast a path farther on.

"I can try." But still Farree was distrustful of those wings.
They were too new, too far removed from all he had ever
knowledge of, for him to truly believe that they could be
successfully used to climb into the sky more than on the short
soarings he had already attempted with more than a little
bemusement and uneasiness.

Purposefully now he fanned them slowly, turned his head
as far as he could to sight their sweep. They were not
feathered—he had already determined that with his hands
reaching behind him—rather they seemed to be covered with
a skin which had a soft, velvety texture almost like close-
shorn fine hair. Now he stood and dared to take a small leap
into the sky using the wings to support and sustain him. He
had discovered a bit of the beat which would lift him and
applied that rhythm.

Up he went into the splendor of the ring-bright night.
When he was sure, having rounded in a circle over the other
two, he ventured out above the growth, fearing to have his
wings fail and let him fall down into the matted vegetation.
But awkward as he was, he was learning with every movement he tried, more and more of what it took to steady
himself in the air, to do what humanoids had always wanted:
reach the clouds.

Only there were no clouds here—just the darkness of that
tangled wood which ringed the lake, the sparkle of the water
which reflected the third ring, and the island beyond.

Out over the lake he beat his way, not trying any high

soaring as yet. Then he was above the island. There was growth here, too, but not a matted wall of it such as grew on the shore. Here were tall plants scattered in clumps, heavy with flowers wide open as if the moon instead of the sun brought them their nourishment. From them came a heavy perfume so that Farree, as he flew over them, felt as though he bathed in the scent. And his mental search brought no hint of life here.

He came in, to settle on the wall which ringed the tower. Now that he was close he could see that time had not struck so heavily here as it had on that castle where the Guild had taken up their den. Rather this surface was smoother than any stone he knew of and it was near white in color, veined darkly with straggling rivers of lines and splotches. There was glitter, too, from points along those paths of darker shades, and when he touched a near one he felt a roughness as if there were some other thing, perhaps a gem, inset in the veining.

Along that wall he walked, using the wings to steady and balance himself, looking down into the interior of the place which was wide open to the glory of Sotrath. There were no other buildings within. Only that tower, and it was thickly agleam with the sparks of fire such as passed beneath his feet.

He had kicked off his boots before he had taken off, and under the long-hardened soles of his feet he felt small sparks of heat, as if every one of those small stones was a flare of a tiny fire. Having made a complete round of the outer wall, he dared to glide down to the pavement below. As he had noted from aloft, here the small bright stones were set in patterns, not following any twist of veining. And each was different. As he landed in one such design, which was a concentric series of circles, there came that which almost sent him soaring again. A flap of wings did carry him upward so that his feet no longer touched the stone, for out of somewhere—

the tower, the very sky above him—there had sounded a
sharp note of sound as if he had struck two knife blades
together.

He waited, his head turned from side to side, watching,
mind seeking. The sound echoed and died. There was no
answer that he could detect. But he was suspicious of those
patterns now—some kind of alarm? Or was it a greeting
meant to assure some people long dead? There had been
Thassa-like caves along the road to the valley, but the tower
seemed unlike their form of building.

The side of the tower which faced him had the dark
opening of a door, though there was no sign of any windows
on any level. To enter so might mean that he was an unwary
smux venturing into a trap.

Smux! He had all but forgotten Toggor during the wonder
of his transformation. But the smux was still with him now,
claws tightly clipping his belt. Having received no intima-
tions of life from the tower he applied touch to Toggor to see
if the smux could pick up something too subtle, too far from
his own species's mental processes to record. But the result
was that Toggor knew nothing.

A wing-assisted leap took Farree from the circle which had
brought forth that answer to the very edge about the foot of
the tower where he noted the patterns did not reach. There he
settled once again. There was a faint reflection of the moon
and ring light. Enough to show him that there was no door
here to bar passage. But the dusk which lay within was
daunting. He had been foolish not to bring with him the
globe. Even if he could see only a few steps ahead, he would
not shrink so from investigating it.

Smux—send Toggor in again? But the creature's night
sight was little better than his own. When he hunted within
the walls for prey he used scent organs. And here the constant small breezes brought the overpowering odor of the
flowers to kill any such clue.

There was no use lingering here—Farree would either
completely explore this structure or he would have to return
with the admission that he had been routed by fear. But he
did not even have the slight advantage his wings gave him in
the open!

Clapping those together and furling them as far as he
could, Farree took a deep breath and started into the tower.
He half expected a second warning of sound, perhaps even
the snap of a trap. But what he did meet was a firm barrier
of—nothingness.

He could not see—he could only feel as he passed his
hands up and down that barrier as stout as any double-locked
door. Yet he saw through and beyond it as far as the light
penetrated and there was nothing—though his hands told him
there was. At last he loosed Toggor but the smux was also
baffled by a barrier he could not penetrate. So—the builders
here had their guards after all. Perhaps this one had been
alerted by his own touching of the pattern in the pavement
without.

However, as he had learned in the Guild fort, there was
always the roof. Urging Toggor to fasten himself once more
to his belt, Farree stepped back far enough to get wingspread
and then leaped upwards, with the beat of the wings indeed
carrying him to where he could grasp the parapet of the
tower.

Here, too, there were patterns on the surface. Farree could
see no hint among them of any trapdoor such as had been his
salvation before. He did not propose to get down and go
exploring, not without knowing more of what he faced. Thus
he set himself to studying the patterns, setting them firmly in
mind.

That done, he sought out with mind reach, and the Lady
Maelen, strong and clear as she had ever been, caught his
cast and answered. He told her of the courtyard below, of the
invisible door bar, and now of these patterns aloft.

"Show me," came her calm answer.

Trying to picture each in turn, he began with the one immediately below his perch on the parapet. It went so and so and so. While the one beyond that was thus, and this, and that. Thus he strove to set up the clearest mental pictures he could.

He felt her growing astonishment, her excitement. "Thus and thus?" came her demand with a newly mentalized design.

Farree looked, but that design was lacking. He returned that message and could sense her disappointment.

"Then this or this?"

Part of that surely—yes! But not as entire as she pictured it for him.

"Below. Look to the court below!" came her order then.

As he had crouched on the wall and surveyed the patterns from a lower point, now did he again, moving with care along the parapet so that he might view all below for her. Some were so intricate in their convolutions that it was difficult for him to sort out their beginnings and endings.

"It is a maze," she returned. "But I must see for myself. I have to see."

"I cannot carry you," Farree pointed out. That his strength had not been great enough to hold her from slipping on the trail was a fact. Also, he did not believe that she and Lord-One Krip could fight their way through that wood and across the water.

"You can carry that which I may use." Back came her answer in a rush. "Come for it, Farree, come for that!"

17.

Farree winged back across the band of tangled vegetation and set foot on the ground not far from the two who waited. Lord-One Krip was busy with that bag which had been clipped to his belt through all their journeying. What he brought out now was not food as Farree had expected but rather a shining square of what seemed to be bright metal, well polished and no bigger than Farree's own hand.

He rubbed his fingers across the upper surface as if to remove some unseen covering and passed it to the Lady Maelen, who held it firmly and looked to Farree.

"Those patterns," she said, "are protective devices of a sort, yet they do not follow those which I have learned. I must see them."

Farree shifted on his perch. The more he looked at the entangled maze of dark greenery before them, the less he could conceive of cutting any path through that without any tools. Perhaps a laser might clear the way but otherwise—

"Look." She was holding up that square of metal. "Have you seen one of these before? The tourists use them for recording sights they wish to remember clearly. It works thus—or better have Krip show you, since this is not a thing of Thassa world.''

He had taken the square back from her and now flipped it over to show two impressions on the back into which a man's forefingers might fit. ''Let the reflection of what you would preserve so show in the mirror and then press here. Wait for the count of five and press again at this other spot and then it will clear and you can move to the next. It is simple and there is room for twenty shots before the power is exhausted and it must be recharged.''

Lord-One Krip held it out and Farree accepted it gingerly. Yes, it sounded simple enough but he was unused to such off-world wonders and he only hoped that he could follow those directions without failure. Also there was something else to mind. He stood up, the picture square in his hands. He did not look to the tower in the lake, the very top of which was visible from where he stood, but rather back along the way they had come. Those who followed—surely they must be nearing now the end of that road through the mountain and might arrive at any moment. What then? Did they have time for such a task as they had set him now? What if those others could crouch in the rubble of the way and take both of the Thassa with their long-range weapons?

''Not so,'' Lord-One Krip answered his unasked question. ''We keep guard and they, as always, will betray themselves by the nothingness their mind shields project.''

''Still they will come—'' Farree was as certain of that as he was now aware that he wore wings. Nor did he believe that even those could carry their prey away from those who followed.

''And we shall go,'' Lord-One Krip returned, ''into that—'' he gestured to the thick growth ahead.

''There is no way!''

The Lady Maelen smiled. ''As long as the third ring holds, I have power, though my people would not have it so.

However, since I have returned I have discovered it is not only the wand which controls, but rather the will and energy of the one who uses such. Yes, we can go but not from here. We shall move on to the north so that we give them no hint of what we have done. But you, winged brother, have that which will serve us best.'' She nodded toward the thing he now held.

Since he had no argument which would stand against her determination and self-confidence, Farree took off once more, rising above the screen of the thick brush and trees, heading for the island in the lake.

Only, as he winged so he felt naked and open to attack by the Guild hounds sniffing on their trail who could easily pluck him down with one laser blast. And he was glad when he settled again on the tower, a point from which he was sure he could record the best.

Slowly and with all the care he could summon he held the square of metal out over the first selection of the patterns below and pressed the depressions, counting aloud. He moved around the parapet of the tower, making sure that his record—if he was truly recording something—took in all those whirls, spirals, triangles, and arcs below. Having made the full circuit which would set those in order, he turned to the ones on the roofs and added them to his store.

They did not have much longer before Sotrath was gone and the third ring with it. Already that was fading into the grayish murk which preceded the sunrise. Clutching the picture taker to him, he arose aloft far enough above the lake as to hope to catch sight of the other two. But there was nothing in the place where he had left them nor anything to be seen along the northern edge of the forest ring. He dropped, to skim just a little above the tallest of the trees in that jungle, looking and then daring to send a mind call.

"The lake," came his answer. "Wait by the lake."

There was a ring of light gravel or sand between the edge

of that jungle and the water. To that he dropped, folding his wings, still being surprised at how completely those crimped into place. There was yet some aching through his shoulders, but he judged that was from the use of muscles which had not been called into duty before and that it would vanish the longer he made use of his new appendages. The silent, undisturbed surface of the lake drew him now and he looked down into its surface as he might into a mirror.

He was— Farree could hardly believe what he saw there. For all his days he had gone misshapen and maimed among other life. Now he was complete. The tips of the wings arose a good five hands above that head which he was able to hold completely aloft. And the wings themselves were not dull but were covered with a satin-shining surface on which were dots and designs of a light green, the color of his skin. They were more magnificent, he thought, with the first swelling pride in himself that he had ever known, than any Lord's cloak of war or office.

He swung out farther over the water to see the better, and knew with every minute, every movement he was more and more what nature had always intended him to be. But what *was* he? Surely he had never been born on Grant's World, or someone in the Limits would have recognized him for what he was. Lanti—had he taken him there? For what reasons? Unless he had been meant to be sold to such as Russtif as a curiosity for showing after brutal training. There was something about his wings which brought a flash of memory. That brilliant scrap which the other Limits rogue had brought to Lanti too late to get an explanation. A piece of—wing! Surely that had been a piece of wing!

He felt cold. Perhaps it was from the predawn wind which had come to ruffle the mirror surface of the lake. But it might have been inside his small, spare body. Winged people hunted for their wings! It would not be the first time according to the legends often repeated in the Limits that a sentient race—and plenty of animals, too—had been wiped out for some special gain on the part of an off-worlder band. Maybe even Lanti had taken him to raise his own pair of wings so when the time came they could be harvested. Perhaps the spacer had wished to impress the Guild with treasure which was a part of Farree. Now that cold filled him, and he dropped back upon the apron of gravel between water and wood. To be hunted for his wings!

"Farree." The sharp mind call alerted him out of that momentary nightmare but he did not take to the sky. Stay on the ground, caution warned him, not let himself be seen by any hunter who had broken out of the mountain ways and now cast about for a fresh trail.

He saw, to his amazement, a quiver in that green wall, a lifting of branch, an uncoiling of vine, and then the Lord-One Krip came out into the open, leading Lady Maelen by one hand. She walked with her eyes open and staring ahead as one might walk mindlessly after some great shock. But she was also singing—a murmur of sound which had in its tempo something of the rustle of leaves, the scrape of branch against branch under a light wind. It would seem that even as her singing had wrought miracles in other places, even among the rocks, here it had tamed the ring jungle enough to let them through.

She pulled free of her companion's grasp and turned to face the woods from which they had just emerged. Now she held both hands out, palm up and empty, and her singing arose through a flight of notes such as might be caroled by a bird, then came to an end.

Lord-One Krip had already reached Farree and was holding out his hand for the mirror picture maker which the other surrendered to him with the hope that his use had been good enough to answer their questions.

The Lady Maelen, once more looking aware of what lay about her, came quickly over the pebbly beach to them.

Lord-One Krip had touched a place on the rim of the mirror, and now there appeared from the side of that square a strip of colored designs which certainly resembled those Farree had aimed to take with his mirror device. As this unrolled, the Lady Maelen laid it out on the gravel, pulling it straight before crouching down to inspect it closely. Sometimes she lifted a fingertip to trace one of those patterns as if to impress it the stronger on her memory.

"It is truly a locking," she observed. "As strong in its way, Krip, as those persona locks off-worlders use for their most precious possessions. Here and here"—she made quick stabs with her finger—"are markings I have knowledge of— these are close to what is so used today. But others." She shook her head. "I can only guess that if one passes over them without proper preparation the result may be perilous indeed."

"What does all this protect?" Lord-One Krip put into words the first question in Farree's own mind.

"Something of the Thassa—but not of our time," she replied. "Here may be what those others have been seeking."

And these traps"—Lord-One Krip swept a hand above the roll of pictures now lying flat upon the ground—"will keep them from entering and finding what they seek?"

She shook her head slowly. "How can we be sure? This was made to warn off those of Yiktor. Will it also work against off-worlders of whom perhaps those who set it never guessed might try their success against the barriers?"

"So what defense have we left against them?" he proceeded.

Her hands arose and sketched a gesture which might have expressed helplessness. "We can only wait and see."

But Farree was not ready to accept that answer—the first he had ever had from her which carried no certainty, only confusion in it.

"How would one unlock this"—it was his turn to gesture—"if it was known?"

"It is a code of sorts," she explained. "One must move from pattern to pattern in a certain sequence and then it will open."

"And that invisible door will be gone?"

She nodded. "But the code was devised by those long gone, and there could be a hundred, even a thousand different sequences—the trying might go on for years, many seasons—and those who searched could come no nearer to success. There is nothing even in the far legends of the Thassa—those which are known to every Singer—which mentions such a find as this."

It was Farree's turn to study the strip of pictures. Those he sought were at the very end. "These four are patterns on the roof—are they any closer to the ones you know?"

She leaned forward. The gray of early morning light since the fading of the rings had deepened, and she squinted and then shook her head. "I cannot tell as yet. There is not enough light."

Lord-One Krip had arisen. "Let us get under cover," he said. "They could not have brought a flitter through the mountain way but they may have a course-setting device with them, and that would give them air support once they set it within this valley."

Withdraw they did under the fringe of trees beyond that ribbon of beach. There they huddled, not too far from each other, easing their tired bodies from the night's labor and travel. They drew lots for first sentry go and Farree had the shortest. He found his wings most difficult to manage, even when furled to the smallest and tightest extent it was possible to set upon them, and he had to push clear to the edge of their cover in order to have room.

The sun arose, almost reluctantly, and the glitter of the water as it had lain under the third ring was now a glare against which he had to shade his eyes. He chewed on one of the strips of journey food, finding it dry and tasteless, and listened intently for any sound of approach by air.

Even though he tried to keep his attention for what lay about and above him, he could not help now and then looking to the tower on the island, wondering if, under the sun, those complex patterns set in the stone were any clearer. Certainly they dared not attempt to solve the code now—the Lady Maelen had pointed out—as that might be a task which would take them long to solve, if ever. He found himself wondering what traps awaited those who did not know the secret at all. He was about to learn.

There were a continued rustling from the layer of jungle as if the plants therein were restless and were changing their positions. But there were no bird calls, no cry of beast, nor chirp of insect. The sullen green growth might have been bare of any life except that of its own.

At times that continued rustling took on the sound of a muttered conversation, one which he could almost follow. Then he shook his head vigorously and moved about a little, thinking that it was lulling him into sleep.

The interruption came from a distance and he had plenty of time to reach out and touch Lord-One Krip's shoulder, the Thassa coming into instant awareness at that warning as if he had been only lying conscious with his eyes closed.

"Flitter!" Farree mind sent as if he could be overheard by the enemy even at this great distance. He jerked a thrust toward the south—that narrow rift through which they had come into this valley.

In turn Lord-One Krip aroused the Lady Maelen, and the three of them drew a little more together, listening. There seemed to be no search pattern on the part of the air craft. By a continued and ever louder sound it was headed straight for the lake, no pattern of circling to pick up a trail.

"Back!" Lord-One Krip urged. The Lady Maelen was already burrowing into the bushes, and under the sound of the flitter Farree thought he could still hear the hum of her voice as if she once more used a Singer skill to help penetrate the jungle growth. That seemed useless—perhaps it would only work under the radiance of the ring—for he saw a branch spring back at her face, and, only because she threw up an arm, were those thorn marks on her forearm instead of across her very eyes.

At least they were under the edging of the wood and the gravel behind showed no discernible track. Though the off-worlders had their own ways of trailing, rumored machines and devices that picked up fugitives by their body heat when they were close enough.

The flitter was out cruising above the lake. Now it circled in a tight orbit around the tower. If they did know where the three lay in scant cover, they seemed to wish to learn more of the building they had chanced upon, for the craft made a third circle. Then it held steady about the tower and a ladder, such as Farree himself had once used to escape, tumbled out of a hatch in its belly.

Down that swung a man while another crouched at the exit, a laser across his arm at the ready, waiting to cover the journey of his comrade. The invader must have made some suggestions, for the flitter swung forward a fraction, and now he was descending past the roof of the tower into the patterned courtyard. He disappeared behind the wall, and a second explorer took his place on the ladder.

Sound—sudden, both sharp and deafening—cloaked even the clatter of the off-world engine. Then a rainbow of light fanned upward. All that glory of the third ring might have been condensed in that.

"No! Do not look!" The Lady Maelen's thought reached Farree and only half-consciously he obeyed, bending his arm across his eyes.

He felt a warmth which was not that of sunlight but rather arose to near the torment of a fire as if he had set his hand to pick up a coal from a brazier, and his wings quivered under that fiery assault. The heat which reached them in such a flash must have been a hundredfold worse within that walled courtyard.

Farree heard a scream that lasted only for a second and then was blasted away by the deafening sound rising to a crescendo. What luck had attended him last night when he might have encountered that same trap!

The heat seemed to hold for a long time, but he heard the sound die away and with it the noise of the flitter, in full retreat after losing two of its crew to whatever disaster was the guardian of the tower.

A scent reached the three under the edge of the wood—not of the moon flowers which had perfumed the night, but a horrible stench of meat burnt to a crisp.

"They are gone," Lord-One Krip said. Farree wondered why he had not tried to track them himself by mind touch, catching that emptiness which was a shrouded mind.

"They will be back," the Lord-One Krip added a moment later. "They will not let this puzzle be."

"Have they anything which can unlock the code?" asked the Lady Maelen. "Have you ever heard of such?"

"No. But that does not mean that they do not possess one. The Guild have knowledge beyond that of any Free Trader such as I was. There are stories enough of what they have achieved."

"Then we must do our best. If this thing which is guarded here is by the will of ancient Thassa, they must not have it!"

She crept on her hands and knees out of the shadow of the bush which had left the scarlet wounds down her arm and reached again for the pictures that had issued from the mirror. Now she turned her attention from those of the courtyard to the patterns Farree had found on the roof of the tower. With her forefinger she traced one design after another.

"They would put their most formidable weapon in the

courtyard," she said slowly. "I do not think that they would much expect any to enter from the air. Thus these are the important ones for us." And her finger went once more over the designs, and she was humming again but not the lazy half-sleepy sound which she had uttered in defense against the jungle belt.

"We cannot dare to try until the moon rises—"

"By then," Farree interrupted, "those may be back with something to open that tower as one opens a bra-crab shell."

She nodded. "That is so. Time lies on their side of the balance. But I cannot believe that the Scales of Molester are so weighed against us who would save patterns of time and space and not blast them into nonexistence. We must wait through the day, save our strength—"

"I cannot carry you to the tower and there is the lake to cross," Farree pointed out. He wondered if they would dare to swim—could they swim? The arid country which seemed home to the Thassa might not have given them any reason for the sport. And though Lord-One Krip had been first a Free Trader spacer, certainly he would have had little enough reason to perfect such a skill either.

"I know," she returned and there was a troubled note in her voice.

"A rope"—Lord-One Krip was looking back into the gloom of the jungle—"one of those lianas, were it tough enough, or a weaving of vines—"

"They live," Lady Maelen told him quickly, "with more of a real life than any rooted thing I have seen before."

"But they also die." He pointed in two places where the full roundness of life had shrunken away and there were brownish loops which were plainly dead or near that state. "Can the dead protest?"

"I do not know," she answered frankly. "It is of importance, this rope of yours?"

"It is the only way, I think, of reaching the island," he

returned firmly. Though Farree could not see any reason for such confidence.

"Ah, well—" She arose and went to where one of those dead coils spanned a tree from branch to branch. Slowly she raised her hand and set it on the brown surface, tugging at it a fraction. Nothing around her moved or strove to make her pay for her audacity. She pulled harder and began her humming song. Within a few moments the arc of the dead vine was free of the branches, looping to the ground and beyond out on the gravel of the beach. Lord-One Krip was on it instantly. So she wrought with two other vines, and they were in time laid along the surface of the beach in lengths beyond the height of the tower itself, or so Farree believed.

"Leaves." Lord-One Krip stood up from stretching the last of those vines in place. "Such a leaf as that." Again he pointed to a bush standing taller than his own head. The bottom leaves of that plant—the ones reaching out over the beach—were also spotted with brown and plainly dying. Their hard, thick sides were rolled up so that they formed a half tube and were large enough for the Thassa to lie upon. "Can these be detached also?"

The Lady Maelen went to the plant and knelt as it towered over her. Her singing became another series of notes, and Farree thought he could almost read a petition into that. Then she leaned forward and set a hand to either side of the leaf and strove to draw it to her. There was no movement save the constant tensing of her body. At least, as it had been with the dead vines, the growth itself made no attack. Then the rotted core of the leaf gave away suddenly so that she sprawled backward, the broken stem dripping with a black liquid which gave off the foul odor of decay.

When a second leaf had been so released from a similar plant Lord-One Krip set them all to work, braiding the tough vine lengths into one knobby rope. When he had done, he took one of the long leaves down to the water and floated it, throwing himself facedown upon it and pushing out a little from the shore. Though it bobbed downward under his weight, yet it supported his head and shoulders above water.

"This"—he indicated the rope—"well fastened to a rock over there"—his wide gesture indicated the island—"can be used to draw us through the water."

He would be trusting a great deal to dead vegetation, Farree thought, but there was a small chance that such might work. His own part of the task was simple compared to theirs. What if they reached the water and the flitter returned?

He had great respect for the Lady Maelen's third ring powers, but this they must do now and the sun gave them nothing but light. However, the trial must be made.

With the end of the coil fastened to his belt he soared up and out across the lake, heading directly for a fringe of rocks before the wall of the courtyard. Once there he hastened to make fast the rope's end to the most slender of those rocks. Lord-One Krip had to wade into the water a little, holding the other end, but it did reach, and he was tugging hard on it, testing its stability.

The Lady Maelen came first, lying in her curled leaf with both hands overhead on the rope, pulling herself along. Against a troubled and current-riven water she would not have succeeded, but the pull across the calm surface, though it seemed to take endless time, was at last accomplished, and Farree flew back with the rope's end to the waiting Krip.

For the second time a leaf made that hardly believable voyage and then, the rope coiled about Farree's arm, the three of them stood before the wall surrounding the courtyard.

18.

Farree crouched on the top of the wall and determinedly did not look to the two twisted burnt things that lay before the invisible door. A laser had fallen from the charred claws of one to skid across the courtyard against the wall not too far away. Could he manage to reach the small strip of pavement there which was free of pattern and retrieve it? The thought of such a weapon for their defense was irresistible. He laid aside the rope which he had carried up and gestured toward the two below, off before they might object.

Down he fluttered, not sure yet of his wing power but impatient to get his hands on the weapon. He made a swoop, gasped suddenly as he lengthened out with his body parallel to the ground, and managed to claw up the butt end of the laser, climbing up into the air and then bouncing over the wall top to the two Thassa below. He offered the weapon to Lord-One Krip, who reached for it quickly.

Now, whether his weight on the end of the rope would be anchorage enough he did not know. In the end he picked that up and did not try to fasten it on the wall but spiralled over to the tower where he could anchor it on one of the jutting bits of the parapet. Then he returned to the wall top where they speedily joined him.

The Lady Maelen lay down and edged along that length of barrier top until she could see the pattern which had been the fatal trap for the Guild men. Farree could sense her aversion to what she saw there, but he also knew that she was driven by duty to consider what manner of trap that was—if she could equate it with something her people still had knowledge of.

"Force released," she said slowly. "After all these tens of tens of tens of seasons that which was set answered."

"But I landed there earlier and nothing happened," Farree commented.

"By luck you must have touched a pattern which was not one set for defense."

He studied the designs carefully. Yes, he had stood at the edge of a crimson circle a foot or so away from the square of wavy blue lines which had been the downfall of the dead men below.

"Dare we cross?" Lord-One Krip wanted to know.

With a pointing finger the Lady Maelen was tracing in the air the patterns between them and the narrow edging of plain stone about the foundation of the tower.

"I do not know. There is a maze there, a curve here, a suggestion of a code. But without full knowledge . . ." She shifted her sight toward the two bodies and shivered. "They will be back," she said then as if speaking thoughts aloud.

"With enough power to blast the place open," Lord-One Krip returned. "Perhaps they will so trigger that as to destroy all of this wholly."

She shook her head. "They want this too much. Or what they think it holds. Remember Sehkmet. They have traced us—some of them—believing we can uncover such another cache for their taking. Now on Thassa world they have found this. Their first defeat was a small one in their eyes. They will be ready to follow through.''

"Look you"—Farree gave a tug to the rope against which he had been pitting his full strength—"can you use this to swing across and land by the tower, then climb?''

Lord-One Krip stood up and eyed the rope and its tower anchor with narrowed eyes. "One can try.''

His hand twitched the rope out of Farree's hold and bent its own strength in a grip which kept it taut, then jerked at it. The rope held. He clasped it tightly and swung down and out across the treacherous pavement, descending so far that Farree was afraid his feet would scrape across the inlaid stones. Then he was at the foot of the tower and was climbing. His feet set to the wall itself, his arms extending one above the other, he used the rope to raise him. They watched him, tense and frozen, until he was at the parapet and over. Then Farree leapt into the air and spanned the distance between them with the aid of his wings, caught the end of the rope, and bore it back to the Lady Maelen.

For the second time he witnessed the dangerous swing past the dead and saw her being drawn up by the man on the tower. He whirred across and was there to meet her.

For a long moment she leaned against the parapet until her breath steadied, but she was staring down at the patterns now revealed below her.

"The third ring," she said slowly. "These are markings very old—if I had time I could perhaps trace a key to this locking. But we must have Sotrath above us when we try.''

Lord-One Krip looked to the sky. "There are hours before we shall have that. They may well be back long before the third ring shines.''

She shrugged. "In that we must take our chance. If they come—''

"He will come." Farree knew that as well as if it had been

announced out of the air above his head. "Their leader will make this his own venture."

Lord-One Krip nodded. "That it seems we must chance. If he is the regular Guild Veep he will make sure of his armament, of no more losses such as he has suffered here. And—"

Toggor suddenly turned from the place he had climbed to on the parapet, his eyestalks out to their full limit, his gaze on the shore from whence they had come. If Farree had caught that message, so had the Thassa. Beyond the maze ring of vegetation the enemy moved. Those who had followed them through the mountain were now prepared to batter a way through the tangled growth.

"Yes." The Lady Maelen nodded. "However—" She, too, had wheeled about to face the growing barrier and now she planted both hands palm down on a curling line of vivid green set with yellow stars of gems which crawled toward them as part of the tower pattern. She knelt so, unable to see now above the parapet, though she faced in the same direction as Toggor.

"Feed me!" she commanded fiercely. "Feed!"

The Lord-One Krip went down on one knee, his hand cupping the point of her shoulder, his other hand reaching out toward Farree. Not knowing just what was to be done, the winged man settled down, awkwardly now because of his wings, but placing one hand within those groping fingers which caught on his with a painful grasp.

Farree gasped. Something was being drawn from his body, flowing on to Lord-One Krip, then presumedly to the Lady Maelen. Her face was so tense and set the flesh seemed but a shallow covering to her bones. She began to sing, first in the low hum he had heard her use to force a path from the growth—then the notes scaled up, grew louder, some ringing out as if she had beaten a gong rather than used her voice to shape them. In the day she sang—would the power without the moon answer?

Though Farree had knelt to take Lord-One Krip's hand, he could see above the parapet against which his shoulder rubbed. Suddenly it was as if a storm cloud had released a wave of wind instead of water. The growth tossed. He could see branches move, vines writhe, some even appearing to unknot themselves and toss loose ends in the air, darting about like the heads of scaled things. This wild rippling ran in both directions. He believed he could even sight bits of leaf and vine which broke loose and wafted along on the surface of that wind out of nowhere.

Farree felt the energy drain from him. Something he had never known existed was being tapped and going through his hold upon the Thassa to sustain that desperate song. He put his other hand to the parapet where Toggor crouched. Now he saw that the smux was rocking back and forth, clacking his larger claws together in part rhythm with the song.

For a while it held loud and steady, and then it began to slow. He could see the drops of sweat running down the Lady Maelen's cheeks, felt her fight to keep on. However, there came an end at last. She swayed and would have fallen had not Lord-One Krip seized her, snatching his hand from Farree and pulling her back against him for her support. A last bit of song, hardly above a whisper, came from her lips and then, eyes closed, mouth gaping, she lay limp in his hold.

The wind or stirring out of nowhere died. Farree tried hard to pick up that nothingness which was the mark of the shielded enemy. There! He had touched one—quickly he searched but there seemed to be no others. Toggor had sunk down, drawn in his eyestalks as he did when he must rest.

Rest! Farree leaned sidewise against the stone, his wings together and folded, an ache in his head and a feeling of emptiness inside him. He was as hollow now as if he had

been squeezed by some great hand and flung aside to lie
without substance.

For how long that lasted he could not tell. There was a
feeble stirring in his mind that they must be again on guard
ready for death coming from the skies. Yet he must have
slept, for he awoke from that place of nothingness with a
hand shaking him, and then Lord-One Krip forced into his
hold some of the rations which they had relied upon so
long—dry and tasteless, yet he choked mouthfuls down.

The sun no longer burned down upon them but sped across
the sky into red sunset clouds, and the Lady Maelen was
sitting up, turning her head slowly from one side to the other
as if she had awakened out of a dream and could not recog-
nize where she was. Then recognition came back to her eyes
and she smiled wearily.

"Let Sotrath rise," she said slowly, "then we shall see
whether, though I am wandless, I am still too lacking in the
Gift to do what must be done. At least this day past I have
wrought more than I would have believed possible. This is
truly a place of power."

"Lacking!" Lord-One Krip burst out. "When you awoke
the woods rang . . ."

Her smile grew a little stronger. "Yes, that I did. I am still
a Singer."

"One of the mighty ones!" Lord-One Krip said forcibly.
"Let them try to deny you your due now!"

"Hush." She put her hand to his lips. "I do what I can,
but to claim full mastery is false." She reached out to touch
that line set in the stones, to fit fingertip to each of the stones
in it. "That this answered the three of us after all the lost
time—that is not *my* mastery but that of those great ones who
set it here."

"And those who hunt us?" Farree sputtered through dry
crumbs.

"Ask that of them." She pointed toward the wood. "They are a greater barrier than even I could guess. Look!"

She pointed now to the eastern sky where the dusk crept down like a curtain. Showing just a tip about it was a thing of glitter which he had come to cherish. The third ring was beginning to rise—the time of the Thassa power at its height was coming!

It seemed to Farree that the dusk came more swiftly than usual. As if the very longing of the Lady Maelen had the power to summon up Sotrath and the moon rings. Yet she did not look to the sky but ran her hands up the curving side of one pattern and down the arabesque of another as if her touch could find what she sought quicker than her sight. Perhaps that was so far; just as she had chosen certain stones to rub when she sang their partnership to the woods, now did she settle at last at the farther side of the roof, waving the other two to the blank border beside the parapet while she settled herself on her knees, leaning well forward so that the palms of her hand each cupped a series of three greenish stones which gleamed the brighter as the third ring crept up the sky behind her head.

Once more she began to sing—this time no hum without words, but rather a chant that accented some syllables with the beat of a drum. That sound gripped Farree and perhaps also the Lord-One Krip, for Farree noted that the spaceman's hands were opening and closing, where they hung by his sides, in time to that beat in words.

Farree had begun to believe that indeed she could accomplish great things by her words alone. He had seen sound shatter crystals once or twice in the Limits, when some sleight-of-hand dealer was showing off skills. Why then could such not pick up the resonance of a voice at proper pitch and be moved by it as was a lock with a key laid into its proper slot? ··

By the time Sotrath itself was showing on the horizon and

the arc of the third ring well advanced, bringing rainbows of light from the pavement, she did indeed achieve what she had set to do. There was another sound across the beat of her voice and before her a dark outline framed a good section of the roof.

Her voice arose in a triumphant crescendo and the block so outlined was sucked downward out of their sight.

Farree gave a cry, clapping his hands to his head. Into his mind there burst such a flash or lash of sights and sounds, of places and people, he felt that his very head would split open, not being able to hold or control this wave of otherness. Lord-One Krip likewise doubled near over as if some mighty blow had sent him reeling, and his hands also clawed over his ears; while the Lady Maelen crouched low, her face drawn and contorted into grimaces, her whole body tensed and resisting.

It was, Farree decided, as if a whole world of different thought had been launched at them. He fought, trying to set in his mind a wall behind which that that was he himself could crouch protected.

Half expecting a company of Thassa or their like to come boiling up through the door, a company the Lady Maelen had sung into their defenses, Farree could see only the dark oblong at their feet, and in that nothing moved nor climbed to meet them.

Wall! Think a wall! Farree's wings moved without conscious thought and he was up—into the night, soaring above the top of the tower. Yet those hundreds, thousands of thoughts (though they were a little muffled) beat at him. He thought a wall, barrier so tight set that nothing could breach it. As he circled on wings about the tower, unwilling to desert those two who did not have his advantage for a quick escape, he was aware that the thought stream was thinning, that now only a trickle of such came through.

The Lady Maelen was on her feet, though Lord-One Krip

still crouched low, his head swinging from side to side as if the very weight of that storm of thought was launched against him in one wave after another. The Lady Maelen held forth the light globe which had guided them through the mountain passage, and that gathered to it the ring's glory until she had cupped a great ball of fire. With that hand stretched before her, she approached the opening, looking down into the depths beneath.

What she saw there Farree could not imagine. When he watched her prepare to descend through that opening he swooped, determined to catch her before she was swallowed up by that maelstrom of mind speech. But he was too late, and, in spite of all his efforts, the clamor caught him again, driving him in self-protection to the edge of the parapet where he strove to shake the Lord-One Krip into action.

Only, it would appear that the man was also still caught in the invisible storm they had loosed. He moaned a little, and his eyes had turned upward in his head so that the whites were visible.

Had he been able to manage the other's weight Farree would have hoisted him up, gotten him away from that perilous open door. Now he could only stay beside him, strive to move in his own mental picture of a wall set against the flood.

The light beamed upward from the opening. He did not think he could have entered, even with his mind at rest. It was not big enough to take his spread of wings no matter how much he could try to compress those. But for the Lady Maelen to go alone into that place! Urgently he shook Lord-One Krip until the other's head flopped forward and backward on his shoulders. Then he felt the other begin to gain control, and a moment later the man's eyes were turned up to meet his.

"The . . . m-minds," he stammered, "they are—"

"Can such a place hold an army?" demanded Farree.
"Whence comes all this?"

"Memories, all the thoughts—of a race!" Lord-One Krip
straightened in his hold, and Farree released him.

"She's gone—down there! I cannot reach her. Can you?"
Farree demanded.

"Not now. If I loose—I am lost."

Yet they both crept on hands and knees, one on either side
of the trapdoor, striving to see what did lie below. Whether
that wave of mind touch that had been building for generations could be loosed suddenly without disaster Farree did not
know, but he felt that the pressure against his mental wall
was less than it had been. And now he could see.

The Lady Maelen stood below a short ladder, and around
her body there was an aura of the light from the globe—perhaps
that served as her defense.

About her also were racks towering side to side, leaving
only the small space where the ladder had given her entrance.
And the racks were filled with a series of blocks which pul-
sated with rainbow colors in a mixture that hurt the eyes
almost as much as the wave of mind touch had near toppled
their other senses. Scarlet, vivid orange, green in five or six
violent shades, blue the same—violet to purple. It was
unbelievable.

She was just standing there, her head slowly swinging
from side to side, her face a mask in which not even her eyes
moved—like one asleep who yet walked.

Before either of them could move, she shifted the ball into
her left hand and with the right she reached out toward one of
the racks.

"No!" Lord-One Krip cried out, and Farree could have
echoed him. But if she heard, that protest had no meaning for
her. Her fingers closed about a cube which was gem-bright in
green, and she plucked it out of the serried ranks of its like
and held it to the level of her eyes. It was as if she both saw

and heard something in its heart which kept her mazed. Then swiftly she stored it back with its fellows and turned to the ladder, coming up to them in haste.

Under the light of the third ring her own gleaming hair, her ivory-pale skin, took on ripples of the lights, but she still walked as one in a trance. Lord-One Krip reached for her as she came within grasping distance, pulled her up toward him as if he needs must draw her out of some great trap.

She did not try to throw off his hold, but she turned with it, holding her globe up to the glory of the third ring and then lowering it to focus its beams on the very stones she had used to open the door. And her chant sounded clear in the night air, the drumbeat of the unknown words harsher and faster as if now she worked against time itself.

Even as that aperture had opened so now it closed. Only when that was done did she look to the two of them as if she knew them again.

"Down. We must get down. To the courtyard!" She pushed away from Lord-One Krip and indicated that treacherous pavement below.

"It is"—Farree swinging upward dared to look again at the two huddled bodies below—"a trap."

"Yes," she agreed. "And it must be reset—reset for greater prey! I must do that, by the third ring!"

With the aid of the vine rope they made it. She waved Lord-One Krip away and pointed to certain lines of the patterns.

"Walk so and so." She motioned. "Get to the other wall and up! We may have very little time. Those others will come." It was as if she had knowledge they did not share.

Lord-One Krip stared at her for a long moment and then did as she had told him. Farree flew to give them an escape route, knotting the vine this time to a hard rock near the shore and feeding the free end into the courtyard. But Lord-One Krip would retreat no farther than the wall itself.

The Lady Maelen was singing again. She did not approach

the part of the designs where lay the dead off-worlders, but
she paced other sections, showing great care where she trod,
and sang the same harsh song she had used to close the door
above. Three times she rounded the tower and each time the
uneasiness in Farree rose. He felt Toggor crowd tightly against
him, and the fear in the smux fed his own.

Then, having trod on the pattern before all the four walls,
the Lady Maelen ran toward them. Lord-One Krip caught her
and tossed her body a little upward so that she clutched the
vine rope at a higher level. Then he was hard behind her as
she climbed and slid down to the other side.

"It is done." She was panting, her body sleekly wet with
sweat, her face drawn and haggard. "And none too soon—
The rocks—those—take shelter—"

She did not have to utter any warning. They had already
heard the beat of the flitter in the sky, saw riding lights like
the eyes of a vast insect coming down the valley even as it
had earlier flown.

They lay belly down behind the screen of rocks, Farree
crimping his wings into the smallest possible space. On the
flitter came, and he heard the Lady Maelen: "They know
something. Surely they would not come under the ring. But
no Thassa would deal with them. What secret has been
betrayed that they hunt so?" It was as if she asked that
question of the world at large.

Over swung the air craft. It hung at hover, and this time
dropped two from its belly onto the top of the tower. At least
they had learned that much from their abortive earlier attempt.

"Yes." The Lady Maelen's voice was only a breath of
whisper, and then she added, "Now, let it be now!"

As to what followed Farree could never afterwards settle in
his own mind. It was as if the rays of the third ring awoke to
life every gemlike stone so that beams of raw and eye-
burning color flashed out. Not only at the men who had
landed on the roof but upwards far enough to transfix the

flitter in turn. Farree thought he heard screams—he was
never sure because it all happened so suddenly.

But the beams of gem light became flamelike and they
licked about the flitter, drawing it down into their heart fire.
Then the tower itself quivered and blazed until he dared not
look at it any longer. It—it melted! There was no other way
he could describe what happened, for its sides grew soft as
thray wax under the sun and spun oddly outward in droplets—
though none of those sped beyond the courtyard wall. But
the tower sank and was gone, and the lights failed so only
that of the third ring held. There came sobbing from where
the Lady Maelen lay, and Lord-One Krip edged closer to take
her into his arms.

"They are . . . dead," she stammered, "they are dead and
with them all their knowledge. It is a second death and
one—one which I delivered to them!"

Farree answered, "But they were Guild and—"

"Not the Guild, those are dead of their own greed. It
was—the ancient memories—those stored lest Thassa need
the weight of them again. But they had their own defense,
and that I set. You do not understand. We were once so great
a people that the Guild, all off-world could not have troubled
us. Then it was chosen that we should take another path. But
there were those who argued that all knowledge should not be
wiped from the face of Yiktor. So they set the memory tower
and each memory was stored there—all the knowledge of
untold time which we cannot count in seasons or Sotrath
rings anymore. All of it gone—and by my doing!" She was
weeping now, and her head fell forward onto Lord-One
Krip's shoulder.

They stood again in the great hall that Farree had first seen
after the landing on Yiktor. The Lady Maelen was a little
before them, facing those leaders of her people, her head
proudly high. There had been a reading of minds, and she it

was who insisted upon judgment. Now it was the elder of the
women who spoke.

"Always you have gone your own way, Maelen. And
always trouble and sorrow comes from it. So the great memories are gone. Well, none can bring them back. Nor"—she
spoke more slowly now—"since there are those who would
take them for a bitter use, can we wish them so. But we say
to you a second time, Kinswoman, there is no place for you,
by three rings or two. You are no longer Thassa but something else—we know not what. Nor can you slip within the
shell of the people. Come to us when you desire but do not
hope to stay—for there is that within you which cannot be
fitted into our life again any more than a flower can be fitted
back into the tight curl of a bud. We do not exile you—"

"No," the Lady Maelen said slowly. "That I have done
for myself. I am grateful that you do not turn from me."

"There is this—" The woman held forth a wand which
one of the men had handed to her.

"No, that I leave also. I am no longer a Moon Singer,
Elder. I sang death to the past—"

"You did as it seemed fit. But, yes, the wand is not a part
of the future for you. And you are wise in your own way.
Where do you go now?"

"Out to the stars!"

"And the enemy who would trace you?"

"Perhaps dead, perhaps alive. But that is a matter for the
future—"

"And you, Krip Vorlund?"

He took a step forward until he stood equal with Maelen to
confront them all.

"Where she goes thus do I also."

The Elder nodded and then looked to Farree, whose wings
moved wide to show the gleaming patches on them.

"And you, little brother?"

He drew a deep breath and voiced it now, just as it had

come to him from the moment that those spans of glory had broken from his ugliness.

"I would find my world—"

"So be it. And we wish you three well. You have done what was to be done—hold it not in your memories as any evil. Time turns awry and straight in many ways. We grant you time as a companion, and may it serve you well."

Farree opened and closed his wings, his head held high now. Time—there was time always ahead, even though a man could hold nothing but now in his two hands. He would have *his* chosen now—he vowed that. Suddenly he felt his hand taken by the Lady Maelen and he realized that his time would be their time also. For the first time in his life he was warmly content.

Norton   cop.1

Flight in Yiktor

Science Fiction